The Coroner's Lunch

Books by Colin Cotterill

The Dr. Siri Series
The Coroner's Lunch
Thirty-Three Teeth
Disco for the Departed
Anarchy and Old Dogs
Curse of the Pogo Stick
The Merry Misogynist
Love Songs from a Shallow Grave
Slash and Burn
The Woman Who Wouldn't Die
Six and a Half Deadly Sins

The Coroner's Lunch

COLIN COTTERILL

Published by
Soho Press, Inc.
853 Broadway
New York, NY 10003

Library of Congress Cataloging-in-Publication Data
Cotterill, Colin
The coroner's lunch/Colin Cotterill

ISBN 978-1-61695-649-3

1. Older people—Fiction. 2. Physicians—Fiction.
3. Coroners—Fiction. 4. Laos—Fiction.
I. Title
PR6053.0778C67 2004
823'.92—dc22   2004048191

Designed by Neuwirth and Associates

Printed in the United States of America

10   9   8   7   6   5   4   3   2   1

With the kindest thanks and lots of love to the following folks:

Pornsawan, Bouasawan, Chantavone, Sounieng, Ketkaew, Dr. Pongruk, Bounlan, Don, Souk, Soun, Michael and his secretary, Somdee, David L, Nok, Dtee, Siri, Yayoi, and Steph.

Contents

The Coroner's Lunch

Tran, Tran, and Hok broke through the heavy end-of-wet-season clouds. The warm night air rushed against their reluctant smiles and yanked their hair vertical. They fell in a neat formation, like sleet. There was no time for elegant float-ing or fancy aerobatics; they just followed the rusty bombshells that were tied to their feet with pink nylon string.

Tran the elder led the charge. He was the heaviest of the three. By the time he reached the surface of Nam Ngum reser-voir, he was already ahead by two seconds. If this had been the Olympics, he would have scored a 9.98 or thereabouts. There was barely a splash. Tran the younger and Hok-the-twice-dead pierced the water without so much as a pulse-beat between them.

A quarter of a ton of unarmed ordnance dragged all three men quickly to the smooth muddy bottom of the lake and anchored them there. For two weeks, Tran, Tran, and Hok swayed gently back and forth in the current and entertained the fish and algae that fed on them like diners at a slow-moving noodle stall.

Vientiane, Two Weeks Later

It was a depressing audience, and there were going to be a lot more like it. Now that Haeng, the spotty-faced magistrate, was back, Siri would have to explain himself every damn Friday, and kowtow to a man young enough to be his grandson.

In the jargon of the Marxist–Leninists, the sessions were known as "burden-sharing tutorials." But after the first hour in front of Judge Haeng's warped plywood desk, Dr. Siri's burden had become *more* weighty. The judge, fresh off the production line, had taken great delight in casting un-expert doubts on Siri's reports and correcting his spelling.

"And what do you put the loss of blood down to?" Judge Haeng asked.

Siri wondered more than once whether he was deliberately being asked trick questions to establish the state of his mind. "Well." He considered it for a moment. "The body's inability to keep it in?" The little judge h'mmed and looked back down at the report. He wasn't even bright enough for sarcasm. "Of course, the fact that the poor man's legs had been cut off above the knees might have had something to do with it. It's all there in the report."

"You may believe it's all here in the report, Comrade Siri, but you seem to be very selective as to what information you share with your readers. I'd like to see much more detail in the future, if you don't mind. And to be honest, I don't see how you can be so sure it was the loss of blood that killed him, rather than, say . . ."

"Heart failure?"

"Exactly. It would have been a terrible shock when his legs were severed. How do you know he didn't have a heart attack? He wasn't a young man."

With each of the previous three cases they'd debated, Haeng had somehow twisted the facts around to the possibility of a natural death, but this was his most creative suggestion. It struck Siri that the judge would be delighted if all the case reports that came through his office were headed "cardiac arrest."

True, the fisherman's heart had stopped beating, but it was the signal announcing his death rather than the cause of it. The newly armor-plated military launch had crashed into the concrete dock at Tar Deua. With all the extra weight, it lay low in the water. Fortunately for the crew, the collision was cushioned by the longboat man standing in his little wooden craft against the wall, with no way to escape. Like a surprising number of fishermen on the Mekhong, he'd never learned to swim.

The overlapping metal deck sliced him apart like a scythe cutting through rice stalks, and the railing pinned him upright where he had been standing. The embarrassed captain and his crew pulled him—his torso—up onto the deck, where he lay in numb confusion, chattering and laughing as if he didn't know he was missing a couple of limbs.

The boat reversed and people on the bank watched the legs topple into the water and sink. They likely swelled up in a few hours and returned to the surface. They had worn odd flip-flops, so the chances of them being reunited in time for the funeral were poor.

"If you intend to cite a heart attack for every cause of death, I don't really see why we need a coroner at all, Comrade." Siri had reached his limit, and it was a limit that floated in a vast distant atmosphere. After seventy-two years, he'd seen so many hardships that he'd reached the calmness of an astronaut bobbing about in space. Although he wasn't much better at Buddhism than he was at communism, he seemed able to meditate himself away from anger. Nobody could recall him losing his temper.

Dr. Siri Paiboun was often described as a short-arsed man. He had a peculiar build, like a lightweight wrestler with a stoop. When he walked, it was as if his bottom half was doing its best to keep up with his top half. His hair, clipped short, was a dazzling white. Where a lot of Lao men had awakened late in life to find, by some miracle of the Lord above, their hair returned to its youthful blackness, Siri had more sensible uses for his allowance than Yu Dum Chinese dye. There was nothing fake or added or subtracted about him. He was all himself.

He'd never had much success with whiskers, unless you counted eyebrows as whiskers. Siri's had become so overgrown, it took strangers a while to make out his peculiar eyes. Even those who'd traveled ten times around the world had never seen such eyes. They were the bright green of well-lighted snooker-table felt, and they never failed to amuse him when they stared back from his mirror. He didn't know much about his real parents, but there had been no rumors of aliens in his blood. How he'd ended up with eyes like these, he couldn't explain to anyone.

Forty minutes into the "shared burden tutorial," Judge Haeng still hadn't been able to look into those eyes. He'd watched his pencil wagging. He'd looked at the button dangling from the cuff of the doctor's white shirt. He'd stared up through the broken louver window as if the red star were sparkling in the evening sky outside the walls of the Department of Justice. But he hadn't once looked into Siri's brilliant green eyes.

"Of course, Comrade Siri, we have to have a coroner because, as you well know, any organized socialist system must be accountable to its brothers and sisters. Revolutionary consciousness is maintained beneath the brilliance of the beam from the socialist lighthouse. But the people have a right to see the lighthouse keeper's clean underwear drying on the rocks."

Hell, the boy was good at that: he was a master at coming up with exactly the wrong motto for the right situation. Everyone went home and analyzed their mottoes, and realized too late that they had no bearing on . . . anything. Siri stared at the sun-starved boy and felt kind of sorry for him.

His only claim to respect was a Soviet law degree on paper so thin, you could see the wall where it hung through it. He'd been trained, rapidly, to fill one of the many gaps left by the fleeing upper classes. He'd studied in a language he didn't really understand and been handed a degree he didn't really deserve. The Soviets added his name to the roster of Asian communists successfully educated by the great and gloriously enlightened socialist Motherland.

Siri believed a judge should be someone who acquired wisdom layer by layer over a long life, like tree rings of knowledge, believed you couldn't just walk into the position by guessing the right answers to multiple choice tests in Russian.

"Can I go?" Siri stood and walked toward the door without waiting for permission.

Haeng looked at him like he was lower than dirt. "I think we'll need to discuss attitude at our next tutorial. Don't you?"

Siri smiled and resisted making a comment.

"And, Doctor," the coroner stood with his nose to the door, "why do you suppose the Democratic Republic issues quality black shoes to its government officials free of charge?"

Siri looked down at his ragged brown sandals. "To keep Chinese factories open?"

Judge Haeng lowered his head and moved it from side to side in slow motion. It was a gesture he'd learned from older men, and it didn't quite suit him.

"We have left the jungle, Comrade. We have escaped from the caves. We now command respect from the masses, and our attire reflects our standing in the new society. Civilized people wear shoes. Our comrades expect it of us. Do you understand what I'm telling you?" He was speaking slowly now, like a nurse to a senile patient.

Siri turned back to him with no sign that he'd been humiliated. "I believe I do, Comrade. But I think if the proletariat are going to kiss my feet, the least I can do is give them a few toes to wrap their lips around."

He yanked open the sticky door and left.

Siri walked home through the dusty Vientiane streets at the end of a long Friday. He usually kept a cheery smile on his face for anyone who wanted it. But he'd noticed that fewer people returned it these days. The merchants along his route who knew him always had a friendly comment, but strangers were starting to misread his expression. *What does he know, this little man? What does he have to smile about?*

He passed government women at the end of their day jobs. They wore khaki blouses and traditional black *phasin* that hung stiffly to their ankles. Each managed to make her uniform unique in some way: a brooch, a different collar, a fold in the skirt that was their own.

He passed schoolchildren in scrubbed white shirts and itchy red scarves. They seemed baffled by their day, too confused to giggle or mess around. Siri felt the same.

He passed dark, half-empty shops that all seemed to sell the same things. He passed the fountain whose spouts had become cave dwellings for insects, and unfinished buildings whose bamboo scaffolding was green with ivy.

It took him twenty minutes to walk home: just enough time to get the annoying image of Judge Haeng out of his mind. Siri was staying in an old French two-story house with a small front garden crammed with vegetables. The building needed just about everything: paint, mortar, uncracked glass, tiles, you name it; but it wasn't likely to get any of them for some time.

As was its way, Saloop lurched out from the cabbages like a crocodile and, even in semi-consciousness, started to howl at Siri. The dog had howled at him and him alone for the entire ten months he'd been there. Nobody could explain what motivated the slovenly creature to pick on the doctor as it did, but there were things going on in that dog's mind that no human could fathom.

As it did every day, Saloop's eerie wail inspired a chorus of barks and howls the length of the street and beyond and, as usual, Siri creaked open the front door to the accompaniment of dogs. He could never sneak home unnoticed. Even the staircase betrayed him. Under his footsteps, its groans echoed in the bare hallway and the loose floorboards announced his arrival on the balcony.

Neither the front door nor the door to his room was locked. There was no need. Crime had stopped. His apartment was at the rear overlooking the little Hay Sok temple. He reversed out of his sandals and stepped inside. There was a desk with books waiting for him at the window. A thin mattress was rolled up against one wall under the skirt of a mosquito net. Three peeling vinyl chairs gathered around a tin coffee table, and a small stained sink perched on a thick metal pipe.

The bathroom downstairs was shared with two couples, three kids, and a lady who was the acting head of the teacher training division at the Department of Education. Such were the spoils of a communist victory. But as conditions were no worse than before, nobody complained. He lit the gas on the one-ring range and boiled his kettle of water for coffee. In a way it felt good to be home.

But this was to be a weekend of strange awakenings. On Friday night he sat at his desk reading by oil lamp until the fussing of the moths got too much for him. His bedroll was placed so he could see the moon emerging from behind one cloud, and the next, and the next, until he was hypnotized into a peaceful sleep.

Siri's dream world had always been bizarre. In his childhood, the images that lurked there constantly interrupted his sleep. The sane woman who raised him would come to his bed and remind him that these were *his* dreams inside *his* head, and nobody had more right to be in there than he. He learned how to walk tall through his nightmares and not to be afraid of what happened there.

Although he stopped being scared, he never did gain control of them. He couldn't keep out unwanted visitors, for one thing. There were a lot of strangers loitering in his dreams with little or no intention of entertaining him. They lurked, laid about, idled, as if Siri's head was a waiting room. He often felt as if his was just a backstage to someone else's dreams.

But the most peculiar visitors to his subconscious were the dead. Since that first mortality, the first bullet-ridden man to die on his operating table, all those who'd passed from here to there in front of him had taken the trouble to pay him a visit.

When he was a young doctor, he'd wondered whether he was being punished for not saving them. None of his colleagues shared these hauntings, and a psychologist he once worked with in Vietnam suggested they were merely manifestations of his own guilt. All doctors wonder whether they could have done more for their patients. In Siri's case, the learned man believed, these doubts came in visual form. Siri was calmed by the fact that in the dreams the departed didn't seem to blame him; they were just bystanders, watching events with him. He was never threatened by them. The psychologist assured him this was a good sign.

Since Siri had started working as a coroner, coming into contact with the bodies of people he hadn't known when alive, these visitations had become more profound. He was somehow able to know the feelings and personalities of the departed. It didn't seem to matter how long it had been since life had drained from the body; his dream world could spiritually reassemble the person. He could have conversations with the completed whole, and get a feeling of the essence of what that person had been in real life.

Of course, Siri hadn't been able to mention these reconstructions to his friends or colleagues. He didn't see it would be to anyone's advantage to admit that he turned into a raving lunatic after dark. His condition did no harm, and it did encourage him to show more respect to cadavers, once he knew the former owners would be back.

With such mysteries going on in Siri's sleep, it was hardly surprising he often awoke confused. On this particular Saturday morning, he found himself in one of those neither-one-nor-the-other dimensions. He was aware he was in his room and that two of his fingers had been bitten by midges. He heard the dripping of the tap. He could smell the smoke of leaves burning in the temple yard. But he was still dreaming.

On one of the vinyl chairs there was a man. The morning light filtered through the cloth curtain immediately behind his head. From inside the mosquito net, Siri couldn't make out his face, but there was no mistaking who he was. He had no shirt and his frail torso was blue with old tattooed mantras. He wore a checkered loincloth, below which two leg stubs rested on the seat. The congealed blood matched the vinyl.

"How are you feeling?" Siri asked him. It was an odd question to pose to a dead man, but this was a dream after all. He became aware of the high-pitched howling of the dogs from the lane out front. All the signs of consciousness were gathering, but the longboat man still refused to leave.

He was sitting, looking back at Siri with a toothless smile smeared across the bottom of his face. Then he glanced away and pointed his long bony finger in front of him. Siri had to sit up against his pillow to see. On the tin coffee table there was a bottle of Mekhong whisky. At least it was a Mekhong bottle, but it contained something darker and denser than it should have. It could have been blood, but that was just Siri's morbid fancy at work.

He lay back on his pillow and wondered how much more aware of his environment he needed to be before the old man would leave. Then the curtain fluttered slightly and more temple smoke puffed in on the breeze. And in the second he was distracted, a doubt was cast. The fisherman's head could have been a fold in the curtain, his body the indentation made by countless backs that had slumped in the chair before him.

As if some conductor had swiped his baton through the air, the dog chorus fell silent and Siri was left with the dripping of the tap. There was no doubt now that he was awake. He marveled again at the magic of dreams, *his* dreams, and chuckled to think that one of his inmates might have been trying to escape.

Suddenly refreshed, and mysteriously elated, he pulled back his mosquito net and got up. He saw the midge that had been trapped inside with him and feasted gloriously on his finger's blood. It flew to the window and out to boast of its coup.

Siri put on the kettle, drew the ill-fitting curtain, and carried his small transistor radio to the coffee table. It was a sin, but one he delighted in.

Lao radio broadcasts boomed from public address speakers all over the city from five A.M. on. Some lucky citizens had the honor of being blasted from their beds by statistics of the People's National Rice Harvest coming directly through their window. Others' houses vibrated to reminders that salt borders would keep slugs off their vegetables.

But Siri was in a blissful black hole, far enough from the PA's for their messages to be no more than a distant hum. He listened instead to his beloved transistor. By keeping the volume down, he could tune into world news on the Thai military channel. The world had receded somewhat on Lao radio recently.

Naturally, Thai radio and television were banned in the People's Democratic Republic. You wouldn't be arrested for listening, but your District Security Council member would knock loudly on your door and shout for all the neighbors to hear, "Comrade, don't you realize that listening to decadent foreign propaganda will only distort your mind? Aren't we all content here with what we have? Why do we need to give satisfaction to the capitalist pigs by listening to their pollution?"

Your name would be added to a list of grade-four subversives and, theoretically, your co-workers would cease to have complete trust in you. But as far as Siri was concerned, the edict only succeeded in depriving the Lao people of some jolly entertainment.

The Thais were devastated that evil communists had moved in next door, in Laos. Their paranoid military could never be accused of subtlety. Siri loved to listen to their broadcasts. He honestly believed that if the politburo allowed free access to Thai radio, people would decide for themselves which regime they'd prefer to live under.

He'd listened to "expert" commentaries on the Reds' inborn taste for wife-sharing, an infirmity that caused such confusion in their society that "incest was inevitable." How communism had led to a dramatic increase in two-headed births he was uncertain, but Thai radio had the figures to prove it.

Saturday morning was his favorite because they assumed the Lao would be gathered by their radios on the weekend, desperate for propaganda. But today Siri was distracted. He didn't even get around to turning on the radio. He brought his thick brown Vietnamese coffee to the table, sat in his favorite chair, and inhaled the delicious aroma. It smelled a lot better than it tasted.

* * *

He was about to take a sip when the light from the window reflected from something in front of him on the surface of the tin coffeetable. It was a circle of water, the kind you get from a damp glass. This was nothing incredible, except that he hadn't put anything on the table that morning. His cup was dry and it hadn't left his hand. And in Vientiane's climate, this moisture could not have been left over from the previous evening.

He drank some coffee and looked at the ring of water calmly, waiting for an answer to come to his mind. He looked up at the chair where the morning shadows had played tricks on him, then back at the table. If he wanted to be perverse, he could remark that the ring was in the spot where the longboat man's whisky bottle had sat. He turned to the shelf on the wall behind him and ripped a sheet of paper from the roll there.

But when he turned back to the table there was no ring of water.

His second strange awakening that weekend wasn't so occult. Miss Vong from the Department of Education had a habit of not knocking on the door until after she'd walked through it. She'd often caught Siri putting things on or taking things off, but she always looked at him as if it was his fault. If he'd done the same at her apartment, he'd be facing a court summons for certain.

But on this Sunday morning, he was still fast asleep when she arrived, so he knew it had to be early. The scent of temple incense had already filled the room, but the roosters were still dreaming of magical flights over mountains and lakes.

"Come on, sleepy. Time to get up."

As she had no children of her own, this annoying woman had taken to mothering everybody. She went to the single curtain and yanked it open. The light didn't stream in, it oozed. It was an early hour indeed. She stood by the window with her hands on her hips. "We have an irrigation canal to dig."

His mind groaned. What had happened to weekends, to free
time, to days off? His Saturday mornings at work invariably
became days, and here they were, stealing his Sunday too. He
pried open one eye.

Miss Vong was dressed in corduroy working trousers and a
sensible long-sleeved shirt buttoned at neck and wrist. She wore
her thinning hair in pigtails and reminded Siri of the Chinese
peasant eternalized in Mao posters. Chinese propaganda
skimped on facial features, as nature had done with Miss Vong.
She was somewhere between thirty and sixty, with the build of
an underfed teenaged boy.

"What torture is this? Leave me alone."

"I will not. You deliberately missed the community painting
of the youth center last month. I'm certainly not going to let
you miss out on the chance to dig the overflow canal."

Community service in the city of Vientiane wasn't a punishment; it was a reward for being a good citizen. It was the
authorities' gift to the people. They didn't want a single man,
woman, or child to miss out on the heart-swelling pride that
comes from resurfacing a road or dredging a stream. The government knew the people would gladly give up their only day
off for such a treat.

"I've got a cold," he said, pulling the sheet over his head.
He heard the tinkle of water filling a kettle and the pop of the
gas range. He felt the tickle and heard the rustle of his mosquito net being tethered to the hook on the wall. He heard the
swish of a straw brush across his floor.

"That's why I'm fixing you a nutritious cup of tea with a
twist of—"

"I hate tea."

"No, you don't."

He laughed. "I thought after seventy-two years, I might know
what I hate and what I don't."

"You need to build up your strength for the digging."

"What happened to all the prison inmates? They used to do all this. Dig ditches, unplug sewers."

"Dr. Siri, I'm surprised at you. Sometimes I wonder if you really did fight for the revolution. There's no longer any excuse for the uneducated and ignorant to be doing all our dirty work. We're all perfectly capable of lifting a hoe and swinging an ax."

". . . and dissecting a cancerous liver," he mumbled under the cover.

"All our ill-advised criminal types are undergoing re-education at the islands. You know that. Now. Are you getting up, or do I have to drag you out of there?"

He decided to punish her for her unsolicited familiarity.

"No. I'll get up. But I have to warn you, I'm naked and I have a morning erection. It's nothing sexual, you'll understand. It's a result of pressure on the . . ."

There was a slight click and the battering of loose boards on the veranda. He peeled down the sheet and looked triumphantly around the empty room.

When he went downstairs, he found two trucks loaded with drowsy silent neighbors, obviously overcome with delight. Area 29C was providing the labor for irrigation canal section 189. It would take the better part of the day, but a sticky rice, salt fish, and *tamnin* ivy lunch would be provided absolutely free.

He shook off Saloop's lethargic charge and climbed onto the rear truck. He'd spotted Miss Vong on the front one, lecturing the young couple from the room opposite his. He nodded and joked with his neighbors as the convoy set off. They nodded and joked back. But none of these good moods could be described as sincere.

Despite having joined the Communist Party for entirely inappropriate reasons, Siri had been a paid-up member for forty-seven years. If the truth were to be told, he was a heathen of a communist. He'd come to believe two conflicting ideas with equal conviction: that communism was the only way man could be truly content; and that man, given his selfish ways, could never practice communism with any success. The natural product of these two views was that man could never be content. History, with its procession of disgruntled political idealists, tended to prove him right.

After clawing his way through a French education system dense and overgrown with restrictions against the poor, he had finally proved that a country boy could make something of himself. He found a rare, benevolent French sponsor, who sent him to Paris. There he became a competent but not brilliant medical student. France wasn't renowned for making life easier for those poor souls born outside its borders. It was every *homme* for himself.

But Siri was used to struggling. In his first two years at Ancienne, without distractions, he was in the top thirty percent of his class. His tutors agreed he had great promise, "for an Asian." But like many a good man before him, he soon discovered that all the potential in the world was no match for a nice pair of breasts. He found himself in third-year pathology concentrating not on the huge blackboard crammed with its neat diagrams, but on the slow-breathing sweater of Boua. She was a red-faced Lao nursing student who sat by the window whatever the weather. He could generally tell from the sweater just how cold it was outside. In the summer, it became a slow-breathing blouse with more buttons undone than was absolutely necessary. He barely scraped through pathology and plummeted into the bottom twenty-percent bracket overall.

By the fourth year, he and Boua were engaged and sharing a room so small, the bed had been sawn short so the door could open. She was a healthy, well-curved girl from Laos's ancient royal capital of Luang Prabang. Her family was blue-blooded Royalist from generations back. But while her parents knelt and bowed at the feet of the passing king and tossed orchid petals before him, she was in her room plotting his demise.

She had learned of the French Communist Party from her first lover, a skinny young tutor from Lyons. At the first opportunity, she set off for her Mecca. Whereas Siri had come to Paris to become a doctor, Boua was studying nursing as a pretext: she was actually in Paris to become the best communist she could be, in order to return to elevate the downtrodden masses in her homeland.

She made it clear to Siri that if he wanted her hand, he had to embrace the red flag also. He did want her hand, and the rest of her, and considered four evenings a week, the odd Sunday, and five francs a month, cheap at half the price. At first, the thought of attending meetings that espoused the fall of the great capitalist empire made him uneasy. He was quite fond of the music of capitalism and fully expected to dance to it as soon as the chance presented itself. He'd been poor all his life, a state he was hoping to recover from as a doctor. But guilt at having such thoughts eventually overtook him.

So it was that communism and Boua conspired to damage his hopes and dreams. By embracing his fiancée and her red flag, he was slowly tearing himself from the grasp of medicine. In order to pass his fifth year, he had to take several make-up exams. By the time he reached his practicum, he had two black stars on the front of his personal file. They indicated that the student therein had to be an exceptional intern if he didn't want to be loaded on an early Aéropostale flight and forfeit his sponsor's fees.

Fortunately, Siri was a natural doctor. The patients adored him, and the staff at the Hôtel Dieu Hospital thought so highly of him that the administration asked him to consider staying on in France and working there full-time. But his heart was with Boua, and when she returned to further The Cause in her homeland, he was at her side.

*   *   *

On Monday, Siri walked down to the Mekhong River and stood for a while. The rains had held on stubbornly that year, but he was sure they were now gone for another five months. It was a brisk November morning and the sun hadn't yet found the strength to dry the grasses on the bank. He let the cool dew soak his feet and wondered how long the Party's shiny vinyl shoes would survive the next rains.

He walked reluctantly along the embankment and kicked up scents from the Crow Shit blossoms that grew there. On the far bank, Thailand stared rudely back at him, its boats floating close to its waterfront. The river that was once a channel between two countries had become a barrier.

In front of Mahosot Hospital, he sat on a wobbly stool beside the road and ate stale *foi* noodles purchased from a cart. Nothing really tasted fresh anymore. But with all the diseases he'd been exposed to over the years, it wouldn't make a bit of difference to his health. He could probably inject himself with salmonella and it would pass straight through him.

With no other excuses to delay his arrival at work, he walked between the shoebox buildings toward his office. The hospital had been put together without style or grace by the French and was basically a village of concrete bunkers. He hesitated in front of his own building before stepping inside. The sign over the door said MORGUE in French. The mat beneath it, his own personal touch, said WELCOME in English.

Only two of the rooms in the blockhouse had natural light. One of these was his office. He shared it with his staff of two, a staff that Judge Haeng rudely referred to as one and a half.

"Good morning, Comrades." He walked into the gray cement room and went over to his desk.

Dtui looked up from her Thai fan magazine.

"Good health, doctor." She was a solid young nurse with a well-washed but rather craggy face and a happy mouth. Her first reaction to everything was to smile, and goodness knows, she didn't have a lot to smile about.

"I doubt whether the Department of Information and Culture would be happy to see you reading such bourgeois perversions."

She grinned at the doctor's comment. "I'm just reminding myself how repulsive the capitalist system can be, Comrade." She held up a badly registered three-color print of a television star wearing a miniskirt. "I mean, can you see me in something like that?"

Siri smiled to himself and raised his eyebrows. A rocking man in the corner of the office attracted his attention. "Ah, good morning, Mr. Geung."

The rocking man smiled when he heard his name and looked up. "Good morning, Dr. Comrade. It's . . . it's going to be a hot one." He nodded his agreement with his own comment.

"Yes, Mr. Geung. I believe you're correct. Do we have any customers today?"

Geung laughed as he always did at Siri's permanent joke. "No customers today, Dr. Comrade."

This was it. This was the team he'd inherited, the job he didn't want, the life he didn't expect to be leading. For almost a year, he'd been the country's head and only coroner. He was the first to confess to his lack of qualifications and his absence of enthusiasm for the job.

The first month of his on-the-job training had been ridiculous. The only Lao doctor with a background in performing autopsies had crossed the river, allegedly in a rubber inner tube, long before Siri's arrival. So, apart from Mr. Geung, who had acquired a massive but well-concealed body of information as that doctor's assistant, there was nobody to teach Siri how to do his new job.

So, once he'd agreed to postpone his retirement, he set about learning his trade from a couple of slightly charred French textbooks. He brought an old music stand from the abandoned American school and used it to hold the books open while he cut and sliced away at his first cases. With one eye on the music stand, he performed like a concert coroner playing away on the innards of the corpses. "Turn," he would say, and Dtui turned the page. He worked through the numbers as recommended by French pathologists of 1948.

He'd performed a good deal of battlefield surgery over the years, but maintenance of the living was a very different science to the investigation of the departed. There were procedures that needed to be followed, observations that needed to be made. He hadn't expected, at seventy-two, to be learning a new career. When he had arrived in Vientiane for the first time with the victorious Pathet Lao on November 23, 1975, there had been something far more pleasurable on his mind.

After the landmark party conference of December 5th, the mood had been higher than a rocket. The celebrations were awash in vat after vat of freshly made Lao rice spirits. Cheeks were bruised from manly kisses.

The crown prince, somber from suit to countenance, had read aloud his father's notice of abdication and, naturally, declined an invitation to join the festivities. The Pathet Lao, after decades of cave-based insurgency, had become the rulers of Laos. The kingdom was now a republic. It was a dream many of the old soldiers, in their heart of hearts, had believed would never come true.

In the spirit of jungle fighters, they moved the trestle tables out of the banquet room and put down straw mats. There they sat in circles relishing their victory. Food and drink were replenished throughout the evening by pretty young cadres in thick lipstick and green uniforms.

Siri figured he'd probably spent more of his life cross-legged on the ground than he had in chairs. He, too, was in a buoyant mood that day, if not for the same reasons as his comrades. He would have returned to his guest house and slept the sleep of the victors if it hadn't been for Senior Comrade Kham.

The tall, gaunt senior party member took advantage of a vacant spot in the circle beside Siri and sat himself down.

"So, Comrade Siri, we've actually done it."

"So it would seem." Siri was unused to rice whisky in such volume, and he wasn't completely in control of his mouth or the tongue inside it. "But I have the feeling we're here to celebrate the end of something rather than the beginning."

"Marx tells us that all beginnings are difficult."

"Nothing you or Marx have ever known could prepare you for the problems you've got coming. But, hell, Kham, you certainly shut the doubters up." He raised his glass and chinked it against Kham's, but quaffed alone. The comrade's eyes were couched deep in their sockets, like snakes looking out at the world.

"You say 'you' as if you don't plan to be helping us with our problems."

Siri laughed. "Comrade Kham, I'm almost as old as the century. I'm tired. I think I've earned my small garden and my slow coffee mornings, afternoons of reading for pleasure, and early nights with a sweet cognac to ease me into sleep." Kham raised his glass to the Prime Minister who sat red-faced and blissfully happy in a far circle. They both drained their glasses and called for another.

"That's odd. As I recall, you don't have any family living. How exactly were you planning to support this decadent lifestyle?"

"I assumed that forty-six years of membership of the party would entitle me . . ."

"To a pension?" Kham laughed rudely.

"Why not?"

Siri always believed, always assumed, that if ever the struggle was won, he would retire. It had been his dream on damp nights in the forests of the north. It was his prayer over the body of every young boy or girl he'd failed to pull back from death. He'd believed for so long that it would happen, he took it for granted that everyone else knew it too.

Kham continued to ridicule his plan. "My old friend, I would have expected you to know better after forty-six years. Socialism means contributing for as long as you still have something to give. When you start to forget where your mouth is and dribble egg down your shirt, when you need to pack towels into your underpants to keep yourself dry, *that's* when the State will show its gratitude. Communism looks after its infirm.

"But look at you. You're still in sparkling health. You have a sharp mind. 'From each according to his abilities, to each according to his needs.' How selfish it would be to deny your services to the country you've striven to free from tyranny."

Siri looked across to the high circle. The President, a reformed member of the royal family, had a sweet, mascara'd soldier on either side of him and had begun to sing them a revolutionary Vietnamese song. He became the focus of attention and conversations hushed around the room. The song finished halfway through the second verse when he forgot the words and the comrades erupted into cheers and applause. A small orchestra of bamboo and wood instruments started up on the stage and the conversations continued in a more dignified manner. Siri hadn't yet been able to shed his disappointment. He waited for Kham to finish a heated conversation to his right and engaged him with more force than the man was used to.

"I take it my situation has already been discussed by the politburo."

"It has. You've impressed us all with your quiet dedication over the years."

"Quiet," Siri took to mean "passive." Over the past ten years, he'd ceased to display the revolutionary passion expected of him and had been shunted off to Party Guest House Number Three, away from all the policy-making and decision-taking in Sam Neua. There he tended to damaged cadres returning from the battlefields and lost touch with the zealous comrades and their politics.

Kham eased his haunches against Siri's and put his arm around him. The doctor was himself a very tactile character but this gesture, in this situation, he considered disrespectful.

"We have allotted you a role of great responsibility."

The words left Kham as a reward but hit Siri like a splintery wooden club across the face. He needed responsibility like he needed another head.

"Why?"

"Because you are the best man we have for the job."

"I've never been the best man for any job, ever."

"Don't be so modest. You're an experienced surgeon. You have an inquisitive mind and you don't take things at face value. We've decided to make you the Republic's chief police coroner." He looked into Siri's green eyes for a hint of pride, but saw only bewilderment. He might as well have told him he was to be the Republic's new balloon bender or unicyclist.

"I've never done an autopsy in my life."

"Ah. It's all the same. Putting them together: taking them apart."

"It certainly is not."

He didn't say this with any aggression but Kham was still

taken aback to be contradicted so brazenly. The senior party members had become used to a level of respect. Siri, although always calm and soft-spoken, had a habit of telling them when they were wrong. That was another reason for his removal to the jungle.

"I beg your pardon?"

"I wouldn't even know where to start. Of course I can't do it. It's a huge job. What do you think I am?"

Even with the glow of whisky still shining from his snake eyes, Comrade Kham was obviously disturbed by Siri's lack of gratitude. He tightened his grip around the old man's shoulders and barked into his ear.

"I think you are a cog in this great revisionist machine which now powers our beloved country. You are a cog just as I am a cog and The President is a cog. Each cog can help our machine run smoothly. But by the same token, one broken cog can jam and stop the works completely. At this important time in our creation, we need all our cogs meshing and coordinated. Don't let us down. Don't stop the machine, Siri."

He gave one last painful squeeze, nodded, and went off to insert himself into another circle. Siri, in a daze, looked around him at the revisionist mechanics. Lubricated by the alcohol, the wheels had already become misshapen. At one point, two wheels had buckled together into a figure-of-eight. There were big important cogs and little insignificant ones, some of whom had gone off to the toilet and not returned. This left large gaps in their wheels. Others were huddled together in small sub-wheels ignoring the big machine altogether.

Siri, suddenly depressed, explained to his wheel that he had to go pee. He staggered in that direction, but walked past the toilet and through the town hall entrance. Guards on either side of the door raised their rifles in salute. He saluted back and yanked his black necktie off. He walked to one of the boy guards and hooked it over the shiny bayonet, where it swung back and forth.

With a grin and thanks, he waved away the drivers of the black second-hand Russian Zil limousines that were waiting to ferry the comrades to their temporary barracks. It was a chilly December morning and there were no stars in the sky, but the way back was a straight line. He walked unsteadily along a deserted Lan Xang Avenue. Ahead of him was the Presidential Palace and a future he didn't much want.

Comrade Kham's Wife

E ven when times were at their hardest in Vientiane, the old stone kiln near the mosque still fired up at three every morning to produce the best bread to be had in the country. Three bare-chested men stoked the wood fire and kneaded the dough into long fingers and laid them out in rows on rusting black metal trays. There was nothing hygienic about it. But there were those who argued it was the dust, soot, sweat, and rust that made Auntie Lah's baguettes the sweetest in Vientiane. Her three sons pulled the sizzling loaves from the kiln with their hands wrapped in old grey towels and put them directly onto her cart.

At six every morning, Auntie Lah wheeled her sweet-smelling bread to the corner by the black stupa. By seven thirty she'd usually sold the lot and returned to the shop for a new batch. These she carted to the corner of Sethathirat and Nong Bon streets, where most of the government departments were. By this time, the baguette trolley had become a customized sandwich deli. Government officials on their way to work could order from the menu of "condensed milk, sardine, or salted buffalo meat," which she lovingly prepared and garnished for them while they waited.

But there was always one sandwich with extras, wrapped in greaseproof paper, waiting for her very special customer to collect every day. Siri never had to order his fancy. He just ate whatever Auntie Lah felt like making for him. It was always different and always delicious. He paid her at the end of each week, and she never asked for more than her standard rate.

When Siri was too busy to come out himself, he sent Dtui, who swore she could feel the old lady's disappointment even before she crossed the road.

"Don't be ridiculous."

"I can. She's got a crush on you." At least seven of Siri's eight pints of blood rushed to his face. Dtui chuckled and handed him his lunch.

"People our age don't . . . well, we just don't."

"Fall in love?"

"Certainly not."

"Rot."

"I beg your pardon?"

"Somchai Asanajinda says as long as your heart can still beat for one, it can always beat for two."

"Then Somchai Asanajinda obviously isn't a doctor."

"Didn't they let you people watch any films up there in the caves? He's probably the most famous Thai film star there is."

"Oh yes? How does a country without any famous films get to have its own famous film star?"

"They have famous films. At least they're famous in Thailand. They make some lovely films."

"All shoot-'em-up violence and cheap romance."

"There. I knew you secretly watched them. Somchai's like this really old person, but he still talks about love and romance."

"What is he, forty?"

"Over fifty."

"Goodness. How do they keep them alive over there?"

"And there's nothing cheap about romance. There isn't enough money in the world to buy love."

Siri looked up from his misspelled report. Dtui was standing with her back to him, looking up through the two remaining slats of the window. Although it was hard to judge from her back, she seemed upset. As far as he knew, she'd never been with a man. Her high standards pretty much eliminated her from the market.

The romance she sought wasn't to be had here in the morgue. It wasn't to be found in the single room she shared with her sick mother, and probably it wasn't in Laos at all. Men were two-dimensional creatures with specific three-dimensional tastes.

There had been eras when large torsos were in high fashion, a symbol of wealth and plenty. Physiology went through cycles. But in the twentieth century, malnutrition was à la mode. Dtui with her laundry-bin build was off the scale. There were no suitors queuing at her door. They wouldn't have to dig deep to find her kindness and humor, but they didn't even bring a spade.

When his report was redone, Siri took his sandwich, some bananas, and a flask of tea down to the river bank. Comrade Civilai was already sitting there on their log, sawing at his own homemade baguette with a blunt penknife. Siri laughed and sat beside him. Civilai sniffed at the air.

"Hmm. What do I smell here? Rotting pancreas? Gangrenous kidney?"

"If you do, they're your own, you old fool. I haven't so much as unbuttoned a cadaverous jacket all morning."

"Ah, what a life." Civilai was still hacking at the stale bread. "Is that what the People's Revolutionary Party pays you for? Sitting around? Flirting with your nurse? Teaching Igor to clap with both hands at the same time? Shit." A chunk of sandwich sprang off his lap and rolled down the dusty bank. He re-wrapped the rest of his meal in its newspaper and gave chase.

When the rains returned in the new year, the water would rise to just a few meters from their log. But it was now some thirty meters to the river's edge, and every foot of dry riverbed had been reclaimed as garden allotments. This was good vegetable-growing dirt.

Civilai began the climb back to their perch, rescuing his crust as he came. He had several lettuce leafs in his top pocket. He was dusty and sweating and hard-pressed for breath.

"I don't know why you don't just eat it in one lump like normal people," Siri said.

Civilai grunted back. "Because," he huffed, "I am a man of breeding." He blew the red clay from his sandwich. "Because I don't want to be caught biting chunks off a log of bread like some caveman. And because my mouth isn't nearly as large as yours." Having made his point, he nibbled politely at the bread.

Civilai was Siri's closest friend in the politburo, and that was probably due to the fact that he, too, was a little mad. But whereas Siri was passively-rebellious mad, Civilai was downright-brilliant mad. He was inspired and eccentric. He'd been the architect of most of the Party's more adventurous ideas.

He was, however, just a little too fast for the plodding socialist system around him. He reminded Siri of a lively dog he'd seen being taken for a walk by a French lady with the gout. The dog ran back and forth panting and drooling, skipping and tugging at the leash, but nothing it did could make that lady walk faster or change direction. Civilai bore more than his fair share of frustration.

He was a bony little man who wouldn't have looked out of place pedaling a *samlor* bicycle taxi. His head had dispensed with the need for hair long ago, and he wore large rimmed glasses that made him look like a big-eyed cricket. He had been born two days before Siri, and thus was barely deserving of the title *ai*, older brother.

"Your mouth could be every bit as big as mine, Ai, if you just used it a little more often."

"Oh, god. Here he goes again."

"I'm ill. I don't think I've got long." He ripped off the end of his baguette with his teeth and spoke through the bread. "I mean, it's only common sense. When the old papaya tree stops bearing tasty fruit, you plant new shoots. You don't wait for it to die first. The party sends off six students to Eastern Europe every three months for medical training. All you need is for one, just one, of those to specialize in postmortem work."

"I'm not the representative for medical services," Civilai shot back.

"No, but you're a big nob. All you have to do is say so, and they'll do it." He took a swig of his tea and handed the flask to Civilai. "I don't want to be cutting up bodies till the day I become one of them. I need this. I need to know when I can expect a replacement. When I can stop. God knows, I could keel over any second. What would you do then?"

"Eat the rest of your sandwich."

"What's the point of pretending to be friendly with a polit-buro member if I can't expect a little help from time to time?"

"Can't you just start, you know, making mistakes?"

"What?"

"As long as they're happy with you, they'll keep you on. If you started to—I don't know—confuse body parts, they might see a more urgent need to replace you."

"Confuse body parts?"

"Yes. Send your judge friend a photograph of a brain and tell him it's a liver."

"He wouldn't know. He's got a liver where his brain should be." They laughed.

"I hope you aren't insulting the judiciary. I could report you for that."

"I've got nothing against the judiciary."

"Good."

"Just the arse that's representing it. How was your weekend?"

"Sensational. Spent both days up in Van Viang at a political seminar. You?"

"Dug a ditch."

"How was it?"

"Sensational. My block won first prize in the 'Uplifting Work Songs' competition."

"Well done. What did you win?"

"A hoe."

"Just the one?"

"We get it for a week each, alphabetically. What's the big news of the month up on the roundabout?"

"Big news? We made it to the top of a world list last week."

"Lowest crime?"

"Highest inflation."

"In the world? Wow. We should have a party or something."

"Then there's the ongoing puppet scandal."

"Tell me."

"The Party ordered the puppets at Xiang Thong temple in Luang Prabang to stop using royal language, and said they had to start calling each other 'comrade.'"

"Quite right, too. We have to show those puppets who's pulling the strings." Civilai hit him with a lettuce leaf. "What happened?"

"Puppets refused."

"Subversive bastards."

"The local party members locked them up in their box, and they aren't allowed out till they succumb."

"That'll teach 'em."

They stretched out their lunch for as long as possible before walking across to the hospital with their arms locked together like drunks. At the concrete gate posts, Civilai reminded Siri he was off to the south for a week and he should reserve the log for the following Monday. They said their farewells, and Siri turned up the driveway.

Before he'd gone five meters, he saw Geung loping toward him. The morgue assistant put on his brakes barely two centimeters from Siri's face. He was excited, and excitement tended to back up his words inside his mouth. He opened it to speak, but nothing came out. He turned blue.

Siri took a step back, put his hands on Geung's shoulders, and massaged them strongly. "Take a few breaths, Mr. Geung. Nothing is important enough to suffocate for." Geung did as he was told.

"Now, what earth-moving event took place while I was at lunch?"

"Comrade Kha . . . Kha . . . Kha . . ."

"Kham?"

"Comrade Kham's . . ."

"Is here?"

". . . 's wife."

"His wife is here." Geung was delighted communication had taken place. He snorted, clapped his palms together, and stamped a foot on the ground. Two country bumpkins were walking past. They stopped to watch Geung's little display. Lao country folk were never too embarrassed to embarrass someone else. One of them turned to the other and said loudly, "A moron."

Geung turned to them sharply. "It takes one to . . . to know one."

Siri was as pleased as the visitors were stunned. He laughed at them, put his arm around Geung, and led him off. "Good for you, Mr. Geung. Who taught you to speak to rude people like that?"

Geung laughed. "You."

They walked on past the administration building with Geung apparently deep in thought. At last he spoke. "But, really I am a . . . a moron."

Siri stopped and turned to him. "Mr. Geung. When are you going to believe me? You aren't. Your dad was wrong. He did-n't understand. What have I told you?"

"I have a . . . a . . ."

"A condition."

"Called Down Syndrome." He recited the rest from one of the endless lists that were stored somewhere in his mind. "In some aspects I am slower than other people, but in others I am superior." They walked on.

"That's right, and one of the aspects you're superior in is remembering things, things you learned a long time ago. In remembering things, you are even superior to me."

Geung grunted with pleasure. "Yes."

"Yes. And another thing you're superior in, is ice water."

"Yes, I am." Since they'd been banned by the director from keeping personal refreshments in the morgue freezer, the nearest refrigerator was in the staff canteen. Geung enjoyed going there to fetch glasses of water for guests, because the girls flirted with him.

"Is Comrade Kham's wife here by herself?"

"Yes."

"Then do you think you could bring her just one glass of ice water? It's a hot day."

"I can do that."

He loped off toward the canteen, and Siri slowed down. He wanted to second-guess Mrs. Nitnoy's purpose for coming here. Her visits invariably spelled trouble, although he couldn't recall doing anything wrong of late. She was a strong, loud woman with a large, menacing chest and hips that rolled at you like tank treads. She was a senior cadre at the Women's Union and carried as much weight politically as she did structurally. Above all else, she was a stickler for rules.

"It has to be the shoes," he thought. Judge Haeng had reported his disobedience, and he'd called in the big gun. She was here to force his feet into sweaty vinyl shoes that would leave him crippled. She'd be sitting at his desk watching the clock to see how late he was getting back from lunch. She'd be superficially jolly and shake his hand and ask after his health, and then humiliate him.

He was feeling sick to his stomach when he walked under the MORGUE sign. He stood at the door to his office and counted to three before confidently striding in. Dtui was alone at her desk reading something she hurriedly stuffed into a drawer.

"Mrs. Nitnoy?"

"In the freezer."

His face went blank and his mind followed. "Wha—?"

"They brought her in just after you left for lunch."

"What happened to her?" He sat heavily on his squeaky chair.

"She died."

"Well, I'd hope so if she's in the freezer. What did she die of?"

She looked up at him and, predictably, smiled. "I'm a nurse. You're a coroner. Isn't that what *you're* supposed to tell *us*?"

"Could you perhaps give me a start? Who brought her in? What did they say?"

"Two drivers from the Women's Union. They said she was sitting having lunch, dribbled a little bit, and keeled over. They checked her pulse and she was dead. The Union doctor told them to bring her here as it was a . . . what do you call it? It was an unnatural death."

Siri was disturbed to find that his first feeling wasn't of compassion for the poor woman, but of relief that he didn't have to wear vinyl shoes. His second feeling was anxiety. This, after ten months, would be his first high-profile case. A lot of senior party people would be looking over his shoulder. He pondered the possible consequences.

"Does Comrade Kham know?"

"He's in Xiang Khouang. They phoned him. He said go ahead with the autopsy. He's flying back this evening."

"I suppose we should get on with it, then." He stood, took a deep breath, and walked through to the examination room. Mr. Geung was already in there, standing in front of the freezer, rocking anxiously, a glass of ice water in one hand, a tissue in the other.

* * *

It was about four thirty by the time all the textbook procedures were completed. She'd been measured, but not weighed because they didn't have a scale. Earlier in the year, they'd experimented with two bathroom scales. Siri and Geung weighed themselves on each, then held up the corpse between them. Due to some obscure law of physics, the body only ever weighed half of what it should have. So they abandoned weighing altogether.

At one point, Siri leaned over the woman's face. He called to Geung.

"Mr. Geung. Your nose is better than mine. What do you smell here?"

Geung didn't need to lean. He'd smelled it already.

"Balm."

"Very good. Let's get the old girl undressed, shall we?"

"And nuts."

"What?"

"Balm and nuts. I . . . I smell nuts."

Siri didn't smell the nuts or know what Geung was talking about, but he got Dtui to note it down anyway.

Once Mrs. Nitnoy's clothes had been inspected and bagged, the body was photographed. The hospital budget allowed one roll of color film per seven bodies, which meant one full-body front, one full-body back, one topical specific to the area of cause. The one or two leftover shots were technically for contentious areas of the anatomy, but often got used up on group photographs of nurses who wanted to send them back to their families in the countryside.

On either side of Mrs. Nitnoy's formidable chest, Dr. Siri made incisions that came together at the base of her sternum and ran down to her pubic bone. Thus the autopsy began.

Everything he did, he explained very slowly, because Dtui had to write it all down in the notebook, and she didn't take shorthand.

Siri used the old bone cutters to get through her rib cage and, one by one, he described, weighed, and labeled the organs, and Dtui jotted down irregularities in her book. Siri then used a fine scalpel to define the scalp, which he pulled forward over poor Mrs. Nitnoy's face. While he began a more detailed inspection of the organs at the examination bench, Mr. Geung set about the cranium.

Although a requisition was in for an electric saw and the hospital board was considering it, in the meantime they had no choice but to use a hacksaw. It was the department's good fortune that sawing was one of Mr. Geung's superior skills. With his tongue poking from the corner of his mouth, he painstakingly and expertly cut deep enough to penetrate the skull, but not so deep as to damage the brain. It was a skill Siri had been unable to master.

The morgue at the end of 1976 was hardly better equipped than the meatworks behind the morning market. For his own butchery, Siri had blunt saws and knives, a bone cutter, and drills inherited from the French. He had his personal collection of more delicate scalpels and other instruments. There were one or two gauges and drips and pipettes and the like, but there was no laboratory. The closest was forty kilometers away, across the border in Udon Thani, and the border was closed to the dreaded communist hordes.

There was an old microscope Siri had requisitioned from the stores at Dong Dok pedagogical institute. If they ever reopened the science department, it would likely be missed. Even though the microscope was an ancient relic of bygone biologists and should have been in a museum, it still magnified beautifully. It was just that the slide photographs in his old textbooks were so blurred, he couldn't always tell what he was looking for.

Most of the results from Siri's morgue relied on archaic color tests: combinations of chemicals or litmus samples. These were more suitable for telling what wasn't, rather than what was. Assuming the necessary chemicals were available at Lycée Vientiane's chemistry department, Siri could usually eliminate fifty possible causes of death, but still be left with a hundred and fifty others.

So it was hardly surprising, when four thirty came around, that he hadn't the foggiest idea what had killed Mrs. Nitnoy. He could give a list as long as your distal tibia of things that hadn't. She hadn't been hit by a train (as there were none in Laos). She hadn't been shot, stabbed, suffocated, or had her limbs severed by an army launch. But as she'd been in a crowded room when she died, these were no great discoveries.

Some witnesses said she'd choked on her food, but the absence of any in her esophagus and the abruptness of her death said otherwise. Without a lab, it was next to impossible to check for poison unless you knew which it was, and as the lady had been eating from a communal table it was quite unlikely she alone would have died.

In the absence of Judge Haeng and his helpful advice, Siri had taken particular pains to establish that she hadn't died from a heart attack. There was no evidence of an occlusion or thrombosis.

He'd read about forensic scientists around the world who reveled in mysteries such as these. He wasn't yet one of them.

Just as Dtui and Geung were leaving for the hospital gardens to do their hour of vegetable tending, the clerk from the director's office came rushing in to tell them that Comrade Kham would be arriving at Wattay Airport at six and they were to wait. Siri told his co-workers he'd stay behind himself and that they should go.

He sat at his desk looking through Dtui's notes. She wrote so small, he considered using the microscope to read them. Instead, he spent the next hour pumping his reading spectacles back and forth in front of his eyes trying to focus on the words. This ultimately gave him a headache and he ended up writing the second half of his report from memory.

It was nine before Senior Comrade Kham turned up, and there was whisky on his breath. His mouth was the only indication of sadness on his face, and it seemed to Siri he was straining to keep a smile inverted.

"I'm so sorry about your loss, Comrade."

"Where is she?"

"In the freezer." Siri stood and gestured for the man to follow him to the examination room.

"Where are you going?"

"I thought you'd want to see the body."

"Heavens no. She's dead, isn't she?"

"Absolutely."

Kham walked past him and sat at Siri's desk, which forced Siri to sit at Dtui's. The Party man thumbed idly through the papers in front of him. "Have you . . . er, cut her open?"

"Mm-hm."

"I'm sorry. You could have made better use of your time. I know what it was that killed her."

"You do? Well, thank God for that. I have no idea."

"I've been warning the silly woman for years it'd kill her. But I suppose if you're addicted, you don't listen to common sense, eh, Siri?"

"What exactly was she addicted to?" He hadn't found any puncture marks on her arms and her liver was pretty as a picture.

"*Lahp.*"

"*Lahp?* Damn." It should have been so obvious, it was embarrassing. As a doctor in the jungle, he'd seen countless deaths as a result of *lahp* or *pa daek* or any of a number of other raw meat or fish concoctions the farmers ate with reckless abandon.

Raw flesh works as a healthful meal only if it's fresh. Bacteria get into it very fast, and the parasites work their way around the body. If you're lucky you may just end up with abscesses, cramps, and chronic diarrhea for the rest of your life.

But there is a strain of more adventurous parasite that lays eggs in the anterior chamber of the eye. From there it either migrates through the retina, or burrows its way into the brain. One minute you're feeling fine and showing no symptoms; the next, you're on a table at the morgue. Siri noticed the comrade was still talking.

". . . eating pork *lahp* since she was a girl. Loved the stuff. It gave her no end of trouble with her guts, but she swore the body eventually built up an immunity to the germs. I detest the stuff, but she couldn't get enough. All our friends could tell you.

"I stopped off at the police department on my way here and told them all about it. There won't be anyone filing an unnatural death certificate for this case."

Siri was still shaking his head. "It was silly of me not to think of it. I didn't imagine a woman like Mrs. Nitnoy eating raw pork."

"Why not? She was just a country girl. You could dress her up but you'd never get the stink of buffalo out of her skin." Siri couldn't really understand why Kham was talking about his wife like this. In generosity he put it down to shock.

"Well, in that case, I'll just do one or two last checks, finish the report, and—"

"Oh, I think you can probably finish the report without disturbing her again. We want to get her cremated as soon as possible. Her family and friends are anxious to give her the last rites. They're waiting for her at the temple."

"But I need to..."

"Siri, my old friend." Kham stood and came over to sit on Dtui's desk, looking down at the doctor. "As a medical man, you're a scientist. But even a man of science needs to show sensitivity to culture and religion. Don't you see?"

This was good, coming from a member of the committee that had removed Buddhism as a state religion and banned the giving of alms to monks.

"I—"

"She's suffered enough indignities for one day. Let her rest in peace, eh?"

"Comrade Kham, I didn't write the law. I can't issue a death certificate until I've confirmed it was parasites that finished her off."

Kham stood and smiled warmly. "I understand that. Of course I do. What kind of a politburo member would I be if I attempted to ignore the regulations?" He walked to the doorway and stood in the frame. "That's why I've decided to have her own surgeon sign the certificate."

"What?"

"I'm so sorry you were troubled today, Comrade Siri. But as there is no suggestion of foul play, there really was no need for an autopsy. I must say, for a man who hates his job so much, you do it quite meticulously. I'm very impressed."

He walked out and left Siri sitting alone at Dtui's desk turning things over in his mind. Kham had known there was to be an autopsy. He'd given the go-ahead over the phone. Now he was saying there was no need. Siri had wasted three hours looking for a cause of death. That time could have been cut in half if he'd known what he was looking for.

He gazed over at his own desk. There was something out of place there. But before he could organize that thought, he was disturbed by a commotion outside. He took one more quick look at his desk before walking out to see what was happening.

He encountered a group of men who were wheeling a hospital trolley that carried a basic but oversized wooden coffin. Kham walked behind them in the shadows.

"You're taking her right this minute?"

The men pushed the coffin past him and into the examination room. Kham followed as far as the alcove. It was dark there.

"The family are all waiting."

Siri looked at the tall man and was overwhelmingly conscious of a dark image some three meters behind him. For some unknown reason it filled him with dread. It wasn't clear, and there wasn't enough light to distinguish features, but its shape reminded him exactly—exactly of Mrs. Nitnoy.

He recalled the longboat man he'd seen in the semiconsciousness of morning. That had been frightening enough. But then he had had sleep as an excuse. Here he was wide awake. This was no dream. He was seeing the outline of a woman who lay dead in the freezer in the far room. She was standing, shaking. She tensed. She readied herself and charged at the comrade's back with all the ferocity of a bull intent on goring him.

She ran at him with her full force, and if she'd been real she would certainly have knocked him off his feet. For a brief second the light from the examination room caught her face. Siri had no doubt it was her, nor did he doubt her look of pure hate. But when her body met her husband's, she vanished.

Comrade Kham shuddered.

"How do you stand this building? The drafts give me goose bumps." He turned to the space behind him at which Siri was still staring. "That the freezer in there?"

Siri's old heart was galloping. He couldn't speak. The best he could manage was to stumble past Kham into the examination room where the pallbearers were waiting patiently. He went to the freezer and with an unsteady hand pulled down the lever that unfastened the door. It opened slowly.

She was still there, still just as dead as she'd been at lunchtime. Siri hadn't really believed he'd find her there. He reached into the freezer and trembled as he pulled back the pale blue sheet that covered the head. The face lay slack across the skull. It didn't wink or give any signs it had been out haunting.

Siri tucked the sheet under Mrs. Nitnoy's body like a shroud to protect her from the rough hands and eyes of the men who had come for her. He pulled out the wheeled platform, stood back and allowed them to take her. Her big feet stuck out like flippers. The men lifted her more gently than they seemed capable of, and lowered her into her box.

"She is all . . . back together, is she?" Kham asked. "We don't want bits of her dropping off on the way home, do we, boys?" The men laughed nervously, more because of who he was than because they saw any humor in what he said. If his insensitivity was to be put down to shock, he must have been deeply disturbed by his wife's death.

But Siri no longer believed this. He looked at Kham, looked directly into his eyes, and the senior comrade turned away, with a hint of embarrassment and something more. Siri didn't speak again. Kham walked outside.

The laborers maintained a respectful verbal silence and tacked the lid on the coffin as quietly as their hammers would allow. They struggled to wheel the comrade's wife back through the door. Due to the extra weight, the wheels yanked the trolley to the right and it crashed into the door frame. The bearers reversed once, but the trolley continued to swerve to the right. It refused to be wheeled out to the yard.

With no small effort, the men were forced to lift the cart and its cargo and carry it through the doorway. Comrade Kham was waiting for them outside, a cheap, fast-burning cigarette between his lips. He had nothing to say either. He walked beside the trolley, frustrated by its zigzag trajectory, and disappeared with it around the end of the building.

Siri stood below the MORGUE sign, his head tilted like a dog listening. But this old dog was paying attention to the debate going on inside his head. He took deep breaths to calm his nerves, but his pulse was still racing.

Half his mind told him to walk away, go home, leave all the doors open, the lights on. Just get out of there and never come back. But the saner half, the scientist half, told him not to be ridiculous. He turned and walked back through the small vestibule and to the examination room.

It was lighted by a flickering fluorescent tube. He stood beneath it in the center of the room and listened. He could make out the moths bouncing against the mosquito netting at the window, and the buzz of the light above. He could hear distant muffled conversations from the hospital and the crowing of a cock rehearsing. But that was all he heard.

A cockroach scurried by his feet and across to the storeroom. There weren't enough disinfectants on the planet to keep a hospital free of roaches in Southeast Asia. Dtui and Geung mopped and scrubbed four times a day and put down poison and sticky traps, but creatures who had survived the freezing of the earth and the meteor were smart enough to survive Siri's morgue.

He followed the creature into the storeroom and switched on the light. A dozen accomplices joined the roach in scurrying for gaps and shadows. Everything in the room was double wrapped or trapped in screwtop jam jars so the vermin had no hope of feasting on the samples that lined the shelves. But the aroma of death pervaded the place and to a cockroach, that was like the scent of jasmine on a warm evening.

The shelves were set out in library rows with only enough space to pass between them sideways. He inserted himself between rows three and four and edged down to the specimen jars. Just above his head, Mrs. Nitnoy's brain hung in a noose of cotton in its own small pond of formalin. The cotton prevented it from becoming misshapen against the bottom of the jar. By the next morning, it still wouldn't be set hard enough to dissect. But perhaps in a few days the comrade's wife would have something to tell them after all.

When Mr. Geung arrived at the morgue on Tuesday morning, Dr. Siri was already at the workbench. The specimen jar was in front of him, empty, and he was about to slice into Mrs. Nitnoy's brain.

"Hel . . . hello, Dr. Comrade."

Siri looked up. "Good morning Mr. Geung."

Geung stood unsteady, staring. "You're here."

"I know I am." Siri understood the problem. Geung was always the first to arrive. He'd never walked in to find the doctor at work this early, and it threw him out of kilter. He needed order and consistency. Despite the illogic of it, Siri asked, as usual, "Any customers today, Mr. Geung?"

Geung laughed and clapped. "No customers today, Doctor." Reoriented, he put his rice basket on his desk and began the morning clean. Siri stooped back to his work.

"Well! Did you lock yourself in the morgue last night?" Dtui was at the door smiling at him.

"It isn't unknown for me to be here early, nurse."

"No. It's not unknown for snow to fall in Vietnam either. But it still makes the front page of the newspaper." She noticed the freezer door open. "She out jogging?"

Siri laughed. "If I'd known you were so funny in the morning, I'd have come early every day. Her husband took her home last night."

"How romantic."

Dtui also went to the office to deposit her lunch on her desk. She bumped into Geung in the doorway.

" 'Good morning, handsome man,'" he prompted.

"Good morning, handsome man," she said.

"Good morning, beautiful woman. Joke?"

"What has two wheels and eats people?"

"Don't know."

"A lion on a bicycle." Geung laughed so enthusiastically, she found herself joining in. Siri in the next room got caught up in the merriment. He felt a sort of fatherly pride that his staff got along so well together. This was obviously a morning ritual he never got to see. He doubted whether Geung got all Dtui's jokes, but he knew he'd still be able to recite them verbatim six months later.

He stared at the brain on the glass tray in front of him. He hadn't given it sufficient time to set properly. It sprawled like a *blancmange*. But he didn't want to wait; for his own peace of mind he had to know. He used his longest scalpel and cut carefully through the brain with one neat slash. He repeated this action several more times until the brain sat in slices like a soggy loaf of bread. He gently separated the sections and used a large magnifying glass to inspect each one.

Dtui, with a surgical mask over her face against the dust, was sweeping in the storeroom.

"Dtui, bring me the camera, will you?"

She looked at him with her brow furrowed. "The camera?"

"Yes, please."

"Well . . ."

"What's wrong?"

"There are only three exposures left on the film."

"That's enough."

"Doctor, Sister Bounlan's wedding party is tonight. I was . . ."

"I sympathize with her. But this is more important. Believe me."

Once he'd saved and labeled the samples, Siri announced he'd be going out for a while. He collected a plastic bag full of liquid, and some vials, and left. He didn't say where he was going.

He walked out of the morgue and past his old crippled motorcycle. It had lain collecting dust and cobwebs in the cycle park for three months. He couldn't afford the new carburetor it needed. He was about to check to see how much money he had on him for the taxi *songtaew* fare when he had an idea. He turned back to the morgue and surprised Dtui reading.

"Dtui."

46   COLIN COTTERILL

"Oh, my God. Don't do that. You scared the life out of me."

"Then don't do things you'd be scared to be caught doing. How did you get here today?"

"Eh? Same as every day. On my bicycle."

"Good. I want to borrow it."

"What for?"

"What for? What do people usually use bicycles for?"

"You aren't going to ride my bike."

"And why not?"

"I'd never be able to forgive myself if you . . . well, you know."

"No, I don't."

"Look, doctor. You aren't a young man."

"Are you suggesting I'm too old to ride a bicycle?"

"No."

"Then what are you saying?"

"That over the age of seventy, the odds of having a heart attack rise forty percent every year."

"God, so I'm already at 120 percent. They aren't good odds."

"Okay. Maybe I got the figures wrong. But I don't want my bicycle to be the cause of your death."

"Dtui. Don't be ridiculous. I swear I won't have a heart attack. Just lend me the bike."

"No."

"Please." His green eyes became moist. That always melted her.

"All right. But on two conditions."

"I'm sure I'll regret this, but what are they?"

"One, that you ride slowly and stop if you feel tired."

"Certainly."

"And two, that you train me to be the new coroner."

"What?"

"Doctor Siri. There you are begging the Health Department to send someone to train in Eastern Europe and not getting anywhere."

"No."

"Whereas here you have a young intelligent nurse, absorbent as blotting paper, enthusiastic as a puppy, resilient as a . . . a . . . brick, already in place, eager to be your apprentice."

"No."

"And then you could say you have this bright girl who already trained as a coroner and she's ready to go to further her education in Bulgaria or some such place."

"No."

"Why not?"

"You aren't the type."

"Because I'm a girl?"

"Because you read comics and fan magazines."

"I need stimulation."

"I can't believe you're even asking. You're a bubblehead. When did you suddenly develop an interest in pathology?"

"I've always been interested. But you don't give me a chance to do interesting things. You treat me like a secretary."

Geung walked in on them with a bucket in one hand and a mop in the other.

"Are you h . . . having a fight?" He smiled.

Siri grabbed the bike key from Dtui's desk. "No. We aren't having a fight. Nurse Dtui is just trying to extort three years of free education and a tour of Europe out of me in return for twenty minutes on her bicycle. That's fair, don't you think?"

Dtui stormed out the door. "Take the damn bike."

Considerably more than twenty minutes later, Siri found himself in front of a small house overlooking the grand yellow stupa. He hadn't ridden a bicycle for thirty years. He should have got off and rested half way up Route That Luang when the air went out of him and his legs began to wobble. But he wanted to show Dtui just how resilient the over seventies could be.

"Hello, Uncle." Teacher Oum stood by the open door and looked at the wheezing old doctor, wondering why he wasn't speaking. She didn't really know what to do to help him get his breath, so she did nothing. She was a scientist, not a nurse.

Oum was a prettily oval teacher at Lycée Vientiane. She was particularly attractive to a man like Siri, who found her worth almost killing himself for, for two reasons. First, she was the last surviving teacher of practical chemistry in the country. Siri was desperate for chemicals, and she had them. If you have the key, the color resulting from the mix of body fluids and chemicals can answer a lot of questions.

Oum had recently returned from Australia, where she'd obtained a degree in chemical engineering and lived with a sexually active Sydney boy named Gary. This left her with a knowledge of chemical compounds unequaled in Laos, a fluent grasp of the English language, and a one-year-old son with red hair.

English was Siri's second attraction to her. He had a handbook from Chiang Mai University that unlocked many of the color-test mysteries. If it had been in Thai or French or even Vietnamese, it would have been invaluable to him in his work. But it was, sadly, in English. The poor doctor could boast a vocabulary of some eleven words in the English language, and those he pronounced so horribly nobody knew what he was saying.

So Siri needed Teacher Oum not only for her chemicals, but also to decipher the text that showed how to use them.

"What's in the bag?"

Siri still had hold of a small plastic bag fastened at the top with rubber bands. His breath and his voice were returning.

"Stomach contents."

"Mmm. Nice. Other people bring soy milk or ice coffee."

"Sorry."

"You had breakfast yet?"

"No."

An hour later, they were at the school. On Tuesdays she didn't teach till ten. By holding on to his arm while he sat on his bike,

she'd been able to drag him alongside her motorcycle. He was
a little stressed from trying to keep his wheels from crashing
into her, or diving into a pothole.

The science lab was poorly equipped. Oum's office was a
walk-in cupboard with shelves reaching to the ceiling, a tiny
workbench, and two stools. The shelves were stacked with hundreds of neat bottles with handwritten labels that boasted they
contained all kinds of sulphates and nitrates. Unfortunately,
most of the boasts were as empty as the bottles. Generous
American donations had long since dried up and the room contained mostly what was available locally. That wasn't much. Oum
had tried to keep a little of everything for old times' sake, but
Siri's visits had seriously depleted her stocks.

Together, they'd submitted proposals through the Foreign
Aid Department, but they knew they were low on the list. There
were shortages of everything. So one Sunday they'd sat down
and painstakingly copied letters in Russian and German, which
they sent off directly to schools and universities in the Soviet
bloc. They'd had no response thus far.

Siri produced the dog-eared Chemical Toxicology lab manual
from his cloth shoulder bag. It was a stapled brown roneo copy
he'd brought back from Chiang Mai. It was only printed on one
side, and his detailed notes from Teacher Oum's translations
filled the blank backs.

"What are we looking for today, uncle?"

"Let's start with cyanide."

"Ooh. Poison." She turned to the cyanide page and looked
down the various tests. "We haven't done poison before. You
don't sound like you're sure."

"You know me, Oum. I've never been that sure of anything.
This is another guess. But there are a couple of clues."

"Tell me." She was pulling down jars from the shelves and
checking to see how much she had left of the various chemicals
she needed.

"Well, first of all, she, the victim, died suddenly without displaying any outward signs of distress. Secondly, her insides were particularly bright red. What are you sniffing that for? They don't spoil, do they?"

"No, I get a little buzz. Want some?"

"No, thanks. Thirdly, my Mr. Geung noticed something strange while we were cutting. He said he smelled nuts."

"Nuts?"

"He couldn't really identify what type of nuts, but my guess is almonds. There aren't that many nuts with distinctive smells."

"Well, surely you and the nurse would have smelled it."

"Not necessarily. A lot of people aren't able to distinguish that particular smell. Some of Mr. Geung's senses are quite well developed. I'm wondering if someone slipped her a pill somehow. The most common one available is cyanide. If I still had the body, there are other signs I could be looking for."

"You lost the body?"

"It was reclaimed by the family."

Oum looked up at him. "That's a coincidence."

"What is?"

"I hear Comrade Kham's wife passed away suddenly yesterday and he went by the morgue and kidnapped the body."

"Really? Where did you hear a thing like that?"

"This is Vientiane, not Paris."

She was right, of course. In Laos, the six-degrees-of-separation rule could easily be downgraded to three, often to two. The population of Laos had dwindled to under three million, and Vientiane didn't contain more than 150,000 of them. The odds of knowing, or knowing of, someone else were pretty good.

"That's true. In Paris you don't have rumor and scandal crawling out of the trash, or up from the drains. If Vientiane folk don't hear anything scandalous for two days, they just make it up to keep the momentum going."

"So, you're telling me the stomach contents you brought to me for breakfast have nothing to do with—"

"Oum, my love. I promise if you don't ask me that question, I won't lie to you."

"Then I won't ask. Let's get on with it. There are three color tests for cyanide in the magic book. I've got the chemicals to do two of them."

Siri pulled two plastic film containers from his bag.

"I have her urine and blood here too, so we'll need to do three samples for each test."

"Yes, sir. You don't have any other bits of the comrade's wife in that bag, do you?"

He looked at her with his angriest and least convincing expression.

"Oum. If I'm right about her, the fewer people who know about it the better. Do you understand what I'm saying?"

"Yeah. I do. Really. Don't worry."

It was lunchtime when Siri returned to the morgue. Auntie Lah had already sold out of baguettes and gone home, but Mr. Geung had kindly picked up the coroner's lunch and left it on his desk. The office was deserted, so Siri went down to the log and sat alone, eating and thinking. He was surprised to hear Geung's voice very close behind him.

"Dtui. She . . . she went home." Siri turned. His lab assistant was leaning over him like a schoolteacher with his finger pointed at Siri's nose.

"Oh, hello, Mr. Geung. Thanks for getting my—"

"You were very bad."

"What?"

"You were very very very bad."

"What did I do?" He felt curiously nervous.

"She isn't . . . isn't . . . isn't a bubblehead. She's a nice girl."

"I—"

"It was very bad to say th . . . th . . . those things to her."

Siri thought back to what he'd said. It hadn't occurred to him anything he said could offend her. He didn't think she was offendable. "Did you say she'd gone home?"

"Yes."

"But she never goes home for lunch. And I had her bicycle."

"She's gone home because she's sad. You made her sad."

"I—"

But Geung was finished. He turned and walked back to the hospital.

"Mr. Geung?"

He didn't look back.

Siri had never been to Dtui's place. It was tucked behind the national stadium in a row of shanties that housed people who'd come down from the north to help rebuild the country. The huts were supposed to be temporary, but no one had yet been rehoused after almost a year. The senior cadres had priority for the new housing that was being built out in the suburbs. The little cogs would have to wait.

As he had no numbers or names to go by, it took him a while to find Dtui's shed. It was latticed banana leaf with gaps at the corners and between the sheets. Lao workmen had a knack for making the temporary look temporary. There was a shared bathroom at one end of the row.

On the floor in the center of the hut's only room, there were two unrolled mattresses with a large woman on each. Dtui was one of them. She was reading a Thai magazine.

"I hope I'm not disturbing you."

Dtui and her mother looked up in surprise to see the doctor at the door, but it was only Dtui who sprang to her feet. She appeared to be devastated that Siri was seeing the conditions she lived in. She didn't say anything at first, perhaps waiting for her boss to complain about her absence from work. But he didn't speak.

"Ma, this is Doctor Siri."

The old lady was lethargic and slow to focus on him. She obviously couldn't move from where she lay. "Good health, Doctor. Sorry I can't get up."

"Ma's got cirrhosis. I told you about it."

"Yes. Good health, Mrs. Vongheuan." It seemed peculiar to be wishing good health to a woman who was clearly not healthy at all. But such was the national greeting. The woman had been ill for years from a liver fluke she had picked up in the north.

Dtui took hold of the doctor's arm and led him outside. Knickerless toddlers ran amok and rolled in the dust. A dog growled instinctively when Siri passed it. Dtui led him up toward the stadium wall where there were no neighbors to overhear. Siri had an apology prepared, but she beat him to it.

"I'm sorry, Doc. I was up all night with Ma. I didn't mean to lose it. I was . . ."

"I just came by to ask you if you'd do me the honor of being my apprentice at the morgue."

"Ah, no. You're just saying that because I went nutty. You don't have to do—"

"I'm serious. I was thinking about it just before I rode your bicycle into the wall of the Presidential Palace."

"You . . . ?"

"I think you need to get those brakes looked at."

"I never go fast enough to need brakes. Did you really . . . ?"

"It's downhill all the way from That Luang, and it didn't occur to me to check the brakes before I set off. I shot through the center of the Anusawari Arch, and I was traveling at about 120 kilometers an hour by the time I passed the post office. It was a bit of a blur."

"Doctor."

"I confess I didn't actually crash into the palace. But that was only thanks to the poor man selling brooms and brushes beside the road. I decided he'd be much softer than the wall. We both came out of it quite well: I didn't break anything, and he sold three brooms to the morgue."

"And the bike?"

"The Chinese aren't very good at making shoes, but they put together bicycles you couldn't destroy with mortar fire. So will you?"

"Will I what?"

"Be my apprentice."

"You're damn right I will."

"Good. Before I leave, I may as well take a look at your mother."

"You fancy her?"

"The cirrhosis, girl. The cirrhosis."

On Wednesday, Siri was the first one at work again. As if Geung weren't confused enough already, he walked out back to the furnace to find his boss on his hands and knees in the concrete trough, putting dead cockroaches into a jar.

"Morning, Mr. Geung. Any new customers today?"

"No new customers today, Dr. Comrade." Geung laughed but stood watching Siri. "That . . . that's dirty. You shouldn't play there."

"Mr. Geung, you're quite right. This is where you put the bags before they get thrown in the furnace, right?"

"Yes."

"The janitor doesn't seem to be around. Do you know if he burned our waste yesterday?"

"He must. He must. It's the rules. He must destroy all hospital waste no more than twelve hours from when it arrives. He must."

"Twelve hours. So what we threw out on Monday evening would have been sitting here overnight?"

"Yes."

"Good. Please put our little friends here in the refrigerator while I go and get cleaned up."

"Ha. Little friends." Geung laughed and ran off inside with the jar.

Siri showered, changed, and again left at about ten without telling them where he was going.

He crossed the road in front of the hospital and picked up his lunch from Auntie Lah. Following Dtui's comments on Monday, he took the trouble to notice a blush in the lady's cheeks. For a second, he believed there may have been some truth in it. They exchanged polite conversation for a few minutes, and then he said "Good health" and walked on.

"The hospital's that way, brother Siri," she reminded him.

"I'm playing hooky. Don't tell the director."

"You should play hooky with me sometime."

He laughed.

She laughed.

There *was* something.

He walked along the river and turned onto one of the small dirt lanes. The Lao Women's Union was housed in a two-storey building whose frontage was overgrown with flowering shrubs. They'd been tended to look natural but were kept under total control. The Union sign had been freshly repainted. A slight dribble of white descended from one letter.

He walked into a bustling foyer where everyone seemed to have urgent business, and he wasn't part of it. He had to throw himself in front of one fast-moving girl to ask his question.

"Do you know where I can find Dr. Pornsawan?"

She was flustered. "Oh, she's around somewhere. Do you have an appointment?"

"No. Do I need one?"

"You should have phoned. It's chaotic here today. The wife of the president of Mongolia's coming."

Siri felt like he'd come to a strange foreign land. So much speed. So much activity. Appointments. Telephones. He didn't feel like he was in Laos at all. His wasn't an appointment culture: you'd turn up; you'd see if the person was there; you'd sit and wait for an hour if he was, go home if he wasn't.

Who were they, these women of the Union with their alien ideas? And why was there so much excitement about the wife of the president of Mongolia?

After flustering two more busy women, he finally found Dr. Pornsawan in the canteen putting up decorations hand-made from plastic drinking straws. There was a huge banner behind the stage that said WELCOME TO OUR FRIENDS FROM MONGOLIA in Lao and French, two languages the president's wife probably couldn't read.

Pornsawan was less flustered and more accommodating than her sisters. She'd heard of the famous Dr. Siri and had some unaccountable professional respect for him. But she still forced him to tie cotton threads to blue and red drinking straws while they spoke. She was a slender lady in her thirties, and she had no eyebrows. She'd briefly entered a nunnery where they had been shaved off and hadn't ever grown back. She was so devoid of vanity, she didn't bother to have new ones tattooed or even to draw them on. It left her with a very clean look.

"You're here about Mrs. Nitnoy."

"Yes. You were at the table with her when she died?"

"Directly opposite."

"And she ate from communal plates?"

"Ah. Now, this is intriguing."

"What is?"

"You've done the autopsy and you still think she was poisoned."

Siri's cheeks became a little more flushed than normal. "I don't have any idea."

"Of course not. Sorry." She smiled at the straws in her hand. "She ate the same food as all of us, and we'd already started when she got here. She took a few mouthfuls of sticky rice, dipped in chili and fish sauce. At about the second or third mouthful, before she could swallow it, her eyes seemed to cloud over. She spat out the rice, dribbled slightly, and collapsed onto the table.

"I tried to resuscitate her, but I believe she died very suddenly. She didn't choke, didn't turn blue. She just died. I tried to massage her heart, gave her mouth-to-mouth, but I didn't feel there was much hope."

"Do you know anything about gnathostomiasis?"

"Yes. I've lost enough patients over the years to parasites. But that's not what killed Mrs. Nitnoy."

"Why not?"

"It's a very painful death. It comes upon you suddenly, but the last few minutes are agony. Mrs. Nitnoy was perfectly normal until a few seconds before she died."

"You're quite right. You seem to have noticed a lot of detail."

"I was talking to her all the time."

"Do you know if she had a headache?"

"Why, yes. It's strange you should ask. That's what we were talking about. She had a horrible hangover. Mrs. Nitnoy liked her beer, and there had been a reception the night before. She'd had a little bit too much and woke up with a splitting headache. If it hadn't been for the preparations for today's visit, she'd probably have taken the day off."

"Did she take anything for it?"

"She had a bottle of painkillers."

"Does she have her own desk here?"

"She had her own office, but you won't find the pills there. She kept them in her handbag."

"That didn't come to the morgue with her."

A supervisor glided through the room yelling urgent instructions.

"No. It was here, but a serious-looking army officer in dark glasses came by to pick it up during the afternoon."

Siri raised his eyebrows. She responded in kind, only to a lesser degree. "He said she had some sensitive documents in her bag and he'd been instructed to come and pick it up."

"By?"

"His superiors. I didn't get any names."

"Did he take anything else? Anything from the desk?"

"No. Just the bag."

"I don't suppose you had a chance to look in that bag?"

"Dr. Siri. What type of woman do you take me for?" She climbed on the chair and hung another chain of decorations. The stage was starting to look like a marquee that had been shredded in a monsoon. "Our design specialist assures us this is all beautiful. Do you think it is?"

"I think it shows a great deal of failed initiative."

She laughed. "I take it your tact got you into the position you find yourself in today."

"Very much so, I'm afraid."

"Don't be afraid. We need more people with the courage to say what they feel. It's getting rarer." She stepped down. "Slippers."

"What?"

"She carried her slippers around in her bag. The Party insisted she wear black vinyl shoes with heels for public engagements. She hated them. They gave her blisters. So she had these soft slippers she put on whenever she could." Siri smiled. "What is it?"

"Nothing. What else did she have in there?"

"Now you think I'm a snoop."

"Snooping's good for the regime."

"Really? All right. Little stuff, mainly. Address book. Keys. Smelling salts. Balm. Name cards. That was about all."

"Did you look at the name cards?"

"Doctor Siri."

"Sorry. No makeup, lipstick?"

"Frowned upon, and quite expensive now."

"So, apart from the address book, there wasn't really anything in there that could be called 'sensitive papers'?"

"No."

"And it was all carried off by the serious officer."

". . . Yes." It was neither a firm nor an automatic "yes."

"Dr. Pornsawan?"

"Almost all."

"Apart from?"

"Well, the reason I know what was in her bag was because I went into it to borrow her headache pills. One or two of the ladies were traumatized by what happened to Comrade Nitnoy."

"And you didn't put them back."

"Medicines are hard to come by. And in all the rush . . ."

"But the ladies you gave the pills to didn't suddenly collapse on the table, so . . ."

"So we may eliminate the pills as potential causes of death."

"I'd like to take what's left, if you don't mind. There may have been some allergic reaction. Not that I have the resources to find out what that might have been."

"I'll go and get them. Can I ask you why you thought she might have had a headache?"

"During the autopsy I noticed the smell of Tiger Balm. It was concentrated around her temples. That usually suggests a headache."

"Excellent. You know, this is all rather exciting. Could you hook this last chain up over the stage? Afraid we haven't got any balloons." She ran off and left him to hang the decoration.

While he was up on the rickety chair hooking the straws over some convenient nails, he thought about what she'd

said. It really *was* quite exciting, this inquiry. He had to admit
he was enjoying the cloak-and-daggery of it all. He was glad to
be out of the morgue talking to live people, exceeding his
very limited authority. It was the first time since the job began
that he could feel his adrenaline pumping.

"There are only three left, I'm afraid." Puffing and blow-
ing, Dr. Pornsawan held out a small brown bottle. "That probably isn't a wise choice of chair, the legs aren't glued." Siri got
down in a hurry, leaving a strand of straws dangling above the
podium. But it was too late to do anything about it.

The frenzy at the Lao Women's Union grew to a riot. Siri
and Pornsawan looked to the door where a small army of men
in ceremonial uniforms was slowly seeping into the almost-
ready dining room. The men took up positions along the
walls.

"Oops. Looks like our guest is early. You may have to join
us for lunch, Doctor."

"I'd sooner not. Why all the fuss about the wife of a
Mongolian president?"

"They're giving the LWU a sizable grant to develop education for girls in the provinces."

Siri wondered what the Mongolians would be getting in
return, but didn't let his cynicism show. He thanked Dr.
Pornsawan and headed toward the one set of doors leading
into and out of the canteen. In the confused scrum at the
doorway, he ran into a small woman whose features had all
gathered at the center of her face. She was surrounded by
larger people in suits and silks. The small woman, assuming,
as he was a man, that he had to be someone important,
reached out to shake his hand.

Siri transferred his baguette to his left hand and returned the
handshake. She had a good grip for a president's wife. She
looked beside her at the interpreter and asked him a question.
He asked a similar question of the Chinese interpreter beside

him, who finally asked the Lao/Chinese interpreter, who asked Siri who he was.

"I'm the official food taster. You can never be too sure." He bowed politely and walked on. By the time the Chinese whisper had made it back to the President's wife, he was already out under the warm midday sun.

The Boatman's Requiem

As he was quite a way from his riverside log, and hungry, he walked down to the nearest point on the Mekhong and found a shady spot under a tree where he could eat his baguette in peace. He particularly enjoyed his lunch that day. He was overcome with a peculiar feeling that, as he didn't feel the way he normally did, he probably didn't look the same either. He imagined himself to be in disguise.

During his stay in Paris decades before, he'd taken delight in the weekly serializations of one Monsieur Sim in the *L'Oeuvre* newspaper. They followed the investigations of an inspector of the Paris police force who was able to solve the most complicated of mysteries with the aid of nothing more lethal than a pipe of tobacco.

By the time he got to Vietnam, Siri was more than pleased to learn that Monsieur Sim had restored his name to its full Simenon, and that Inspector Maigret mysteries were now appearing as books. The French in Saigon had shelves of them, and a number found their way north to be read by those communist cadres who'd spent their formative years in France.

Siri had been able to solve most of the mysteries long before the detective had a handle on them—and he didn't even smoke. Now, below the swaying boughs of the *samsa* tree, he felt a distinct merging. The coroner and the detective were blending. He liked the way it felt. For a man in his seventies, any stimulation, should it be kind enough to offer itself, had to be grasped in both hands.

He walked back along the river, but when he reached the intersection that would have taken him back to his morgue, he responded not to obligation, but to instinct. He flagged down a *songtaew*, one of the dwindling number of taxi trucks plying the Vientiane streets. He told the driver where he wanted to get off, and squeezed amid the zoo of villagers already crammed inside. The *songtaew* followed the river east, away from the town. It was never so full it couldn't pick up more passengers.

Twenty minutes later, Siri was helped down by a strong girl who held a cockerel under her other arm. He paid his fifty liberation *kip* to the driver, crossed the road, and stood for a moment in front of the newly christened Mekhong River Patrol, wondering what he was doing there. The MRP, a navy of sorts in a landlocked country, had the near-impossible task of policing the long river border.

The pilots of the hurriedly converted river ferries were army men, trained in two weeks to operate boats that were so noisy you could hear them a mile off. Anyone crossing the river illegally, unless they were stone deaf, could easily hide themselves until the armor-plated craft chugged on by.

Siri was directed out back to the boat captains' dormitory. There, the night-shift skippers sat playing cards, or stood in circles kicking a rattan ball back and forth. He was in luck. Following an unfortunate accident, the person he sought had been transferred to the night patrol. Siri found Captain Bounheng rocking back and forth on a cane chair, like an old man. He was only in his twenties.

Siri introduced himself and shook the young captain's hand. "Do you mind if we take a walk?"

Bounheng was confused but followed Siri out across the dry rice fields. "Is this normal?"

"For a coroner to follow up on cases? Oh, yes. It happens all the time. I spend as much time interviewing as I do looking at dead bodies. It's all very mundane. Reports. You know."

Bounheng seemed a little more at ease after that. "He never should have been there."

"The longboat man?"

"We were docking. He was fishing in an illegal spot." The captain was deliberately striding ahead of Siri, who was hard pressed to keep up with him.

"I understand. The old fool. These fishermen are an ignorant crowd. Never do what they're told." He jogged round in front of the fleeing man. "Can I ask about you?"

"Me?"

"Yes. How long had you been . . . in control of your boat?"

There was a long hesitation. "I mean, this is a new unit. Only just been set up."

"I understand. So? Months? Weeks?"

"A week."

"And I imagine it's really stressful work."

"Stressful?"

"I'd say so. Patrolling against attacks from anti-communists from across the river."

Bounheng laughed involuntarily. "Dr. Siri, I'd been up-country fighting hand to hand for two years. This is a holiday cruise compared to that. No anti-communist in his right mind's going to launch an armada across the river in a built-up area. The most stressful thing we ever see is villagers swimming across to Thailand. With the river this low, there are plenty taking their chances."

"So what you're saying is that it's a bit of a slack posting."

"It's very peaceful."

"How fast do you travel?"

"Ten knots. That's the rule."

"What a good job. I should apply."

Bounheng laughed again a little nervously.

"But I . . ."

"What?" the captain asked.

"No, it's not important. I've got enough for my report. It doesn't matter."

"No. Come on."

"Well, if you were traveling at ten knots and coming in to land . . ."

"Yes?"

"Why didn't you have time to stop when you saw the long-boat man?"

Bounheng immediately broke eye contact and set off again on his escape across the fields. "Like I said, he shouldn't have been there."

"But you'd have had a pilot, watching. Right?"

Bounheng was obviously used to having a wristwatch that had somehow taken leave of him. He looked at the back of his wrist and swore unnecessarily and loudly when he noticed it was missing. "I've got to get back. Like you say, you've got enough for your report."

"Of course, I'm sorry to keep you so long. Thanks for your cooperation."

On the walk back, Bounheng slowed down a little and regained some of his composure. That was until he noticed Siri was no longer beside him. He turned back to see the doctor standing stock-still in the middle of the dead paddy, looking down at the unwatered stubble.

"What is it, Doctor?" He went back to see what Siri was looking at. But the doctor wasn't actually looking at anything. He was putting together a hypothesis. When he started to chuckle, the captain felt uneasy. "Doctor?"

Siri gazed up at him, and then looked him directly in the

eye. "All right, son. Here's my theory. It may just be the foolish imagination of an old man, but hear me out. It seems to me, there's a lot of smuggling goes on across the river. Most of the cigarettes and liquor we get in Laos come from Thailand."

"What are you . . . ?"

"Just listen up." Siri noticed how the remaining friendly color had bleached from Bounheng's face. He stood with his hands on his waist. "I believe you boat captains are . . . tempted to turn a blind eye from time to time. Maybe even change your schedule."

"Are you suggesting . . . ?"

"I'm suggesting for every two hundred crates of whisky you don't see cross over . . ." Bounheng turned his back on Siri ". . . one crate may very well find its way aboard the river patrol boat as a sort of thank-you. I'm suggesting that on the evening the longboat man lost his legs and his life, the crew of your boat and its skipper were pissed as newts. I'm suggesting you were all so drunk, you had not a brass *kip* of control over your vessel; over the boat you'd only learned to operate a week earlier."

He saw a slight shudder pass across Bounheng's young shoulders and walked closer to him. "I'm suggesting the longboat man wasn't in the wrong place, but that you were. And by the time you realized it, you were so close to the wall of the bank that you had no time to pull up. I'm suggesting Mekhong Whisky killed the old fisherman."

He turned to see Bounheng's face. Tears were rolling down his cheeks and his mouth was contorted with pain. Siri stood there, silent and overwhelmed at his own revelations. The adrenaline had sunk to his stomach, and it fluttered there like moths trapped in a jar. It was some minutes before the young man was able to speak. He couldn't look at Siri. "Which . . . which one of them told you?"

"Them?"

"The crew."

"No, son. I haven't talked to your crew, or to any witnesses."

Bounheng faced him, his eyes red with tears.

"It was the longboat man himself that told me."

The captain dropped his head and sobbed as if the weight of the river were crushing his chest. Siri, too embarrassed to merely stand back and witness the man's suffering, stepped up and put his arms around him. He felt Bounheng's body throb with grief, and could understand how much the boy had already suffered for his foolishness. There was nothing to be said.

By some miracle of timing and history, he'd avoided man's justice. But for many years to come, he'd suffer the justice of remorse, the nightmares of guilt. A soldier may kill a thousand of the enemy in battle and not feel a thing. But the death of one innocent man lodges itself in the conscience forever.

When he could stand it no longer, Siri pulled himself away and searched for a pen and paper in his shoulder bag. On the back of an old envelope, he wrote down some information he remembered from his autopsy report. He forced the paper into Bounheng's hand.

"Boy. This is the name of the fisherman, and his home village. I believe they have a small altar there. It might help you to go there and talk to him."

Siri walked slowly back across the fields toward the road. Step by step, the significance of what had just happened pulled him down below the surface of common sense. His old heart started beating like a giant catfish caught in a net. Somehow he'd known. Somehow, the longboat man's visit had told him. But where was the logic in that? What was the scientific explanation?

He felt no gloating, no pride in what he'd just been able to achieve. He was walking a narrow path between fear and excitement, between power and powerlessness, between sanity and . . . He didn't want to think about what was happening to him.

Two, then three *songtaews* went past him on their way back into town. They beeped their hoarse horns begging him to climb in, but he let them go. He sat under a jackfruit tree and went over the meeting in his mind. He went over it, and over it, and over it. But if he'd hoped for an explanation to come to him, he was going to be disappointed.

"Oh. Good to see you. We assumed you'd died of old age."

Mr. Geung laughed at, and repeated, Dtui's irreverent comment.

"We, ah . . . ah . . . ah . . . assumed you died of old age."

It was after three, and Siri had been missing for over five hours. The army sergeant had asked them where he was. The Nam Ngum Dam security chief had asked them where he was, and Judge Haeng, on the telephone, had asked them where he was. But no one could answer. The staff consensus was that he was now in serious shit.

But, here Dr. Siri was, smiling, in the office doorway. There was a cheeky, somewhat youthful expression on his face. He strode in and went to his desk as if everything were normal.

Everything certainly was not.

"Any new customers, Mr. Geung?"

Geung searched for stock answer number two. "We have a guest in room number one."

It wasn't the answer Siri was hoping for. He wanted peace. He wanted to go home. He had enough on his mind already without yet another body in the freezer.

Dtui waltzed over to his desk with a bigger grin than usual on her craggy face. "I probably don't need to tell you how upset Judge Haeng was to find you out of your office during working hours. As your loyal assistant and official trainee, I was planning to lie and tell him you'd just stepped out for a minute. But he already had a couple of witnesses in his office saying you'd been gone most of the day."

Siri didn't seem to care. He continued to smile. "What did he want?"

"He'd love it if you could phone him back before nightfall, because he has several questions to ask you about our new guest."

"Don't tell me it's another celebrity."

"Nobody knows who he is. But he's certainly got a lot of people interested in him. They all want to know what he died of."

"Mr. Geung." Siri looked over, and Geung stopped rocking. "You saw the body?"

"Yes, Dr. Comrade."

"What'd he die of?"

"Drowned."

"Excellent. There you have it, Dtui. If Judge Hinge-face calls back, that's the initial diagnosis. Tell him I'll be in touch in the morning."

He started to claw through the papers on his desk as if he were missing something important. Dtui and Geung looked at each other, mystified.

"Have you two moved anything from here in the last couple of days?"

Geung shook his head violently. Dtui looked indignant.

"I wouldn't dream of touching your desk."

"Then where's the . . . ?" He cast his mind back to the day of Mrs. Nitnoy's autopsy. He'd been working on the report till late, until . . . That was it. That was the "something different." On the night Comrade Kham sat at his desk and talked him out of doing any more tests on his wife, the report had been there in front of him. The bastard had stolen it.

"Like a common thief."

"Who is?" Dtui was looking to defend her honor.

"Not you two. We've had a nasty low-life in here 'borrowing' reports. Dtui, you still have your notebook?"

"The autopsy book?"

"Yes."

"Yeah. It's here in the drawer." She pulled it open and produced the notebook.

"Good girl. I'll borrow that, if I may, and start a new report on Mrs. Nitnoy." He walked over and took it from her.

"Do we know what she died of yet?"

"Not quite. But she certainly didn't die of *lahp*. And neither of you can mention that outside this room. Got that?" They nodded. "It's starting to look like somebody wants this case closed in a hurry. We, my children, are no longer common coroners. We are investigators of death. Inspector Siri and his faithful lieutenants. All for one and one for all." He walked over to the doorway, turned back to his team, clicked the heels of his sandals together, and saluted. He smiled and chuckled his way out the main door and into the carpark. Through the skylight, they could hear him singing the French national anthem until he was finally out of earshot.

Inside, the office was silent. The cockroaches were quiet. For once, Dtui didn't know what to say. Even Geung, from his other dimension, could recognize the abnormal when he saw it.

"The Comrade Doctor is . . . is nuts today."

Tran the Elder

With all the excitement, it was a wonder that it was still only Thursday. Siri arrived at work refreshed and packing new energy. Again, he was the first there. He unlocked the building, opened the windows, and sent more cockroaches scurrying for cover.

Before embarking on the great telephone adventure, he went to visit the guest in room one. He wasn't a pretty sight. The puffy skin had begun to shift, as if it had been removed and replaced in a hurry. It was beginning to develop a waxy brown texture that suggested, without any further investigation, that the body had been in the water for two to three weeks. Siri pulled the cover back completely and noticed a thick tourniquet of plastic twine several layers thick around the left ankle. The skin had been worn completely through from the tightness of it. He made a mental note that the blood had settled at the back of the body and around the legs. If he'd been floating since he died, hypostasis would have been evident at the front of the corpse. But there was none.

He noticed all these things but replaced the sheet and set off to find the expert who understood the magic of telephone technology.

A pretty girl was filing. She turned to see who had come in.

"I need to call the Justice Department."

"The phone's on the table behind you, Doctor. Just write the number in the book, who spoke to who, and for how long."

She turned back to the cabinet. Siri stood there uneasily, not yet ready to look at the telephone. She glanced back over her shoulder to see him still in the same position.

"I thought *you* might do it," he said quietly.

"Do what?"

"Make the telephone call for me."

"No. It's just a regular phone. You don't need an operator."

He looked around at the somber black machine and walked tentatively toward it. Its numbers peeked out at him from the portholes of the dial. He studied it for a while and carefully picked up the handset. He held it to his ear and listened to the warm buzz.

"Hello?"

There was no response.

"You *have* used a telephone before?" She'd deserted her filing and come to stand behind him. It was the moment of truth. He confessed.

"No."

"Doctor?"

It did seem rather hard to believe that in seventy-two years, Siri hadn't once handled a phone. But Laos wasn't a phone culture. There were fewer than nine hundred working telephones in the entire country, and most of those were in government offices. Even during Laos's dizzy heights of corruption, only the very well-off families had had their own phones.

To a poor student in France, a phone had been out of the question and, besides, there had been nobody to call. But even then he'd had a phobia about the things. So it was hardly surprising, for a man who'd spent most of his life in jungles, that the skill of manipulating the dreaded machine had passed him by.

"I've spoken into field walkie-talkies, but there was always a technician there to twirl the handle." He smiled.

She was obviously a charitable girl, because she became teary-eyed to find herself in the presence of such a disadvantaged elderly doctor. She took the handpiece from him and smiled back. "What's the number?"

"Number?"

After a while, she found the Department of Justice in the very slim telephone directory and taught him how to steer the dial around the face of the machine. It was all annoyingly uncomplicated in the end.

As he'd hoped, Judge Haeng had just left for court to preside on another divorce case. The man had a file jam-packed with domestic disputes and paternity suits, but nothing that could in seriousness be called a crime. Haeng's clerk, Manivone, assured Siri that the judge was livid and expected to find the autopsy report on his desk when he came back from court that afternoon.

Siri asked after her new baby and her husband's pig problem, and slowly grew quite comfortable with the telephone in his hand. The girl virtually had to tear it away from him in case anyone was trying to get through.

So, Siri had achieved two major feats before the day was barely underway: he'd used a telephone virtually by himself, and he'd communicated with the Justice Department without actually having to talk directly to the annoying little man in the flesh. Unfortunately he wasn't able to complete the trifecta with the autopsy.

Dtui, more enthusiastic than ever, stood with her notepad poised as Siri restated his previous observations. He noticed several other odd indicators on the ill-fitting skin. Most obvious of these were what looked like burn marks around the nipples and genitalia, but nowhere else.

Dtui quite rightly pointed out that the string round the ankle indicated that he'd been tied to something heavy and sunk. But she made one other observation that Siri hadn't thought of. "Why didn't they use cord or wire or something?"

"What do you mean?"

"Well, if you're going to the trouble of weighing the guy down, you shouldn't use crap string like this. Everyone knows this cheap Vietnamese nylon stuff doesn't last very long in water. They used to use it to tie up bamboo for scaffolding. Then in the rainy season it would all fall down 'cause the string rotted."

"Hmm. Maybe it's all they had handy. They might have been in a hurry. But that's a good point. Write it down." She did so, proudly.

The last note they made, before Siri started to cut, was of the expression on the man's face. The jaw was locked open and there was a look of horror that none of them had seen before on a corpse. It was unlikely to have happened postmortem.

Once he was inside the corpse, and they'd recovered from the unpleasant stench, there were one or two more surprises waiting for Siri. With the body so deteriorated, it would have been very difficult to categorically state that drowning was the cause of death. But the opposite wasn't true. There were ways to show that it wasn't.

It takes some four minutes to drown in fresh water. In that time, about half the circulating blood is suffused with this intaken liquid. The water, and the algae it contains, will have been pushed into the far recesses of the lungs if the victim was still breathing when he entered the water.

Siri took samples from the stomach, lungs, and arteries, but his first instinct told him that the corpse was already dead when he went into the water. Nothing indicated he'd still been breathing or that his heart had been beating. But Mr. Geung could be forgiven for his assessment of the previous day. All the other signs were there. The man had spent two or three weeks in the water. That was certain.

Secondly . . .

A man with an extremely loud voice suddenly appeared in the

doorway. He had a cloth over his mouth and looked at the team as if he'd caught them being naughty.

"What's all this bloody stink you're making in here?"

Siri didn't look up. "Get out."

"Not until you stop making this wretched stink. What's that you've got there? A body, is it?"

"Mr. Geung. Could you remove that very rude person from our morgue?"

Geung went at him, but the invader retreated to the alcove before he could do any damage. Still he shouted. "I'm going to report you all to the hospital director I am. Damned stink. It's not good enough."

Siri laughed, none the wiser. "Where were we?"

"Secondly . . ."

"Right. Secondly, there seems to be some anomaly around the chest cavity. There's livor mortis around the main artery, which suggests heavy internal bleeding."

"What causes that?"

"No idea. We'll look it up later."

He found nothing else. The liver showed the effects of alcohol, but not enough to have killed him. The heart and brain gave nothing away. While Dtui and Geung sewed up, Siri checked the skin samples under the microscope.

"Dtui, do you want to come and take a look at this?" She hurried over to the bench and lowered her eye to the lens. "What do you see?"

"Ehhh, green? Little shiny bits?" She moved the slide. "Black? More shiny bits? It's very pretty. What is it?"

"Well, this is skin from the area around the nipple that looked burned. The green section could have been caused by copper. The shiny bits are probably metal deposits."

"Which means?"

"I'll have to do some chemical tests at the lycée, but I'd say these were electricity burns."

"Whah?"

"Electric burns to the nipples and testicles. What does that say to you?"

"Ouch."

He laughed. "Can you try something more detective-like?"

She thought about it for a few seconds. "Torture?"

"That's what it looks like to me. You don't accidentally electrocute yourself on the nipples and genitalia. I can't think of any other explanation."

"So he was tortured, tied to a rock, and thrown into the reservoir. He must have been a popular lad. You think the torture might have killed him?"

"There's no evidence it was terminal, as far as I can see. I suppose the blood in the chest cavity might be connected, but I doubt it. I'll spend some time with my textbooks. Do you want to write up the report?"

"Me?"

"Why not? You've seen enough. Just make the letters big enough to read this time."

"You want me to type it?"

"You can *type?*"

Geung laughed. "She h . . . h . . . has skills."

"So it would appear. Don't you need a typewriter?"

"It helps. There's one over in the admin office that they let me practice on."

Siri shook his head and tutted. "You know? I think it was very wise of me to choose you to become my new apprentice. Anyone know who that was that came in here and yelled at us?"

"No."

"No."

The report was typed, spelled correctly, and on Haeng's desk an hour before he got back from his domestic tinkering. The body was back in the freezer and the morgue was spick and

span. Siri promised not to ride into any walls or broom sales-
men, and Dtui let him use the bike. He cycled directly to the
lycée.

Teacher Oum was teaching a class, so he sat outside and
enjoyed the sounds of Russian, new history, and political ide-
ology being taught by converted French, English, and ancient
history teachers in the various rooms around the quad. They
read directly from the Department of Education printouts,
and the students copied down what they heard. There were
no questions, because the teachers probably didn't have the
answers. But apart from these few additions and subtractions
to the curriculum, life hadn't changed that much for the students and teachers who had stayed behind in the capital.

It had been a quiet transition from what the president
called "a bastardized version of America" to a Marxist-Leninist
state. The Lao People's Revolutionary Party, formerly the Lao
Patriotic Front, had planted the seeds of rebellion long
before December '75. Villages already had sympathizers in
place and ready to implement new policies. The Pathet Lao
already had seats in Parliament and a Party office just a brief
swagger from the US Embassy.

Underground unions at all the major utilities were ready to
stop work as soon as they were given the word, and by the time
that word arrived, the police and the military were so short of
superiors that there was no one to give orders to quash the
rebellion. By then, most senior officers had swum or floated
across the Mekong to refugee camps along the border.

The people of Vientiane were indifferent. They'd lived
through the heady days of dollars and corruption and rib-
aldry, and benefited little from the American presence. Those
who got rich during that period didn't share their ill-gotten
wealth with the common folk. Before the Americans had been
the French, and the general feeling was: the less said about
them, the better.

No, many of the Lao that stayed on in the capital after the takeover were supportive of the new regime. The feeling was that they couldn't do much worse than their predecessors, and Lao people were sick and tired of being a foreign-owned colony. If they were to be mismanaged, it was time to be mismanaged by other Lao.

When the bell rang for the end of the day, the scene became one of happy escape rather than departure. Siri passed the smiling teenagers, and they saluted him with their hands together in a polite *nop*. Until they got used to the faces of the new administration, it was good policy to *nop* everyone over fifty.

Teacher Oum looked up from her theoretical chemistry notes. "Ooh. Two visits in a week. You must be busy."

"I think Buddha's testing me to see whether I've abandoned him too."

"What can I do for you?"

"I'm sorry, Oum. Can we try that cyanide test again?"

"What on?" He pulled out the headache pill bottle. "I'm hoping we'll find some residue in here. But I think the pills themselves are just aspirin. Then there are these." He produced a small jar with two dead cockroaches in it.

She laughed. "Don't tell me you're handling murder inquiries for the insect community now. You know we don't have a lot of chemicals left for these tests?"

"Then let's make it count."

And count it did.

The Chicken Counter

On Friday morning, the mystery of the loud-voiced man was solved. Siri and the team were closing up an old lady who'd drunk toilet bleach to relieve her family of the burden of having to look after her. Because it happened in a hospital bathroom, there had to be an autopsy.

The hospital director, Suk, came to the door and called Siri into the office. The loud-voiced man was standing there with his arms folded high on his chest. The director was another administrator who'd been given authority too young in life and felt obliged to use it. He, too, was threatened by Siri's disrespectful personality.

"Siri, this is Mr. Ketkaew." Siri held out his hand but the man refused to shake it. "I assume you've noticed the new structure at the rear of your building."

"No." There wasn't much need to go round to the back of the morgue when there had been nothing but a deserted lot.

"Then I suggest you come and take a look."

The three of them marched around the corner of the morgue building, where they were confronted by a small bamboo hut. It contained a desk, a chair, a filing cabinet, and a blackboard. Over the door was a hand-painted sign that read *KHON KHOUAY* REPRESENTATIVE.

The *Khon Khouay* were the neighborhood spies, lovingly known as "chicken counters" by the locals. It was their function to keep a rein on affluence and extravagance. Usually, they were part-timers who accepted their role reluctantly on top of other responsibilities. That Mr. Ketkaew had his own office and a real sign suggested he was taking his position seriously.

"Mr. Ketkaew has been assigned to area 18. As the hospital is in the center of that area, we have the honor of allowing him to set up his office here." The way he said "honor" suggested to Siri that it was anything but. The hospital, far from being wealthy, was struggling to make ends meet. The last thing it needed was a chicken counter, particularly an enthusiastic one.

Ketkaew spoke up. He was a man with no volume control. "So I'm not having any more of those stinks coming out of your place. You understand?"

Siri didn't really know how to react. He'd seen these officious little men before, sampling their first taste of power. At best, they could be annoying. But there were times, if you got on the wrong side of them, that they could be downright dangerous. "Mr. Ketkaew, perhaps you could suggest to me how to stop dead bodies from smelling bad."

Ketkaew had to think about it. "Can't you spray them with something?"

"You mean like air freshener?"

"Something like that."

Siri laughed. Even the director suppressed a smile. "I'm afraid we aren't legally allowed to do that. The law clearly states you cannot spray anything sweet-smelling on a body that affects the natural odor. It's an infringement of human rights."

"Well, I suppose you'll just have to close the windows then. I can't be expected to work with such a damned stink."

"You want us to close the windows? In that case, we'll have to spend scarce hospital money on an air conditioner. You do want us to breathe, don't you?" Ketkaew shrugged his shoulders as if he didn't care. "The best solution would be for Director Suk to move your office somewhere else so you don't have to put up with it."

Suk cut in. "No. No, I'm afraid this is the only spot we can provide in the hospital grounds. There are one or two sites *outside* the—"

"Absolutely not. I insist on being on-site in order to do my job to my maximum efficiency."

It all became clear to Siri, then. The hospital didn't want Ketkaew there, but couldn't really refuse. So they put him behind the morgue, hoping the smell would drive him out. As far as he could see, Siri was likely to be the one to suffer most. Why did these things always happen on Fridays! He began to observe them creeping up on his calendar with feelings of dark foreboding. And he still had Judge Haeng to look forward to.

It was difficult for Judge Haeng to discuss Siri's "attitude" at the second burden-sharing tutorial because they weren't alone. In the second guest chair sat a dapper man in his forties who probably hadn't looked much different in his twenties. He had an amusing, softly handsome face and was built for speed. He didn't say much.

Judge Haeng introduced him formally. "I should like to introduce to you Inspector Phosy of the National Police Force. The inspector has just returned from a very successful training period in Viengsai. He is now ready to return to his responsibilities as a senior investigator here in Vientiane."

Siri leaned over and shook Phosy's hand. It was a long handshake that seemed to be extracting information from him. Most people shook hands in Laos, and a person developed a sense of what to expect from different types of shakes: sincerity, impatience, weakness. Siri wondered what he'd just given away.

He thought about the policeman. "Away for training in Viengsai" meant re-education. All of the students at the Police Academy and their superiors had been invited to the north for training when the Pathet Lao took control, partly to establish where their loyalties lay. If Phosy had only just returned, he'd been in the camp for a year. Siri wondered how that would affect a man. So far, he'd laughed at all Haeng's jokes and agreed with everything he said. It was starting to annoy Siri. Haeng coughed.

"I wanted to have you both here to talk about the bodies that were retrieved from Nam Ngum," Haeng started.

"Bodies?"

"Yes, Doctor. There were two."

"Nobody told me that. Why did we only get one at the morgue?"

"All in good time, Siri. Phosy, did you get the copy of Siri's report that I sent to your department?"

"Yes, Comrade Judge. It's right here. It was very thoughtful of you to send it."

"It was no more than the courtesy we expect between different arms of the legal mechanism. If I'd got it earlier, so would you have." He glared at Siri who smiled, undamaged.

"Excellent, sir." Siri was beginning to wonder how long it would be before the policeman walked over and polished Haeng's fly buttons.

"Where's the other one?" Siri asked.

"At the Vietnamese Embassy."

"I didn't know they had a freezer there."

"They don't. I believe they have him on ice."

"What for?"

"Until their own coroner can get here."

"Their own . . . they don't trust me?"

"It isn't a question of trust, Siri. If they find the same evidence of torture on their man as you did on yours, this could become a very embarrassing international incident."

"What makes him 'their man'?"

"This." Haeng held out a small folder, expecting Siri to come and get it. Instead, the puppy-dog detective leaped to his feet and handed the file to Siri. He remained standing at Siri's shoulder and was first to comment when the photos of the corpse came into view.

"Traditional Vietnamese tattoos. Very distinctive."

"Yes, very distinctive indeed," Siri agreed. He was quite surprised at just how clear they were. "At what point was he rerouted to the Vietnamese Embassy?"

"Someone at the dam recognized the tattoos. They called the embassy, who sent one of their advisers." There was no shortage of Vietnamese "advisers" around the capital. Cynics—and Siri was one of the founding fathers of cynicism—suggested that there was so much advice from Hanoi being passed around, it wouldn't be long before the official language changed to Vietnamese. "You can imagine how delicate the matter is," Haeng droned on. "A Vietnamese national being interrogated and tortured in Laos. The cabinet discussed it yesterday. We're going to request that you be allowed to observe their autopsy and compare notes."

"Request? Why request? This is Laos. Shouldn't we be insisting?"

"It isn't as easy as that."

"It should be. We aren't her next province yet, you know."

"Siri, if you're going to spend time with the Vietnamese, I suggest you watch your mouth. They aren't quite as understanding as we are."

The meeting went on longer than usual, as Haeng felt obliged to outline all the cases that he and Siri had "cooperated" on. But as long as the doctor kept his mouth shut, it was comparatively painless. Things seemed to be winding down—Siri looking toward the door and escape—when Haeng coughed again.

"I've been thinking, Doctor. Now that the work of your department is being recognized by the police, I believe it's time for you to get rid of the moron."

Siri shuddered. "The moron? Oh, I don't know. I know he has his off-days, but I don't think that's enough reason to kick

Director Suk out of his job. He has a family. Please give him another chance."

"Director . . . ? Goodness, no, Siri. I'm talking about the retard you have as your morgue laborer. I'm prepared to offer a full salary for that position now."

"I'm so pleased. Mr. Geung will be delighted when I tell him he can have a living wage."

"Pay attention. I'm telling you to get rid of him and hire a normal person."

"I can't get rid of him. He's the only one there who knows what to do."

"He's mentally deranged."

"Aren't we all?"

"I'm beginning to wonder in your case, Doctor."

Siri sighed. "Judge Haeng, Mr. Geung has a mild strain of Down Syndrome. His condition makes him ideally suited for repetitive work. My predecessor spent a good deal of time teaching him his job. He isn't going to forget it. He isn't dangerous or clumsy, and his condition isn't likely to offend any of the clients we get passing through our place.

"He's been at the morgue for three years, so when I say he knows the work better than I do, I'm not being facetious. He's constantly reminding me of procedures I've forgotten, and where things are stored. He has an amazing memory, and my nurse Dtui and I love him very much."

Haeng was becoming agitated. He tapped his pencil on the table so hard the lead broke. "I'm overwhelmed with emotion. I can barely keep my eyes dry. But now let us return to rational thought for a second. Can you imagine how this would look if a visiting dignitary came to tour the hospital?"

"And I wasn't wearing my plastic shoes, and Dtui forgot to put on her underwear—"

"Doctor!"

"Visiting dignitaries don't go anywhere near morgues; and if by some miracle they did, they'd be struck by the compassion our great and farsighted republic shows by hiring three minority groups to work together in the same office. You have women, retarded, and horribly old people, all there on show."

Phosy, who had been silent and unflinching throughout this embarrassing confrontation, suddenly cleared his throat loudly and offered: "I have a Mongoloid cousin. He doesn't do any harm. He even fries us bananas every Friday. Most of the time we even forget he's nuts."

Siri and Haeng turned to look at the policeman, who wasn't making eye contact with either of them.

That simple comment poured oil on the troubled waters in Judge Haeng's office. It also let the judge know he was out-numbered. He agreed that Geung could stay on, pending an external assessment, but that he certainly wasn't qualified for the raise Haeng had mentioned.

With that, the meeting ended. Siri and Phosy shook the judge's hand and walked to the door together. But before fol-lowing Siri into the hall, Phosy turned back.

"Comrade Judge, I feel compelled to tell you that today's meeting has been a great inspiration to me. I hope it won't embarrass you too much if I say that my confidence and my faith in the socialist system become re-ignited whenever I meet people such as yourself. I'm so happy that my country has figureheads like you to look up to."

Hearing this from his spot in the hall, Siri felt like throw-ing up. When the policeman eventually joined him, they walked in silence along the concrete passageway to the carpark. This was the man they'd given Siri to work with, so, like it or not, he had to be polite. He watched him put his notebook into the pannier at the front of his old French motorbike.

"So, does your cousin live with your family?"

The policeman looked down at his boots. "What cousin's that?"

"Your banana-frying Mongoloid cousin." There wasn't a reaction. "You haven't got one, have you?"

Inspector Phosy straddled his bike. The slightest of smiles creased his lips. "I've got a sister with hemorrhoids." He kick-started the bike four or five times before it engaged. There was a fearsome noise from the engine. Black smoke belched from the exhaust and neither rose nor dissipated.

Siri, in its midst, threw his head back and laughed, and at that second he made a decision. It was the fastest and potentially most dangerous decision he'd made for a long time. "I need to talk to you about a case."

"It can wait till Monday."

"No. No, it can't."

The inspector looked deep into Siri's green eyes and nodded. "I'll come to your rooms this evening."

"You know where I live?"

"I'm the police."

Without bothering to explain, Phosy sped off through a shoal of bicycles, leaving the riders choking in black smoke.

Phosy somehow managed to negotiate the stairs to the landing outside Siri's door without making a sound despite the loose boards. So when he knocked, Siri jumped. "Come in."

The policeman let himself in. He'd already left his shoes outside. He was casually dressed and was holding a bottle. You couldn't help but respect a man who turned up at your door with a bottle. Siri looked at it. "I hope that isn't a urine sample you want analyzed."

Phosy came inside, quickly located the glasses and started pouring. "It's only Thai brandy. I should have asked if you drank." He handed a glass to Siri, who nodded to his generous guest.

"Is this a service of the new police force?"

"I was taught to show respect to my seniors."

"You don't have to suck up to me, you know."

"I know."

"Good luck."

"Good luck." They both drank.

"It seems you learned a lot at that camp."

"It was a valuable experience. I can recognize seventy-three varieties of vegetables. I could tell you how old a rice shoot is, or how many months pregnant a buffalo."

Siri laughed. "Good luck."

"Good luck."

They finished the first drink, and Siri took the bottle and poured a second round.

"So, they didn't convert you to communism?"

"They made me aware of the values of the socialist system and the worthy eff—"

"Okay, okay, I won't ask you any more questions about the camp. Tell me about Phosy the man."

Over the next hour, Siri learned that Phosy had been married and had two children. While he was in the north, they fled across the river; he hadn't heard from them since. He came back to a house empty of family and furniture, and was currently living in one room.

Phosy learned that Siri had been married and faithful to only one woman in his life. She had been unwilling to interrupt her contribution to The Cause, so they had never had children. This made loneliness all the more difficult when, eleven years earlier, she'd been killed under mysterious circumstances, leaving Siri with little enthusiasm for life, work, or the furtherance of the Communist Movement.

It was amazing what two strangers could learn in a short time with the aid of Thai brandy. Interesting, too, that each had weighed up the other so quickly and decided he was to be trusted.

"So, did you really have a case to discuss, or were you just hoping I'd turn up with some booze?"

Siri knew he'd gone too far to back out now. He lowered his voice. "I can tell you, but I don't know if you'd be interested in doing anything about it."

"Why not?"

"It could get you in trouble."

"What about you? Aren't you afraid of getting in trouble?"

"I'm permanently in trouble."

"Who told you you could trust me?"

"Your Mongoloid cousin and your hemorrhoidal sister."

They laughed and drained the last dregs from their glasses.

"You don't want to believe them. They've got big mouths. You got any coffee?"

While Siri prepared the aluminum filters and spooned in the rich coffee, he reviewed the official version of Mrs. Nitnoy's passing for Phosy. But when he'd put the steaming cups on the table, he went over and closed the window shutters.

Mr. Ketkaew's arrival at the hospital had reminded him there were ears everywhere: in the temple, in the house, in the next room. The Junior Youth League was being trained to listen to the idle talk of their parents and report it. Area security monitors like Ketkaew were lurking by open windows, listening for treason and Thai radio broadcasts. The Lao had been the most easy-going people in the region, but this mistrust was slowly turning them paranoid.

Siri dragged his chair over beside Phosy's. His story had arrived at the Tuesday tests. He spoke in a whisper. "There wasn't a shred of evidence in the brain that she'd been killed by parasites. Nothing. To go that suddenly, there should have been cysts."

"Couldn't the parasites have set up home somewhere else?"

"If they had, she would have been in agony for some time. The brain was the only location that might have caused her to switch off suddenly like that. So we did tests at the high school. We found a high concentration of cyanide in the stomach."

"Cyanide?" They were both sobering up quite quickly.

"A lethal dose. I'd siphoned off some stomach fluid for the records but hadn't kept any solids. The waste was all thrown out on Monday. By the time it became clear it could be useful, it had all been incinerated.

"My guess is that not all of the tablet had dissolved in her stomach. What hadn't been absorbed into the blood before she died gave off fumes in the furnace. It isn't airtight. The janitor who does the burning was off sick the next day. He showed distinct signs of cyanide poisoning. I found some dead roaches around the furnace and we tested them. They were positive."

"Why do you assume the cyanide was in a tablet?" Phosy was leaning forward. He hadn't touched his coffee. Siri told him about Mrs. Nitnoy's hangover and the pills.

"I was hoping we'd be able to find traces of cyanide in the bottle but, actually, we struck oil."

"Another pill?"

"There were three tablets left in the bottle. One of them was cyanide. It had been filed down to look exactly like the others. The other ladies at the Women's Union had been very lucky."

"So, someone put two cyanide tablets into a bottle of headache pills. They didn't know when she'd take them, but I suppose that wasn't important. Have you told Comrade Kham all this?"

"Ah, now, this is where things start to get complicated." He told Phosy about the comrade's visit to the morgue on Monday and the disappearance of the report. He didn't mention that Mrs. Nitnoy had briefly come back to life.

The detective whistled long and low and drained his coffee cup. "This is a fine mess."

"I was thinking of waiting to see whether my unfinished report turns up as the official statement."

"Was it signed?"

"Not when it left me."

"Good, yes. That would be very incriminating. I don't think you should make this official until we know more about it. The Justice Department doesn't have a great deal to do these days. Something like this would float up through the system in no time. What do you suppose your friend Haeng would do with it?"

"That's just it: I don't know how anyone would react. When we were in the north, justice sort of took care of itself. There was an honor system. But now that we've become civilized, a lot of people seem to be assuming roles left over from the old regime. I don't know who to trust."

After another coffee, the two men went downstairs. Saloop was on the night shift. It was eleven and he was wide awake. He bounded up to Siri's leg and barked at it with his nose inches away from a potential kick in the jowls. He seemed unaware of the danger.

"What's with the dog?"

"Doesn't like me. Loves everyone else. Dogs have always had a problem with me. Never known one that didn't act like this."

"That's odd."

He looked up. The wooden shutter of the front bedroom window creaked shut. Siri followed his gaze.

"Night, Miss Vong." She didn't answer. He knew she'd want to get a look at whoever had been getting rowdy with Siri upstairs. If she had any romantic yearnings at all, she would be impressed by this good-looking policeman.

As he was getting on his old bike, and the dog-howl chorus struck up in the streets around them, Phosy leaned close to Siri's ear. "Give me some time to think about this case before we do anything."

"We?"

Both men smiled as Phosy kicked the motorcycle to life and sped off. Siri was left alone in the middle of the lane in a bank of smog, susceptible to dog attacks. Despite all the threats, he'd never been bitten by a dog, not once. Miss Vong's shutter was slightly ajar again.

"Night, Miss Vong."

"Go to bed, Dr. Siri."

On Saturday, Siri was deservedly dull-headed. The chair squeaked when he leaned back from his thick forensic pathology text. He put his hand on his forehead and scoured the French department of his memory for a word. He knew it was in there. He'd put it in almost fifty years before and hadn't had cause to remove it. But for the life of him he couldn't find it.

Tearing in the main chest artery could be caused by high speed collision, or precipitation. What the hell was *precipitation*?

The pages of his French dictionary had become welded together after a typhoon the previous year, and he hadn't been able to get his hands on a new one.

"It'll come," he said. He leaned back as far as his chair would go, with his hands behind his head. "It'll come." He looked to the doorway and was startled to see a thin person in a much larger man's uniform standing there. It was a uniform he knew very well, that of the ex-North, now entire, Vietnamese army. But he couldn't recall seeing one so sparingly filled. It brought to Siri's mind the monster body suits he'd seen in Japanese science fiction films. The man's neck emerged from a collar that had space for three other necks. The rest of the uniform hung off him as if it were suspended from a hook. He spoke to Siri in Vietnamese.

"I'm looking for Dr. Siri Paiboun."

Siri's Vietnamese was heavily accented but otherwise fluent.

He'd spent fifteen years in the north of that country, training at first to be a revolutionary. But finally, when they realized his limitations as a guerrilla, they had him working in field hospitals with the Viet Cong.

"You've found me."

The man smiled with relief and walked uncomfortably over to the desk. He blushed and shook Siri's hand. "I have to apologize for the . . ." He looked down at his own chest.

"The uniform? Did you lose a bet?"

The Vietnamese laughed. "No. It was the only one they had available at the embassy."

"So why wear it?"

"I was brought in as a military adviser. The ambassador's afraid that if I walked around in civilian clothes I could, technically, be shot as a spy." Siri laughed. The story was even funnier than the uniform. "I'm Doctor Nguyen Hong."

"Then drape yourself over that chair and tell me what I can do for you."

Nguyen Hong smiled and sat opposite Siri. "I believe you had an alleged drowning victim in here this week."

"Ahh. The twin. You're a forensic scientist."

"Just an old coroner, actually."

In the doorway he hadn't looked so old, but close up Siri could see the hair was a little too black, and the teeth were a little too large for the mouth. He was probably the same age as Siri, but with some renovations.

"What can I do for you?"

"I was hoping I'd be able to take a look at your victim. I suppose there's an official way of asking, but I prefer the 'front up and try' method."

"Me too."

"Good. There is every reason to believe your chap's Vietnamese as well. But without the tattoos we had no right to claim him. I don't suppose you'd know what a fuss this is all causing back in Hanoi."

"What kind of a fuss?"

"The story's going around that you've kidnapped and tortured our citizens. They're eager to find out how official it was."

"Why would anyone assume it was official? It could have been a drug deal or—"

"We've identified our man. He was a government representative, Nguyen Van Tran. He was part of a delegation that disappeared after they crossed the border into Laos at Nam Phao. They were on their way here to Vientiane, but never showed up. Their mission was top secret."

"How many of them in the delegation?"

"Three. Two officials and a driver."

"And you ID'd your man from the tattoos?"

"No, we have fingerprints and dental records, and there was a ring."

"He was still wearing a ring?"

"Yes. His father's name was engraved on the inside. There wasn't anything about the tattoos in his military file, so he must have got them after he enlisted."

"Do you have the records of all three men?"

Nguyen Hong folded back his long sleeve and reached into his satchel. He produced three manila folders and put them on the desk in front of Siri. "Help yourself."

Siri opened the three files and looked at the photographs. The second was familiar.

"I reckon this is ours."

"Then that's the driver. His name is Tran as well."

"All right, Doctor. I suggest we take our respective files and reports to the canteen, have a bite to eat, and swap stories. I don't suppose you'd like to shed that uniform and borrow a white coat, would you?"

"I'd love to."

Nguyen Hong changed, and Siri put together his carbon copy of the autopsy report. Then the two set off for a real coroner's lunch in the canteen. Given the topic of their conversation, they were guaranteed a table to themselves.

Autopsy Envy

"**W**ord's on the streets, I go away and leave you for a couple of days and you're already in bed with the Vietnamese."

"I knew you'd be jealous."

It was Monday, and Siri and Civilai sat on their log washing down their rolls with tepid southern coffee. They looked out at the sleek white tern flying a foot from the surface of the river. It swooped down for a fish, thrust its beak in too deep, and crashed, somersaulting with the current.

"I bet that hurt."

"Does the committee have a problem with me consorting with the Viets? They are still our allies, aren't they?"

The battered tern, its feathers flustered, broke triumphantly through the surface of the water with the fish in its beak. The two old friends put down their plastic cups and applauded.

"There are allies and there are allies, Siri. There's how we see them and how they see themselves. To us, the advisers are resources we can use or ignore as we see fit. They believe they've been allocated to this or that department to steer our policies closer to their own, to make us more dependent on them.

"The more advisers we allow in, the more Hanoi sees us as an appendage. That's why we have a deliberate but unofficial policy of ignoring 40 percent of what they tell us."

"Even if it's good advice?"

"We don't throw it out completely. Rather, we store it away until the chap's gone off, frustrated at our non-compliance; then we dig it out and pretend it was ours all along."

"How does my flirtation with the Vietnamese coroner fit into your unofficial policy?"

"Well, as long as we're getting something out of it . . . He *is* sharing information with you, isn't he?"

"Everything he knows, I know. The only problem is that we have different results for our two bodies."

"That's undoubtedly your mistake. You aren't really very good, are you?"

"I assumed I'd messed up when I saw his results. My fellow was apparently the driver, Tran. He was in worse shape than the Tran they had on ice at the Vietnamese Embassy."

"Are they all called Tran over there?"

"Only the ones that aren't called Nguyen. Anyway, our Tran had been laid out at the local temple for a couple of days while they worked out what to do with him. But then they found the other Tran, the one with the Vietnamese tattoos, so naturally they contacted the Vietnamese Embassy.

"Once a body's out of the water, it deteriorates quite rapidly, so my Tran was in a horrible state when I got him. They packed their Tran in ice and waited for Nguyen Hong to come and take a look. The ice made a mess of their corpse too. So neither of us had optimal material to work with."

"Excuses accepted. Did you two agree on anything?"

"We're both quite certain they didn't die from drowning. We also agreed they'd been weighted down."

"So they weren't supposed to be found?"

"That depends on whether you adhere to the Dtui theory."

"Which is?"

"If they'd really wanted the bodies to stay down, they would have used flex or wire, something that doesn't dissolve that fast."

"Brilliant. So if we accept the Dtui hypothesis, whoever

dumped them in the water wanted them bobbing back up. Do you know what they died of?"

"Well, mine appears to have had a major trauma in his chest artery. Nguyen Hong's seen it often in motorcycle victims: high-speed collisions."

"And as he was the driver, we could surmise that their car had an accident."

"Could be."

"Did you get to see his Tran as well?"

"I'm sneaking in to the embassy this afternoon when all the dignitaries are at the reception. You people are never short of receptions, are you?"

Civilai rolled his eyes. He was obviously slated to meet the Cuban delegation too.

"That's why it's called the Communist 'Party,' and not the Communist 'sit down and get some work done.'"

Siri laughed.

"What about the rumors that these fellows had been tortured?"

"True as far as I can tell. Both of them."

"How peculiar. Why would anyone want to torture a driver?"

"This case has more questions than answers, I'm afraid.

According to Nguyen Hong, his man may have died from the torture."

"No connection with a high-speed collision?"

"None he could tell."

Rajid, the crazy Indian, was walking along the bank toward them. He wore his only sarong, a threadbare old thing. He was an unkempt but very handsome young man who was kept alive by the generosity of the shopkeepers who'd known him since he was a child. They'd never heard him speak.

He sat cross-legged a few feet from the old men and started to play with his penis. The log where they sat was just as much the Indian's as theirs.

"Hello, Rajid."

"Hi, Rajid." But he had better things to do than respond.

For some unfathomable reason, Civilai lowered his voice to continue his interrogation of Siri. "Any indication from your friend as to why the Viets are accusing *us* of this, rather than the Hmong? If they drove through Borikhumxai, they were asking to get themselves kidnapped by their old enemies."

"Right. But there are two reasons why they don't think that happened. And I won't charge you for all this free intelligence you're extorting from me. One, they had an armed escort all the way to Paksan. From there, the road was well policed and considered secure. They were last seen at Namching, just sixty kilometers from Vientiane.

"Second, if they didn't make it to the city, why would the kidnappers go to the trouble of driving them through all the roadblocks, through Vientiane and eighty kilometers north to dump them in the dam? There are plenty of bodies of water in the south, even the river.

"So the skeptics in Hanoi are suggesting that they did make it to Vientiane, but were picked up by our security units, arrested, or something."

"For what?"

"They haven't told me yet."

"Who?"

"The spirits."

As always, Civilai fell about laughing at the very mention of Siri's spirits. The doctor's ongoing burden was just a long running joke to Ai. He was too much of a pragmatist to take any of it seriously. He got nimbly to his feet, put his arms straight in front of him, and began to hop up and down like a Hong Kong ghost. "Ooooh, Doctor Siri, help me. The Pathet Lao electrocuted my nipples because I didn't stop at the traffic light."

Siri laughed reluctantly at the ridiculous sight of his friend prancing around like a ghoul. They never saw him like this at politburo meetings.

The joke was, of course, topical in that the Vientiane administration was at that moment debating whether to invest in a seventh traffic light and who should operate it. The volume of traffic didn't warrant such a major investment, but they were worried about the image a lack of lights might project overseas. The Department of Transport had acquired a report that showed that of all capital cities, only Bujumbura had fewer traffic lights. At the meeting, Civilai had brightened the ridiculous proceedings by suggesting the costs could be halved due to the fact there were so many red lights left over from the old regime. They'd only have to buy green ones.

"You old fool. Sit down and act your age. Forget I said anything."

Civilai, laughing but winded, sat himself back on the log and swigged at the coffee Siri held out for him.

"You don't waste any time, older brother."

"What 'any time' don't I waste, little brother?"

"You only got back yesterday. Your meeting with Haeng could only have been this morning."

"What makes you think . . . ? Aha, what a mind for one so old and feeble. You didn't tell me about the electric nipples, did you? I wouldn't make much of a criminal, would I?"

"You just aren't used to dealing with a supreme intellect."

"Well, supremo, what's the next stage in your investigations?"

"Nguyen Hong and I are taking the bus up to Nam Ngum."

"Honeymoon?"

"Fishing trip."

"The third body?"

"There's a chance all three were planted there together. Maybe Hok just hasn't had a chance to escape his rock yet. If he's still under water, his body should be better preserved than the Trans. It could tell us more."

"You taking your snorkel?"

"I can't swim."

"So *that's* why you're still in Laos!"

They finished the coffee and did their best to ignore Rajid making whoopee with himself along the bank.

The Pathological Rebel

Dr. Siri,
  You are to go to Khamuan as soon as possible. Contact me
for details.

Haeng.

"What?" Siri looked up at Geung, the harbinger of doom, who looked back at him blankly. "Where did you get this, Mr. Geung?"

"A ma . . . ma . . . man on a motorcycle."

"What's happening to this job? For nine months we plod along nicely: a couple of old ladies, the odd electric shock, and a bicycle fatality. No murders, mysteries, or mayhem. Then, all of a sudden, the body business explodes like an atomic bomb. I've got corpses coming out of my ears."

Geung looked at Siri's ears but didn't see the corpses. The doctor briefly considered using the telephone, but opted instead to walk across the street to the Justice Department. He waited forty minutes till Haeng was free.

"Siri, come in. The army has . . . sit down, for goodness sake. The army has contacted us for urgent assistance in Khamuan. You'll be leaving tomorrow."

"But I'm—"

"It appears there has been a series of mysterious deaths

amongst the upper ranks of military personnel working on an agricultural—"

"I—"

"—an agricultural development project down there. Neither the army nor the police have been able to ascertain the cause of death. Until they get an official appraisal, they can't begin to know if it's natural or whether a crime has been committed."

Siri still hadn't sat. He stood waiting for Haeng to look at him, but the judge was reading a report, or pretending to. "That's all. See my clerk for the details."

"Are you telling me to drop the Vietnam case and run off to the south?"

"Case? Case? Case?" Siri wondered whether the record had stuck. "Siri, you're a coroner, and not a very good one at that. You're sent bodies. You examine them. You send me the results of your findings.

"Coroners don't have cases. *Judges* have cases. *Police* have cases. You, Siri, have dead bodies. You have two such bodies waiting for you in Khamuan. I'm getting a little tired of you putting yourself above your station. Don't start getting too big for your . . . old brown sandals." He smiled minutely at his own cleverness, but still he hadn't looked Siri in the eye. "Now get out."

Siri stood a while and collected his thoughts. He turned and walked to the door. Judge Haeng listened for the sound of it opening and closing, but instead he heard the click of the lock. Something dropped suddenly in his chest. He glanced up to find Siri looking back over his shoulder at him.

"What are . . . ?"

Siri walked back to the desk, rounded it, and sat on the corner a few centimeters from Haeng's shirtsleeve. The young judge was looking confused, somehow vulnerable. Siri grabbed the annoyingly tapping pencil from his hand and pointed it at him.

"Listen, son. I know you have to seem to be what you are. I know you're probably nervous, lost from time to time. I understand how overwhelming all this must be for you. But I don't intend to put up with your insecurity anymore."

"How dare—"

"Don't. Don't say anything that might make me state my opinions as to your qualifications to be doing this job." The judge squirmed slightly in his chair. He seemed sulkier, younger, with every word Siri quietly spoke.

"Even though I happen to know you got this position because of your relatives—"

"I—"

"—you undoubtedly have skills, otherwise they wouldn't have taken the chance with you. You wouldn't have survived the USS.R."

"I—"

"But *I'm* doing a very difficult job too. I'm doing it reluctantly, and I'm doing it poorly because I don't have the right facilities or resources or experience. You, boy, aren't making it any easier for me.

"Whether you or I like it or not, I'm the head coroner. From now on, I shall handle the 'cases' that come through my office as I see fit. I shall follow up on them whenever I deem it necessary, and I shall send you reports that state my opinions when I'm ready to. Once they're signed, there will be no amendments made to suit your statistics. Close your mouth, for goodness sake."

Haeng put his lips together. They appeared to be quivering.

"If my talking honestly like this offends you, I'm very sorry. I apologize to your mother, who probably loves you in spite of everything. I apologize to her for the fact that I have to remind you to be respectful to your elders.

"If I've succeeded only in driving the thought of revenge into your head, let me remind you that I'm seventy-two years old. I'm twenty-two years beyond the national life expectancy. I've exceeded. I'm on overtime. In my natural life, I've already experienced any form of punishment you could come up with.

Basically, there's nothing you can do to me to fill me with even a smidgen of dread.

"I'd be delighted if you fired me, absolutely ecstatic. Sending me north for re-education would be heaven. I'd be packed before you could shake a pencil. It wouldn't even be much of a loss to end up in front of a firing squad. Now, I imagine that puts you in a difficult situation, because I no longer intend to take your rudeness.

"Here's what I'm going to do. Tomorrow, the Vietnamese coroner and myself are going to Nam Ngum Reservoir. We'll spend a night there, maybe two. I'll come back here and run tests in my morgue, and consult with Dr. Nguyen Hong. Then, when I'm certain I can't do anything else in Vientiane, I may very well consider a trip to Khamuan.

"By that time, you will have arranged travel papers for me, and negotiated a flight south on one of the military transports. I'm too old to drive down there on roads full of holes. I'll also need a small per-diem in case of eventualities. You'll have reminded the military that there's only one coroner and he has a very full caseload. As far as I know, the Justice Department isn't subordinate to the military in peacetime. We're doing them a favor.

"I'm leaving now." He stood and handed the pencil back to Haeng. "Naturally, I won't tell anyone we've had this little talk. Whether you discuss it is up to you. In the future, you'll treat me with civility, and I shall offer you my experience and cooperation to help turn you, bit by bit, into the type of judge you should be."

Haeng had stared into his powerful green eyes the whole time, hypnotized. Siri nodded, turned, walked to the door, and polished one sandal on the back of his trousers before leaving the eerily silent room.

A Little Fishing Trip

"Well, I must say this is a lot more civilized than the bus."
Siri and Nguyen Hong sat in the back seat of the black
limousine looking at the driver's thick neck crammed into a
tight Vietnamese military uniform. Nguyen Hong was wearing
something that fit him better for the trip.

"The ambassador wouldn't dream of letting me travel anywhere
on public transport. He says there are bandits everywhere."

"And he thinks we'd be safer in a big expensive car?"

"There is an escort." They looked out through Siri's window
at the short but jolly armed escort on his post office motorcycle.
A hunting rifle was slung over his shoulder. An ambush would
wipe the lot of them out in seconds.

"I don't think your ambassador gets out much."

"Siri, I've been reading up on the resilience of the sphincter."
Siri chuckled.

"And they say the Vietnamese aren't a cultured race."

"You know we were wondering whether the bowels could
have filled with reservoir water naturally over two weeks?" Both
bodies had what they considered to be an abnormally large
quantity of water in them. "Given the minimal fish and algae
damage to the internal organs, the books say the muscle con-
traction would likely have made the bowels relatively watertight.
There shouldn't have been that much water inside."

"Come on, Hong. Don't we have enough mysteries already?

Perhaps they were thirsty and drank a lot of lake water before they were killed."

"None of that water had passed through the kidneys."

"Then, what are you saying?"

"Have you ever been waterskiing, Siri?"

"Oh. All the time. I often hook up the line behind the yacht when I'm on a cruise."

Nguyen Hong laughed. The driver looked at Siri in the rearview mirror and despised him for his wealth.

"Don't tell me you have?"

"I had a privileged youth, before I saw the light."

"Goodness. So, what's it like?"

"Waterskiing? Invigorating."

"And there's a connection between that and the sphincters of Tran and Tran?"

"I'm not sure. There may be. You see, I wasn't the world's best waterskier. I spent more time falling down than skiing. And there's no better way to give yourself an enema than to . . ."

"I get the point. So, do we assume the Trans were merrily waterskiing on Nam Ngum Reservoir?"

"Hardly. But if they'd been dragged behind a boat . . ."

"The effect would have been the same. Very clever. And that could have been part of the torture. God, I hope the torturers got something out of them. They certainly put a lot of effort into getting them to talk. You think they really had anything that important to say? You aren't keeping anything from me, are you?"

"I've told you all I know. And I'm certain the driver knew nothing. All he could have disclosed was how many kilometers to the liter his jeep did."

"Well, if I was the driver I would have told them that at the first sign of danger. Wouldn't you, driver?" The driver ignored him and concentrated all his energy on rounding potholes and scattering pedestrians.

At the reservoir they met the Nam Ngum district chief, who introduced them to the two fishermen who'd found the Trans. The second of these two poor fellows had been sitting in his boat minding his own business, when a Tran came shooting up out of the water like a missile. The brown, misshapen face looked right at the fisherman before flopping back down. It almost gave him a heart attack.

When Siri told the district chief what he had in mind, he knew there wouldn't be a long queue of volunteers. Even the best divers in the district would balk at going down in search of a three-week-old corpse. There was a healthy tradition of folk-lore and superstition around the lake villages, and the discovery of two bodies had shaken most folks up. But in a fishing community there's always one old-timer who'll do anything for a couple of *kip*. In this case it was Dun. Dun couldn't even afford a boat. He usually just waded into the lake to his waist and cast his oft-repaired net into the water a few dozen times. He lived on the low-IQ sprats and water vermin that didn't have the savvy to avoid him.

"Sure, I'll do it . . . for five hundred *kip*."

Since the devaluation in June, the *kip* had settled at two hundred to the US dollar. He was pushing his luck to ask for such a huge sum, but he fully expected the city fellows to bargain him down. They didn't. They gave him half in advance. It was his lucky day.

The second fisherman took Dun out to where he'd been frightened by the sudden appearance of Tran, and Siri and Nguyen Hong stood on the shore with the chief. Dun put on the goggles Siri had brought from town and slid over the side of the boat still wearing his shirt. He wasn't down for more than five seconds before he came up gasping for air. The chief explained it was a result of all the smoking he did. While Dun dove, and choked, dove and choked, Siri got the chief to fill in some of the details of the day they'd found the tattooed man.

"Exactly who was it that identified the marks as Vietnamese?"

"Oh, I was quite certain myself. But it was confirmed by this military chap. He said he'd been stationed over there in Vietnam, and he recognized the tattoos straight away."

"Is he still around?"

"No. He wasn't from here. He was just doing a survey."

"On what?"

"Boat traffic back and forth to the rehabilitation islands, he said."

They could see the two islands in the distance: Don Thao for the male villains and addicts, and Don Nang for the ladies. Siri dreaded to think what type of rehabilitation was going on there.

"Did you see his orders?"

"Goodness no, Doctor. People in uniforms don't like to be bullied by laypeople, and he did have a big gun, so I didn't ask."

Out by the boat, old Mr. Dun was starting to look like a drowning victim himself. Nguyen Hong was concerned.

"Do you think we should call him back in? I don't think he's going to make it." Siri nodded and they were just about to yell to the fisherman, when Dun stopped coming back up.

"Oh, shit." They shielded their eyes from the glaring sun and scanned the water for any sign of Dun. The surface was smooth as glass and the man in the boat seemed unconcerned by what horror might have been going on below him.

Both doctors knew that in fresh water the diver had a little over four minutes. Nguyen Hong had been checking his watch. "Three. Why doesn't the fisherman go down and help him?" Siri asked the chief.

"He says he's not a very good swimmer. No point in losing both of them."

It was a little over the four-minute mark when Dun popped out of the water, his face smiling and purple. It was dramatic last-minute stuff, like Houdini. Dun held up his hand to wave and to show he was holding something. It seemed to be the end of a rope. When he yanked on it, first a foot, then a leg rose out of the water. Hok had been retrieved.

In order to get at the body before the air had a chance to speed up the decomposition, the two coroners set up a makeshift morgue in an empty concrete room behind the dam. The chief's wife kept running in and out with tea.

The findings for Hok were similar to those of the second Tran, but for two major discrepancies. Although there were signs of shock, there was also a huge wound, apparently from a gun fired at close range. It entered his chest a few centimeters from his heart, and exited by the shoulderblade. Nguyen shook his head.

"This really makes no sense. This wound alone should have killed him."

"You don't think it did?"

"Well, it couldn't have. Look."

Siri leaned over the wound and saw what had confused his colleague. The point of entry was still open and angry. But there were clear indications of scabbing around the exit wound. There was no doubt that Hok's bullet wound was an old one, one that was still healing when he died.

"What's he doing running around with delegations with a big hole in his chest? He should have been recuperating somewhere."

"Question one," said Siri. "And then there's question two. Explain this to me." He held up the rubber-coated electric wire that he'd just unwound from Hok's ankle. "It just gets more and more weird."

"You mean, if they had this stuff, why didn't they use it to tie down all three?"

"There's enough on this fellow for a whole regiment. Do you suppose it all means something?"

"That we're being left clues?"

"Perhaps."

"Then, no offense, but I fear they've badly overestimated us. I don't have any idea what it all means. Do you?"

"Not yet. But I will. When we're finished here, I think we should go have another chat with Mr. Dun."

Dun was sitting happily on the veranda of his packing-case bungalow, smoking and drinking his earnings. The thought of offering the doctors anything didn't enter his mind.

"It was a bomb."

"What kind of bomb?"

"The type the shithead Americans used to blow us all to nirvana and back. There was three of 'em down there, half-buried in the muck. They had writing on 'em."

"Do you know what language it was?"

Dun laughed at the idea that he might have ever been blessed with the ability to read. "No. But I tell you what. There was a Chinese flag on one of 'em."

"It isn't my job, I tell you. I don't have to do this. I'm putting in an official complaint to the embassy. This won't be the end of it."

Siri wondered whether there'd be an end to the complaining. The Vietnamese driver hadn't stopped since they left Nam Ngum. Siri had to put up with the brunt of it because he was sitting beside him in the front of the limousine. "It isn't . . . natural."

"I know. Watch that bicycle, will you?"

The trunk of the car might just have been large enough, had it not been for the spare tire and the eight liter cans of petrol. The armed guard had positively refused to have him on the motorcycle pillion. So there really had been no choice.

Mr. Hok, wrapped tightly in canvas but still dripping, leaned stiffly against the back seat beside Dr. Nguyen. Even with the air conditioner full on, the smell was quite overpowering. The driver had half a roll of toilet paper stuffed up his nostrils. Siri turned to Nguyen Hong.

"Do you speak French?"

"Some. It's a bit rusty."

"Driver, do you?"

"Ha. Where do you think I would have earned the privilege of a French education? I'm a pauper. I'm a man of the earth. The soul of the new regime."

"Good." Siri switched to French. "Any theories yet, doctor?"

"Hundreds, but not a one that makes any sense. You?"

"Let's try this. Tran and Hok were here on a mission that was so urgent Hok didn't even wait for his bullet wound to heal. Let's assume it was something damaging to us, and we picked up the delegation before it could reach its destination. They were brought out here to the islands with all the other criminals, tortured until they talked, then dumped in the lake and weighted down with old Chinese ordnance.

"But our people wanted your people to know we'd caught them, so they used dissolving string. They knew we'd then go looking for the third man and discover the Chinese shell casing which, given the chilly relationship between you folks and Beijing, would only serve to rile you even more. How's that?"

"Sounds like a perfect incentive for an international incident. Probably enough to make us break off relations," Dr. Nguyen opined.

"It's exactly the kind of thing our respective hot-headed politburos would latch on to."

"You don't sound very convinced."

"I just feel, I don't know . . . I feel that if something's so clear-cut that *I* can work it out, there obviously wasn't that much effort spent on trying to cover it up. Maybe they didn't expect us to figure out this much. If it had been left up to the police, they'd have put in a report that would have gone straight to the committee. If it hadn't been for the news getting to your embassy, the Vietnamese wouldn't have heard anything about the incident. It would have been covered up and denied.

"It was either an amazing coincidence that someone identified the tattoos, or it was set up step by step. There just happened to be a military person on hand who just happened to recognize the tattoos? I can't believe our side would go to so much trouble to break off ties with Vietnam."

"What do you think we should do?" Dr. Nguyen asked.

"Look, I have to go south for a couple of days. Do you think you could stretch out your official autopsy till I get back?"

"I don't write very fast."

"Good. I'd feel better if we didn't start another war until we knew exactly what was happening," Siri said.

"I agree."

Assassination

They took Hok directly to the morgue, where Siri introduced him and Nguyen Hong to the team. He explained that while he was away in the south, Dr. Hong would be doing tests on Hok and using the office. As Nguyen Hong didn't speak Lao, and apparently Dtui and Geung didn't speak anything else, it wasn't likely to be a chatty few days. But Siri had a feeling they'd all get along nicely.

With the unknowing assistance of Mr. Ketkaew, they put together a bamboo platform on short legs from what was left over from the *khon khouay* office construction materials. By placing it carefully around Tran, they were able to slide Hok into the freezer above him as if he were lying on a very shallow bunk bed.

Siri went to clear a space at his desk for Nguyen Hong and found a large sealed envelope with his name on it propped up against the plastic-skull pencil holder. He assumed it was from Haeng, so he decided not to open it. Now that he was enjoying his work, he didn't really want to be sacked. What he'd said to the judge was all bluff.

But after the Vietnamese doctor left, and Dtui and Geung were out tending their hospital papaya and mango trees, he could put it off no longer. He sat and slit open the plain brown envelope. Inside was a typed note, and it was indeed from the Justice Department. He wondered whether the committee would let him retire peacefully or if he'd be punished again.

He looked down at the signature and was pleased to see the name of Manivone the clerk. She explained that Siri had a seat on the early flight to Khamuan from Wattay Airport at six the following morning. The words "if convenient" were added, probably at Haeng's insistence, as a postscript. He would be met in Khamuan by a Captain Kumsing. Fishing in the envelope, Siri found his travel papers and three thousand *kip* in large notes.

A satisfied smile spread across his face like lard on a hot wok. He stood at his desk and did a little jig around the chair.

"What's her name, then?"

Siri looked up to see Inspector Phosy leaning against the doorframe grinning.

"Claudette. Claudette Colbert."

"Sounds foreign."

"You see? That's the investigative mind at work. Normal people wouldn't have picked up on something like that." Phosy came over to the desk and they shook hands warmly. "How's life for a policeman in a city without crime?"

"Lots of interesting meetings and political seminars. In fact, there's only one case that's causing me any trouble, and that's your friend Mrs. Nitnoy."

Siri put his finger to his lips and nodded toward the open window. "I'm just off for a walk. Want to come?"

"Pleasure."

Siri packed everything he'd need the next day, locked up the morgue, and walked with Phosy down to the river.

In front of the Lan Xang Hotel was a makeshift outdoor bar that had seen better days. People didn't have the money for wining and dining. This little bamboo affair only really did business at sunset. Then the out-of-towners, the government advisers, the "experts" and Party people, came down to enjoy the sunset. Locals gave themselves a treat once a month and sat nursing one soft drink for an hour.

As there were no walls or rules, customers could move the

rickety tables wherever they liked to get a view of the sun taking its leave. Phosy and Siri carried their chairs almost down to the water's edge, and the grunting bar mama lugged the table after them. She was delighted when they ordered half a bottle of Saeng Thip Thai rum and some quail eggs. Siri did have three thousand *kip* in his pocket, after all.

"You probably weren't going to talk about Mrs. Nitnoy at all," Siri said at last. "But the hospital's got its own chicken counter camped right behind our morgue. I get the feeling everything we say in there is on record somewhere. Were you? Going to talk about Mrs. Nitnoy?"

"I was. You sure we can trust the frogs down here?"

Siri laughed. "I didn't ever think it would get to be like this. I know there's no great system of eavesdropping agents and spies. I know it's all in our minds, but a mind is a powerful thing."

The mama came jogging down to the water with a tray. On it were the rum, drinking water, little speckled eggs, and, miracle of miracles, ice. They looked at it as if it had just landed from a different planet.

"Where did you get this, mother?"

She lowered her voice in case there were any police around.

"I've got friends in the kitchen, over there." She nodded toward the austerely tacky frontage of the country's premium hotel. It was a hostelry unlikely to gather ratings stars on the international circuit, but the Lan Xang was the pride of the capital. It seriously overcharged and the staff could only have been trained by Mack Sennett, but at least it was somewhere to put up foreigners.

"I don't suppose they could rustle up some steaks for us, could they?" Phosy asked.

"If you don't mind 'em raw. You'd be shocked if you knew what they've got over there in that friggin' kitchen. Makes you wonder who's got the money to afford any of it. Wine and all, they tell me. Wine!"

"Disgraceful."

"Yell if you need me." She waddled back up the bank.

They poured themselves drinks and were generous with the ice while it lasted.

"So. Mrs. Nitnoy?"

"It's been difficult. I couldn't just stroll up and interview people. You can imagine. But from rumor and hearsay, and goodness knows there's no shortage of that, everything pointed to your comrade having a minor wife."

"H'mm. That's very traditional of him."

"It turns out she's a hairdresser, Mai, at a salon up at Dongmieng. She's from Sam Neua, didn't come down here till early this year."

"You suppose she followed him down?"

"It looks that way. She's only a young thing, about twenty-one. But according to the girls at the salon, she—"

"You went to the salon?"

"I needed a trim and a massage anyway. She was off the day I went. The girls think young Mai has very high ambitions. She doesn't take this hairdressing training seriously at all. According to the others, she said she wouldn't have to be a hairdresser for long."

"Planning a step up."

"Looks like it."

"You think that's enough reason for the comrade to bump off his wife?"

"Why not?"

"Why? He was getting the best of both worlds. He had his official wife for show and official engagements, and his hairdresser for—"

"—in-depth analysis of *Das Kapital.*"

"Exactly. *He* had nothing to gain from it. But *she* did."

"Ah, you're a devious man, Dr. Siri. How would she get access to pills?"

Siri looked across the water, imagining himself with a pipe. "What if she wasn't working on this by herself?"

"Meaning?"

"A boyfriend. I mean a *real* boyfriend. Or what if she's a member of some anarchist movement? It would be to everyone's advantage to get the minor wife into the comrade's house. This is a small world. They just needed to get someone close enough to borrow her pills, slip in the cyanide."

"Someone at the Women's Union?"

"Or at a reception. She liked her beer."

"It still doesn't make sense. If Kham wasn't involved, why . . ."

"You boys all right there?" the mama yelled from the bar. They signaled they were fine.

"Why would he go to so much trouble to cover up the murder? Why would he submit a false report?"

"He did?"

"I got into the files. Your report is the official autopsy document."

"But it wasn't finished. It wasn't signed."

"It is now."

"Bastard. Well, can we get him for that? For forging an official document?"

"We don't know it was him."

"I do. He stole it from my office. Right under my nose."

"Your word against his."

Siri took a long swig of his rum and almost choked on an ice cube. Phosy slapped him on the back.

"Thanks. So what do we do now?"

"What we do is continue to keep quiet. I'll see what I can get on the hairdresser, and make discreet inquiries about Kham. We still don't have enough to make an official complaint, not even if we knew who to submit it to."

"This stinks. I thought we'd taken over so we could clean up society. But all we're doing is changing the variety of the corruption."

"Don't be so negative. This is just one isolated case. Things are better, you know that. The country the way it is now is a much healthier place to bring children into."

"Is that re-education talking?"

"No. It's me. I believe it. Laos is doing all right."

They watched the sun land somewhere in Thailand and the pink sky turn to purple, then mauve. On a rock down by the water, a boy with regulation short hair and a girl with regulation long hair sat two feet apart. They weren't allowed to hold hands.

The rum was gone and Phosy refused to let Siri walk him back to the hospital to get his bike. They shook hands in front of the hotel, comrades in crime prevention. Siri held on to the hand after it was shaken.

"Thanks for doing this. I know you're taking a risk."

"Me? No. I'm a born-again communist. Nobody's watching me anymore. But your friends need to be careful. Who else knows about this?"

"Only Teacher Oum at the Lycée. She did all the tests."

"Well, you tell her to be careful. She should tell nobody else."

"She knows."

"Good. I'll keep in touch."

Siri walked back through the deserted streets. It was only 8 P.M., but Sethathirat Road was as quiet as the grave. Only an unlit bicycle passed him on his way home. Small pyres of burned rubbish were smoldering on street corners. A rat emerged from a drain and chased a skinny cat through the portal of Ong Teu temple.

These were streets that used to ignore time. Clubs and bars that closed only when the last drunk fell out into the street. Whores and addicts had littered the sidewalks. He'd heard about that other extremity, and here he was at this one. He couldn't bring himself to believe there wasn't something safe and joyful between the two.

Even before he reached his lane, the dog howls struck up. After the quiet of a Vientiane night, he felt responsible for disturbing the peace. The uneven surface of the unpaved road caused him to stagger once or twice. The rum had affected his balance. He wanted it under control before Miss Vong spotted him from her curtain observatory. He turned onto his front path, where Saloop crouched, growling, in front of him.

The curtain quivered.

"Good night, Miss Vong."

There was no response. He looked down at the dog. Perhaps if he made an effort, perhaps if he could befriend this mangy critter, word would get around the neighborhood that he wasn't such a bad human after all.

Instead of walking around the animal as he usually did, he stepped directly toward it. He uttered soft sounds to calm the beast. For every step Siri took forward, the confused mongrel took one backward. It was scared, but it growled on. This tango continued until Saloop was backed right up against the front door.

Not wanting to lose a finger, Siri cupped his hand as if he were holding a treat and crouched down to offer it to Saloop. Instantly the dog barked, and there were two sharp cracks like the sound of a whip. Siri looked around, not sure where the sound had come from, and the dog used the diversion to scurry off into the vegetables.

Siri stood, looked back toward the pitch-black lane, then back up at the house. The only light came from a gas lamp in an upstairs window. There was nothing to be seen but shadows. Something unnerved him about the sound, but there was nothing he could do. He walked inside and closed the door.

With his alarm clock set for four thirty, Siri showered and went to bed early. Even before the musty smell of the kapok pillow reached his nostrils, he was asleep.

Tran, Tran, and Hok were walking with him along a busy city street. It was the West: an English-speaking country. There were cars and throngs of impatient people. It was evening, and the

neon lights all around flashed and glowed, spelling out words
he couldn't read.

The three Vietnamese were huddled about him like security
guards around a corrupt president. Whenever someone from
the street tried to approach Siri, one of the men would step
between them and push the person off roughly. Even though
many were twice the size of the little Vietnamese, they yielded to
the bodyguards.

Every now and then, Siri recognized passersby and tried to
greet them. There were friends from the north, colleagues,
even Dtui and Geung were walking along that street. But he was
embarrassed, because every time they came to say hello, the
Vietnamese fought them off. Tran, Tran, and Hok looked as
they must have looked in life. They seemed happy, enjoying
their rude work. They didn't speak, just shielded Siri and hurried him along the road.

A child in the crisp elementary-school uniform of the republic stood in front of them. He looked nervous and held a pencil
in one hand and a pad of paper in the other. Even though Siri's
entourage could have trampled over him, he bravely stood his
ground and held out the pad. He wanted Siri's autograph. The
four men stopped.

The doctor reached forward. He cupped his fingers as if he
were holding a treat and crouched down. The child smiled; what
teeth he had were red with betel nut. He took a step forward, but
before Siri could take the pencil from him, the Vietnamese
pounced on the child and beat him. They kicked and trampled
him. Siri was appalled. He tried to pull the men off, but they had
immense strength.

Through the hole that passed through Hok's chest, he
could see the boy's face. He was dying, but he was changing
also. The childlike face peeled away to reveal the face of an
old man. The guards stood back and the man, now dressed in
the uniform of the People's Liberation Army, lay dead in a pool

of blood. Beside him was a broken syringe; Siri had mistaken it for a pencil. The acid it contained bubbled and hissed on the sidewalk. A crowd had formed of the people who'd passed them earlier. Each of them held a syringe that dripped with acid.

Siri snapped awake from his dream and was suddenly fearful of the silence and darkness around him. There was no moonlight. Although he could see nothing, he had a feeling there were people in the room. He could sense their movements.

"Who's there?"

There was no answer. He pulled his mosquito net to one side and held his breath. He concentrated on the blackness, trying to pick out familiar shadows in the room, movement, but he couldn't even see the outline of the window.

The dog chorus rose gradually in the distance, pained, high-pitched howls. And out of that chorus came the voices. He knew whose they were. There were three, speaking Vietnamese. Chanting, rather: "The black boar is still here. The black boar is still here."

And Siri woke again. This time the alarm clock yanked him conscious. It was still dark, but some dull natural light now bled through the window. The luminous dials of the clock confirmed that it was indeed four thirty. He felt like he hadn't slept at all. The mosquito net was off him, and the insects had feasted on his blood.

He dressed clumsily, grabbed his bag, and walked downstairs in some sort of trance. He used his flashlight to illuminate the way. The front door creaked open, and he shined the beam out along the path. Saloop wasn't on duty, and the house seemed oblivious to his leaving. He closed the door and used the light to inspect it. It was about twelve centimeters thick and must have been magnificent when the house was still loved and the hinges oiled, the panels varnished. Now it was clumsy and crooked.

He felt a chill when the light of the torch found the two bullet holes at chest level. There was no question what they were. The shells hadn't been able to pass through the solid teak. If Siri hadn't bent down when he did, he was certain those two shells would now be in him.

To Khamuan by Yak

The Yak-40 lifted uncomfortably, like an overfed goose. Like the two Soviet pilots sitting at the controls, it wasn't pretty to look at. Siri couldn't imagine what deal had been struck to make this clumsy airplane and its original crew available twenty-four hours a day to Lao VIPs. Neither could he think what the pilots must have done wrong to be punished so. But for six months it had ferried generals and ministers around the country, courtesy of the Soviet Union.

Siri was the only passenger. The co-pilot pointed to a bench seat and the safety harness when he came aboard, and grunted. That was the end of the in-flight service. But he was glad to be alone. He needed time to think. He'd been in battles, been shot at often enough. But assassination was a different matter altogether. It was personal and rude. He was more angry than afraid.

On his way to the airport he'd made two stops. He'd awakened Nguyen Hong and warned him to be careful. He suggested he write down everything they knew and leave it in an envelope at the embassy, to be opened in case of any "accident."

Then he'd stopped at Dtui's. She was already awake. Her mother was in a bad way. Neither of them had slept. This was hardly a time for more bad news. He didn't mention getting shot at, but he told her if anyone came by to ask, she should deny all knowledge of any case having to do with any

Vietnamese. She was a cleaner and Geung was a day laborer, and they wouldn't know a head from a pair of feet. From his tone, she could tell he was deadly serious.

The plane growled its way south, the Mekong to its right, the rising sun to its left dazzling through the tiny portholes. Siri felt like there were hornets in his head. It wasn't just from the vibration of the fuselage: so many ideas were buzzing out of order in there, reality and fantasy were getting jumbled.

He tried to interpret last night's dream. The Vietnamese were obviously protecting him. Perhaps they were warning him not to trust anyone. Who was the boy with his blood-red smile? What had Siri discovered that made him dangerous enough to kill? Or, more likely, what did they suspect he'd discovered? And who were "they"?

It was clear that he was getting close to an answer, close enough to make one side or the other nervous. He just hoped he could work it all out before they managed to do away with him. How frustrating it would be to spend eternity in the afterlife with an unsolved puzzle.

The Yak bounced along the makeshift Air America air strip in Khamuan as if they'd forgotten to put wheels on the thing. It kicked up clouds of dust and jerked to a stop just as the runway came to an end. The co-pilot came back to open the door and virtually pushed Siri through it. They weren't stopping. The plane was on its way to Pakse to collect the prime minister and the Cuban delegation.

Siri ran off the runway to avoid being decapitated by the pirouetting Yak, and watched as it hurled itself into the morning sky. Once the engine sounds had faded, there were no others to replace it. He stood at the end of two hundred meters of straight earth surrounded by lush jungle vegetation, alone.

The only comfort he could derive from the situation was that this was Khamuan. This was the province he'd apparently been born in and lived in for the first ten years of his life. He hadn't been back since. Nothing he saw now brought back any memories. Jungle looked pretty much the same everywhere.

Twenty minutes later, he heard the sound of a vehicle searching for the right gear. It got closer. He left his shady spot and walked out to the strip. An old Chinese army truck lurched through the vegetation at the far end of the runway and stopped there. Siri stood at his end and the truck stayed at the other, like gunslingers weighing each other up.

When it was obvious he wasn't going to walk to them, the truck sped down the strip and skidded to a halt in front of Siri, leaving him with a coating of dust. Two soldiers jumped down from the truck and saluted.

"Dr. Siri?" Given the circumstances, he wasn't likely to be anyone else.

"Captain Kumsing?"

"That's me." The other man, the one standing back and wearing an unmarked uniform, spoke. "It's nice of you to come so soon. One more day and the bodies would have been walking around." It was a joke, but Mrs. Nitnoy, sprang to Siri's mind.

"Yes. They tend to do that."

In the truck on their way to the project base, Captain Kumsing did his best to summarize what had been happening out there in the wilds. This, he explained, was a military program. It was a pilot development project to rehabilitate the struggling Hmong districts devastated by years of war. At the same time, they hoped to wean the Hmong off their dependency on their opium crop.

He neglected to mention that the Hmong comprised some 10 percent of Laos's population and many of them had been on the other side, fighting the communists alongside the Americans. Siri's immediate but unasked question was why the military would give aid to the Hmong when many other Lao areas were in an equally desperate state.

Captain Kumsing explained that the project had begun in July and was initially under the command of Major Anou, a veteran of Xepon and Sala Phou Khoun. Siri remembered Anou as an ambitious man with relatives in France. He was about fifty and had been in excellent health when they'd met. Siri had given him a medical exam a few years back. That's why he found it hard to believe that the major had died of a heart attack after only a month at the project site. He had died in his sleep, and the camp medic could find no suggestion of foul play.

They buried the major, as was the custom, and the Vietnamese adviser, Major Ho, took over while they waited for a Lao replacement. After two months, this second major vanished. He wandered off into the jungle and didn't come back. But few people were surprised. By then he'd already started to talk to himself and act oddly. When he left, he'd been wearing a crown of *pak eelert* leaves. The Lao assumed he'd been eaten by tigers.

In September, after a period without a commander, two young officers arrived from the north. Both had been newly promoted. The senior of the two took over the role of project director. But after two weeks he developed mysterious stomach cramps. He was in such pain that they flew him to Savanaketh for a checkup. The doctors there could find nothing wrong with him.

He came back with a clean bill of health, and died a week later. He was thirty-four.

His colleague took over. He'd been doing fine until a week ago. He hadn't had any physical or mental problems. Everyone thought the curse was ended. Then one day he was driving out to view the project site. He liked to drive the jeep himself. There were two other men with him. They warned him he was going a little too fast, considering the state of the road, but he didn't take any notice. It was as if he wasn't really himself.

He told them he was going home. He cut across a cleared area of land and stood, actually stood, on the gas pedal. He sort of froze. He was headed straight for this big old teak tree on the far side of the clearing. The men tried to wrestle the wheel from him, but he was solid—like cement, one of them said. When it was clear what was about to happen, the men threw themselves out of the jeep. They had no choice. One of them didn't make it. He hit his head on a stump and died instantly. The other broke both his legs. He'd looked up in time to see the jeep smash headlong into the tree. His boss was still standing up with his foot on the gas. He flew through the air and hit the tree like a sparrow flying into a pane of glass. Didn't stand a chance.

Siri was amazed. "Who's next in the chain of command?"

The captain sucked his teeth. "Me. But we aren't announcing that. As far as anyone outside knows, there's nobody in charge. The commander's office is empty, and we've passed the word around that we're waiting for a new officer from Vientiane."

"You think that'll make any difference?" The truck was bobbing along a furrow that had been churned through the thick jungle. It was barely a road, and Siri held on to the dashboard to keep his teeth from being shaken loose.

"Of course. We don't want them to know who's in charge. It's obvious they're targeting the leaders."

"Who's 'they'?"

"Well, it's obvious."

"Not to me."

"The Hmong, of course."

"The Hmong? But I thought you were helping them."

"Well, yes. Most of them see it like that. But, of course, in every community you'll find capitalist sympathizers who hold a grudge because they lost."

"And how do you imagine they're knocking off your leaders? Surely a bullet or a grenade would be easier than what you've described."

"Ah, they're cunning. They know that would start a land battle. No, they do it all with their potions."

"They have potions?"

The captain lowered his voice and was almost inaudible
above the sound of the engine. "They're heathens. They practice witchcraft, Doctor. They have all these poisons and hallucinogens. All they need to do is drop some of these drugs into
the water supply or the food."

"The Hmong are poisoning you to stop you from developing
their community?"

"It's revenge, Dr. Siri. They were brainwashed, you see? The
Americans convinced them that us communists would never do
anything to help them if we came to power. They don't realize
that we're all brothers. The Americans managed to make them
believe that they aren't Lao."

"They're not."

"Not technically, Comrade. But they're family. They may not
have been born to Lao parents, but we all live together in the
same homeland. A dog or a cat isn't a human being, but think
how many families treat their dogs like a member of the family.
It's the same thing."

"H'mm. Good point. So you think the dog's biting the hand
that feeds it?"

"In a way, yes. Not the whole pack, Doctor. Just one or two
rabid strays. But until we know what poison they've been using,
we won't be able to round them up. That's why we need you."

They pulled into a sprawling military complex with machinery
and vehicles all over. To anyone foolish enough to believe the
captain, this would have seemed a humanitarian effort to
exceed even the most extravagant of the U.N.'s follies.

Under a makeshift palm-leaf shelter behind the empty command office, two large caskets lay side by side. Bare-chested soldiers carried them inside and placed them on trestle tables that
wobbled under their weight. The men pried off the lids to

reveal Kumsing's predecessor and his companion. They were wrapped in natural tobacco leaves and garnished with herbs. This reduced the smell and kept the bodies in remarkably good condition. There was minimal insect damage.

The camp medic was a twenty-year-old, trained as a field nurse on dummy patients without blood. He and a middle-aged woman from the mess tent were assigned to help Siri with the autopsies. If he'd ever had doubts as to his good fortune at having Geung and Dtui at the morgue, the following six hours dispelled any of them. These two were worse than hopeless.

Even before the bone cutters had begun their cracking of the first rib cage, the boy was throwing up through the open window. He repeated this trick a dozen times during the day. The woman didn't stop gabbing the whole time, asking silly questions, getting in Siri's way to get a better look at the fellow's insides. She had to get it all right to tell the girls back at the canteen. With those two, and the huge flying insects that buzzed in his face like little helicopters, the ordeal was a nightmare.

It wasn't even a nightmare with a happy ending. He wanted very much to find clear signs of natural causes of death, but he couldn't. Neither was there anything to suggest foul play in either man. The junior officer's collision with the tree had made an awful mess of him. Some thirty-eight bones were broken and the skull was shattered. But it was all postmortem. He'd died some time before his jeep hit the tree.

Both men had been in prime physical condition, strong and healthy; but, for some reason, they'd simply stopped living. He couldn't understand it, and he knew that wasn't an answer Captain Kumsing would want to hear. The only other option was, indeed, that someone had used a toxin that left no obvious signs.

Siri put the men back together as best he could without assistance, and soldiers came to replace them in the caskets. It was usual, with deaths such as these, that didn't result from natural causes, for the bodies to be buried as soon as possible without any ceremony at the graveside. They couldn't be cremated, because the belief was that their souls weren't yet ready to go to heaven.

Superstition, religion, and custom often overlapped in Laos, and even Siri, who had no spiritual beliefs, found nothing strange about such a practice. It was just the way it had always been. The bones would be left to commune with the earth until the family decided a fitting period had passed. Then the body, if the family could find it, would be dug up and cremated withfull ceremony.

Siri went to see Kumsing in the project office that he shared with five enlisted men. He was sitting at a far desk, the smallest desk in the office. Siri noticed how the thin man twitched as he worked and wondered whether the tic was a result of the stress he was under. He wore a white T-shirt as a disguise for his rank and had forbidden anyone to salute him. Siri decided that if the Hmong didn't get him, he'd probably worry himself to death.

He took the captain outside and explained what he'd found and what he hadn't. They walked together across the clearing. Even in Vientiane, Siri had never seen so much earth-moving equipment in one place.

"So, are you saying they died of natural causes?"

"No, I'm saying I found no evidence they died of unnatural causes. But neither did I find indications of natural death."

"But the captain crashed into a damn tree. Don't tell me that didn't kill him."

"He was dead before he hit it."

"That's not possible. The men said he was standing up with his foot on the accelerator, yelling his heart out. You must have got it wrong."

"I'd feel a lot better if I did get it wrong. But there's no doubt in my mind. The tree didn't kill him, and a heart attack didn't kill his mate. I couldn't see any evidence they'd been poisoned by anything traditional. But I've heard of potions that can kill a man without leaving obvious signs. It would take a lifetime to test for all of them."

This debriefing obviously wasn't pleasing Kumsing, whose tic became more pronounced the more he heard. He thrashed the side of his fatigues with a sprig of young bamboo.

"Have you interviewed the locals?" Siri asked.

"The Hmong? They just deny everything. They aren't likely to give up one of their own. They're peculiar people, all that spirit-worship mumbo-jumbo. It wouldn't surprise me if they have one of those witch doctors with his own factory turning out poisons and crazy drugs."

"How far is it to the nearest village?"

"Four, five kilometers. Why?"

"I need to go and talk to them."

"Oh. That won't do you any good."

"Captain, the only way we can isolate the drug, if there was a drug, would be to find out what varieties they use out there. Get samples and take them back to do tests in Vientiane. Until that happens, we won't know the cause of death, and you can't arrest anyone. Are you with me?"

"I suppose so."

"Good. I'll need a driver."

"You want to go now?"

"No time like the present."

"But it'll be dark in a few hours."

"Then it's just as well that I'm not afraid of the dark, isn't it?"

They were driving along an overgrown gully similar to the one by the airfield. Siri suspected these tracks couldn't be seen from the air, and were probably set up by smugglers. The Ho Chi Minh Trail was just like this, a tunnel through jungle. It was no wonder the Americans had been unable to shut it down. The Hmong must have learned the trick from their enemy.

Captain Kumsing had opted not to come along on this journey. He'd sent Siri with a driver and a younger captain. The driver was the friendlier of the two.

Siri asked whether they'd be able to see the project site on the way.

"No, sir. It's over that way about thirteen kilometers."

"Really? Seems a bit odd you'd set up a crop substitution project so far from the villages you're helping."

The driver laughed. "Yes, sir. It does, doesn't it?"

The captain glared at Siri, but it didn't stop him smiling. In fact he kept smiling until a large black shape came hurtling at the windscreen with a thud. The shape flapped against the glass and flew up over the roof of the cab. Siri and the captain both shielded their eyes, but the driver seemed used to it.

"Damn thing."

"What on earth was that?"

"Crows, sir. They get sport out of buzzing our transport."

"Crows? Is it normal to find crows this far from cities? I thought they were flying rats."

"I'm not a bird man, me. I know a lot about fish, but—" The crow came at the truck again, this time at the side window where the captain slapped at it. He fought to get the window up, and the angry bird bloodied his hand with its beak.

"Shit!"

Siri helped fight it off until the window was up and the bird flew back into the trees. The driver wound up the window on his side.

"Never seen one as frisky as that. Must be the time of day. You know, I say crows, plural, but I guess there might just be the one. Those brown chest markings, I recognize them. I've seen that fellow before."

The captain sucked at the blood on his wrist and mumbled under his breath. Siri reached into his pack for antiseptic.

"You want me to look at that?"

"It's nothing." And he didn't mean it wasn't a serious wound. He meant it was nothing. He held up his wrist and in spite of the blood they'd all seen, there wasn't a mark.

The driver whistled. "Now, that's odd."

As they neared the village, they passed an army guard post. The sentry waved them through. The road opened into a clearing where thirty or forty bamboo-and-grass huts sat on either side of a small stream. Narrow paths criss-crossed in all directions, and at every intersection there was a small structure like a bridge, too small for even a child to cross. The newer ones were decorated with flowers and incense sticks. Older ones had been ignored and left to fall into decay. The driver saw Siri looking.

"They're bridges so the lost souls can find their way back to their bodies." He laughed.

"Heathens," the captain muttered. Every tree on their way in to the village was circled with colored cloth and white strings. Many had trays of offerings and piles of stones in front of them. Siri thought it was all rather charming, and somehow familiar.

Two more armed soldiers came to meet the truck. The army appeared to be providing very generous security to the villagers of Meyu Bo. One of the soldiers was holding a walkie-talkie and was telling headquarters that the doctor had arrived.

Half a dozen village elders had been herded together into a reception committee for the eminent guest from the capital that they didn't want. They were to stand a few paces back until called upon to offer a sincere welcome.

"Don't expect anything in the way of manners," the captain told Siri when they were out of the truck. "They're an ignorant lot."

One of the guards led Siri to the elders, who stood counting their toes like schoolchildren. They knew not to speak until they were spoken to.

"Elders of Meyu Bo, this is Dr. Siri Paiboun."

Despite their own status, the four men and two women held their palms together high in front of their faces as the army had instructed them. They were surprised when Siri returned the *nop*, beginning even higher and with a deeper bow. That was when they bothered to look at him, and that was when they noticed. They *all* noticed. They stood transfixed by the sight of the little doctor who stood in front of them.

The elders looked sideways at each other to be sure they were all seeing the same miracle. Siri and the soldiers began to feel uneasy. The captain spoke.

"Don't just stand there like buffalo. Don't you have something to say to your guest?"

There was another embarrassing silence before the village headman, Tshaj, took one hesitant step forward. His hands were still pressed together in front of his face. His Lao was strongly accented.

"It is you, is it not?"

"I hope it is," Siri said. He stepped forward to shake the headman's hand, but the old man retreated back to the others.

"Heathens," said the captain. It was obvious he felt no compassion for the proud race that had been his enemy for over a decade.

The elders were huddling and chattering nervously in Hmong. They were plainly confused about something, their *nops* still frozen in front of them.

The driver stepped forward and shook his head. "I've seen 'em nutty before, but they're breaking all the records today. They usually can't wait to get all this official stuff over and done with and get back to whatever fool thing it is they do here."

Siri attempted to take another step forward, but this time all the elders retreated together. He didn't know what to make of it.

"Is there something wrong?"

"How did you come here?" one of the women asked.

"Yak-40." There was silence. "I flew."

The elders chattered again even more excitedly. Then the same woman boldly ventured forward from the group and reached out for Siri's arm. Her hand was shaking. She seemed relieved when she found flesh and bone inside his shirt sleeve. She reported back to the others, and the atmosphere automatically changed.

They all gathered around Siri, touching him, smiling, asking questions in Hmong as if he was a long-lost friend. The military men didn't know what to make of it. The captain called out to him. "You been here before or something?"

"Never," Siri smiled.

"Mad, all of 'em."

The elders half-led, half-carried Siri off to the meeting hut. He was baffled but enjoying the attention. They sat him in the place of honor on the floor facing the doorway, and brought water and sweets for him to eat. The soldiers, they just ignored.

Again and again they tried to ask him questions in Hmong. Each time he told them in Lao that he didn't speak the language. They laughed. He laughed. The soldiers yawned.

Finally the elders settled in a circle around him, leaving a few respectful meters either side of him. Their numbers had swollen now to about twenty. They all introduced themselves, but the only names he remembered were Tshaj, the headman, Nabai, the woman who had inspected him for flesh, Lao Jong, a tall, grinning, toothless man, and Auntie Suab, the second lady elder, who was tiny. She smiled so sweetly that Siri could tell she'd broken many hearts in her life. The captain sat unsmiling inside the doorway with his boots pointed at the circle.

Slowly the light dimmed as more and more villagers came to peer at the amazing sight in the meeting hut. They blocked out the light in the doorway and the windows. The eyes of the children filled the gaps between the banana-leaf walls. Siri could have led them on longer, but he started to feel guilty for taking advantage of this mistaken identity.

"This is all very pleasant," he said. "But it's true what the *soldiers* said." He was surprised to hear himself use the Hmong word for soldiers. He must have picked it up somewhere. "I really am Siri

Paiboun from Vientiane. I'm the coroner [he used the expression 'ghost doctor' to help them understand] at Mahosot Hospital. I'm sure I look like someone you know, but I'm afraid I'm not him."

They didn't reply, just stared at him, smiling. He wondered whether they understood.

"Just who do you think I am?"

"You are Yeh Ming," the headman said without hesitation. The villagers all around them gasped.

"I wish I were," Siri laughed. "He must be *quite a warrior*. What does he do, old Yeh Ming?" The expression *quite a warrior* was a Hmong phrase he didn't remember knowing.

Auntie Suab spoke quietly and seriously, as if this were some type of test. "Yeh Ming is the greatest shaman."

"Yeh Ming has supernatural powers," Tshaj added. "One thousand and fifty years ago, you . . . he . . . drove back twenty thousand Annamese with just one ox horn."

"A thousand and fifty years ago?" Siri laughed again, and all the Hmong laughed with him. They were a good audience. "It's true I am beginning to show my age, but a thousand and fifty years? Don't be cruel to an old man."

Nabai spoke. "This isn't the body you used then. You couldn't fight off half a Vietnamese with the body you have now."

"*That's very kind of you.*" That was another Hmong expression. It was obviously a very simple language if he could pick it up just by being around these people. "But if I've changed bodies, how do you know it's me?"

The captain finally lost interest in this fiasco and went off to eat with the guards.

"A body is easy to shed," Tshaj explained, "but the eyes will always be there. You can't replace the river-frog emeralds. Zai, the rainbow spirit, turned two river frogs into emeralds to thank the first shaman for giving him more colors. They're passed from body to body."

So it was his eyes. It all came down to the fact that he had green eyes. Through the course of the discussion and the meal that followed, he wasn't able to convince them he wasn't a one-thousand-year-old shaman, not even by showing them his motorcycle license. Even when they'd persuaded him to stay the night with them, and the captain and the driver had gone back and left him in the charge of the permanent village guards, he still wasn't comfortable. He felt embarrassed to be receiving food and lodging on the strength of his similarity to Yeh Ming. But he was having a good time.

The business he'd come to resolve had been shuffled to the side somehow. But he thought that as a respected imposter, he'd eventually get more answers than the captain. He was sitting at the edge of the village under a rustic pavilion with the senior men. They were into the second bottle of the most delicious fruit-flavored rice whisky he'd ever tasted.

"I want to tell you all why I'm here," he said.

Tshaj interrupted him. "We know why you're here."

"You do? Why, then?"

"You're here for the dying soldiers."

"That's true. Can you tell me what killed them?"

"Yes."

Sweet Auntie Suab arrived at the crucial moment. She was a maker and distributor of amulets and she carried a large collection to the table.

Tshaj was annoyed. "Suab, this is a men's meeting."

"I'm so sorry, brother. But this can't wait until morning." She dumped the assortment of pendulums and amulets and religious and sacrilegious artifacts on the table in front of Siri and stood back. Siri laughed.

"Oh, God. Don't tell me I have to wear all these." The others laughed too.

Suab shook her head. "No, Yeh Ming, only one. I blessed one of them with your spell."

"Which one?"

"You'll know."

"How?"

"It'll come to you."

Siri raised his eyebrows and looked down at the thirty-some-thing medallions in front of him. He'd pick the wrong one and perhaps they'd take him more seriously as a coroner. The odds were in his favor. He knew it would dispel the magic of the evening, but perhaps that was a good thing.

He reached across the table for the largest amulet. It was an ugly, dust-covered lump. He felt sure if Suab had blessed an amulet for him, she would have doused it, or anointed it, or at the very least dusted it off. This was easy.

But as he reached across, the ever-dangly button on his shirt cuff became anchored on something. He lifted his arm to find he'd hooked a small black prism on a leather thong. The amulet was so old that any characters or images that had once been etched on it were now rubbed away.

"Yes." Auntie Suab said with a sigh. "Yes."

"No, wait. That wasn't fair. Best out of three?" But it was over.

Suab gathered up the failed medallions and, with a satisfied smile, walked off to leave the men and the blessed amulet to their business.

"That was weird," Siri conceded.

"Aren't you going to put it on?" one of the men asked.

"Certainly not. I'm not about to start believing all this non-sense."

"Then you won't be pleased to hear how the soldiers died," said Tshaj.

"Don't tell me it was voodoo." He disguised his unease with another giggle, but noticed how Lao Jong and a man so dark Siri could barely see him exchanged a guilty look. Because it was one of his duties as head of the village, Tshaj assumed the role of story-teller. The others refilled the glasses and leaned back in their seats.

"The soldiers came half a year ago. They said they were coming to help us. They said they needed to clear forest land so we'd have somewhere to plant crops to replace our opium.

"We've always grown opium. We don't do much with it ourselves. Use it as medicine sometimes, eat it when there's no food. But it was our only cash crop for a long time. It was good enough for the French. They bought every kilo we could produce. And the Americans refined it in Vientiane and sold it to their own troops in Saigon.

"But the good People's Democratic Republic decided it was a terrible thing. They said we have to substitute something else for it. Something healthful. If you ask me, I'd say they just wanted to keep our income down, so there's no chance of our funding an uprising.

"We've been watching the soldiers clear the forests, and we've been waiting and waiting to see what substitute crops they were going to plant for us. Hectares and hectares they've cleared."

Siri nodded. "I thought as much. Do you know where they're selling the timber?"

"Oh, yes," the dark man said. "It goes through Vietnam and gets shipped off to the enemies of the Chinese, to Formosa."

"Really? I wonder just how much of those profits is being shared with the government."

"It doesn't make any difference to us," Tshaj said. "If the army gets the profit, or the government gets the profit, it's all the same to us out here. *We* don't get anything."

Lao Jong spoke up from the far end of the long table the Americans had left as their only memento. "The animals are fleeing from the saws, so we have to go further to hunt. Some of our young men are away for weeks at a time, looking for game. The water in our stream is polluted by the silt that's running down from the hills. But these are just physical problems."

"Yes, they're only physical problems," Tshaj continued. "We've suffered many physical ills over the years and survived. That's not what frightens us here. It wasn't physical things that killed your soldiers. As you know well, Yeh Ming, powerful spirits abide in the jungle. [Siri rolled his eyes.] Most are kind, helpful spirits, but there are many malevolent lost souls out there. They leave the bodies of the troubled dead and reside in the trees with the nymphs and the ghosts."

"A bit like sub-letting, you mean?"

Tshaj ignored the smiling doctor. "When we cut down a tree for our huts, or to make space to plant crops, we ask for permission from the tree spirits. We make offerings, sacrifices sometimes, as our own shaman sees fit. Usually, the spirits will move on without blaming us. After all, we have to live together, share what resources we have. That's the way it has always been.

"Some of the trees in these parts are as old as the land itself. The spirits have become powerful here. When the soldiers came, they didn't ask permission. They didn't show any respect. They didn't sacrifice a buffalo or consult a shaman. They just started cutting. And they cut and cut and hauled the timber away in trucks. They cut hundreds, thousands of trees.

"Can you imagine? Even the most benevolent spirits have become evil. They all seek revenge."

"The tree spirits killed the soldiers?" Siri knocked back his liquor and his glass was refilled. "How did they do that, exactly? Lightning?"

"Possession."

"Oh, come on."

Toothless Mr. Lao Jong leaned forward onto the table and looked into Siri's eyes.

"You, of all people, should know about that."

"I should?"

"Think of your dreams."

Siri shuddered. "What do you know about my dreams?"

"I know you can't keep the spirits in anymore."

"I—"

"Mr. Lao Jong is our *Mor Tham*, our spirit medium. He can see. He knows you're a shaman."

"I am not." Lao Jong's uninvited intrusions were beginning to get as annoying as his gummy smile.

"The dogs know it."

"What dogs?"

"They all know who you are. They know what lives inside you."

"The only thing living inside me is nausea. This stuff is making me feel ill."

"It shouldn't. It's all from the forest."

The crowd of men around Siri was beginning to blur. The alcohol was deceptively strong, and the topic of conversation was giving him the willies. But deep down in his agnostic scientific soul, he wanted all this talk of ghosts and mediums to be true. He wanted there to be something else, something illogical. He'd been confined and restricted by science all his life, and he was prepared to break free.

But this? This was all talk: all superstitious claptrap from a bunch of old drunk village Hmong. They got lucky. Everyone has dreams. The dog comment was just a guess. Basically it was all crap. He stood shakily, excused himself, and asked to be taken to his bed. The whisky was beginning to make him confused. Two of the men came smiling to prop him up from either side and began to lead him off. But before they had gone far, Tshaj called out to him.

"Yeh Ming." Siri and his props turned back. "I speak a few words, just enough to get by. But no one else at this table tonight speaks Lao."

That was the last thought to enter Siri's swimming head. They walked him to the guest hut and laid him down, but he wouldn't remember any of that. He was unconscious long before.

It shouldn't have surprised him, given all the talk and the setting and the whisky, but his dream that night was a spectacle.

He was dressed as a Hmong of a thousand years hence. For reasons known only to the Great Dream Director, he was riding Dtui's bicycle through a fairy-tale jungle. He didn't see the trees as trees, but rather as the spirits that inhabited them. They twirled together from the roots to high up in the sky. They were kind and welcoming, just as Tshaj had described them. Many were women, beautiful women, whose long hair curled into, and became, the grain of the wood.

It was a happy place; he seemed to know all the spirits, and they liked him. But the bicycle was squeaky and its noise awoke a black boar that had been asleep behind the bushes. Its fangs were still bloody from a kill. The tree spirits called out to Siri, warning him, but he seemed unable to move. The bicycle was locked with rust. Heaven knows why he didn't get off and run for his life.

The boar charged. He looked up at the spirits but they couldn't do anything to help. When he looked back, a small woman was standing between him and the boar. She seemed fearless, even when the boar leaped from the ground and soared through the air toward her. Before it could strike, she held up the black amulet in front of its face, and it turned from muscle and fur into a black sheet of burned paper. It floated harmlessly to the ground and crumbled.

She turned to Siri. He'd expected to see the sweet face of Auntie Suab, but instead it was the same old man's face with its betel-nut red mouth that had lain dead at the feet of the Vietnamese in his previous dream. (He must have been making a guest appearance.) He ignored Siri and went from tree to tree ripping down the spirits and the nymphs and putting them into a Coca-Cola bottle. Even before the bottle was full, the trees were empty of spirits, and he vanished. All that was left was Siri on his rust-locked bicycle surrounded by trees that were now just wood.

He heard the sound of chewing, and looked back over his

shoulder to see that the jungle floor behind him was a vivid green. The color seemed to vibrate as it reflected in his eyes. And as he watched, the carpet of green spread closer and closer to him. And when it was close enough, he could tell that this was a swarm of green caterpillars. He looked back; everything in its path had been destroyed, devoured by the hungry insects.

The bark of the trees around him was stripped away, the leaves were gone in seconds, and slowly the tree trunks were leveled. When there were no more trees, the caterpillars caught sight of Siri. They crawled all over him and Dtui's bicycle, and just as they'd eaten everything else, they began to chew their way through him as he watched calmly. It tickled. Very soon, Siri could feel himself inside the caterpillars.

A flock of crows swooped down and ate the caterpillars that contained small bits of Siri. Then whales somehow managed to eat the crows. And the whales were swallowed up by volcanoes and suddenly Siri, or at least bits of Siri, was in every creature and every geological feature on Earth. It was one hell of a good finish.

"Yeh Ming."

Siri knew neither where nor, momentarily, who he was. He looked up to see the pretty face of a girl like a tree nymph looking down at him.

"The elders wish to invite you to breakfast."

She was speaking Hmong, and he understood. She blushed at his smile and left him alone. He was on the floor of a simple hut on a mattress of straw. He felt immaculate, invincible, and incredibly hungry. When he sat up, he felt something at his neck. It was the black amulet. He didn't take it off.

The jeep came to pick Siri up after ten. The guards had called through to headquarters earlier and warned them that the doctor was acting oddly. They were afraid he might have been doped. They reported the previous night's proceedings.

At headquarters, Siri jumped from the jeep like a young man and strode into the hidden commander's office. The men there looked up at him; he thought he detected some mistrust in their eyes.

When he saw the doctor, Kumsing rose and walked over to him. "Outside." He took Siri's arm roughly and led him through the door. When they were far enough away from the building, Kumsing spoke angrily. "All right. Suppose you tell me just what your game is."

"Well, I used to box."

"You know what I mean. What exactly have they sent you here to do?"

"They sent me to answer your request for a coroner."

"And I suppose it's just a coincidence that you speak fluent Hmong?"

"Given that there's only one coroner in the country, you'd have to assume yes, it is a coincidence."

"Why didn't you see fit to mention it to me?"

"Well, firstly because it's none of your business. And secondly because I didn't know."

Kumsing looked at him in amazement. "Didn't know? You didn't know you could speak Hmong? Don't insult my intelligence, Doctor."

"I promise you, when I arrived in Saravan, I couldn't speak a word of it. But I believe there may be a scientific explanation for that."

"What's that round your neck?"

"It's a magic amulet."

"My men tell me you've been here before. The Hmong knew you. You omitted to tell me that, as well."

"Well, I probably forgot. It was a long time ago. About a thousand years, to be exact. At that time I defeated twenty thousand Annamese with an ox horn. I have to assume it was a rather large one."

Kumsing's expression turned from anger to concern. "They haven't . . . done anything to you, have they?"

"You mean hypnotized me and turned me into a lunatic? No. I don't think so. This is the way I've always been. It was quite an amazing visit, mind you."

"Did you get the samples?"

"Their potions? No. They didn't use any. Captain Kumsing, I suggest you come to your office with me and listen to a most strange tale. Twenty-four hours ago, if someone had told it to me, I would have had them committed to an asylum. But, like me, I think you'll eventually come to believe that there may be only one way to save your life."

The Exorcist's Assistant

The village elders were dressed in their Sunday best and standing at attention when the jeep arrived that evening. As per instructions, only Siri and Kumsing were on board. Kumsing had driven. The village guards had reluctantly pulled back to the post on the road. The two visitors were at the mercy of Meyu Bo Village. Kumsing was already having doubts.

Siri and the elders greeted each other in Hmong. He'd explained his theory to the captain that morning. Siri had been born in Khamuan. He'd lived there for the first ten years of his life. He knew nothing of his parents. When he was about four, he went to live with an old woman. But if his mysterious family had been Hmong, or if they'd lived in a Hmong area, he would have absorbed a lot of the language and spoken it.

His scientific explanation was that the language had remained dormant for all these years, but was reawakened by this exposure to Hmong people. Kumsing found it hard to believe, but Siri felt a good deal more comfortable with that explanation than with the alternative. He'd check its likelihood with the professors at Dong Dok College when he went home.

The elders led the two men to Lao Jong's hut, where an ornate shrine had been set up facing the door. An ornamental sword was embedded in the earth in front of it. Two trays sat on the altar. One was decorated with a banana-leaf cone, other banana-leaf origami, and flowers. An unshelled chicken's egg sat proudly at the summit of the cone, defying gravity. The second tray contained small portions of foodstuffs, alcohol, and betel nuts all shrouded in white unspun cotton threads.

Tshaj went up to the captain. "You bring?"

Kumsing displayed all the outward signs of calm skepticism, but when he spoke, his voice trembled. He handed over his old uniform shirt. "Here, but I don't want candle wax and ash all over it."

Tshaj took it from him and folded it flat. Lao Jong's wife lifted the second tray on the altar. It had been sitting on a third, empty tray upon which Tshaj placed the shirt. The woman then replaced the tray of offerings on top of the shirt. Kumsing's essence was now present in the ceremonial paraphernalia.

The elders retied the long white cotton threads that looped down from the wood rafters, circled the altar, and fanned out to the door jambs.

"Please wait, sir." Tshaj sent Kumsing to sit with Siri on the ground.

An audience was gathering slowly. It was important that everyone in the village attend this evening. It was the only way to discover who harbored the malevolent spirit; the *Phibob*. The *Phibob* could not possess its victims directly and inflict harm on them. It chose a living soul to hide in. This allowed it to channel evil from all the aggrieved spirits toward the aggressor. The hosts rarely knew they carried the *Phibob*.

"I don't know about this, Siri. If the men found out . . ."

"If the men found out, I bet they wouldn't be surprised at all. They weren't born soldiers. I bet a lot of them would recall rites like this from their own villages. Anyway, I'd also bet they know already."

"What makes you think this isn't just a plot to discover who's commanding the project now? Why should they want to help me?"

"Survival."

"What do you mean?"

"If the commanders of the project continue to die, what do you suppose the army will do?"

"They'll assume we have been attacked by the Hmong."

"And wipe them out."

"We aren't barbarians, you know."

"Really? You'd be surprised what your army's doing in the name of rooting out insurgents. Chemicals are being rained down on villages suspected of harboring Hmong resistance. One more little village wouldn't make much difference. That's why. They want to be spared. The only way to do that is to placate the spirits and keep you alive. If it works, you'll have to beg forgiveness for every tree you cut down from now on."

"I'd be a laughingstock."

"Better a live laughingstock than a dead unbeliever. But it's up to you." It was hard for Siri to convince him of something he wasn't convinced about himself. He didn't know why he believed this was Kumsing's only chance. He hadn't expected that his description of his night in the village would have been enough to persuade the captain to accompany him. But the young man was so desperate, he would have tried anything.

Siri looked around at the unlikely cast of this night's drama. It all seemed so ridiculous. Lao Jong, dressed all in red, was attaching tiny cymbals to his fingers. His wife was tying a hood around the top of his head. Tshaj was lighting the tapers and candles. The sickly sweet scent of the incense mixed with the smell of the beeswax lamps.

Auntie Suab was working the crowd, handing out amulets like a peanut seller at a soccer game. Most of the village had arrived already. The elders and key figures were on the floor inside, the rest standing or sitting on benches outside. Despite the numbers, there was no sound. Even the babies lay silent against their mothers' breasts.

"Is this dangerous?" Kumsing whispered.

"Don't know. Never been to one before. You'd better shut up now."

Lao Jong, with his hood still pulled back from his face, knelt at the altar and offered up the tray of snacks and liquor to his own teacher and all the teachers before him, way back to the time of the first and greatest shaman. His wife lowered his hood, and he gently tapped the finger cymbals together in a slow rhythm. His wife took up a gong and began to beat in time to his rhythm with the thigh bone of a wading bird.

Lao Jong slowly began to chant a mantra that was in no language Siri had ever heard, yet somehow he seemed to know it. Somehow he seemed aware that Lao Jong was calling for the great gods, the angels, the good spirits to come to him, to use him. He rocked gently back and forth next to the altar and summoned the spirits. For thirty minutes he chanted, and no one grew restless. People seemed hypnotized by the rhythm and the movement. There was still no other sound.

Only Captain Kumsing huffed in frustration again and again. The smoke was irritating his eyes. The gong and the cymbals were buzzing in his ears. He thought he was going to throw up.

Then, almost undetected at first, the repetition of the mantras grew faster, and the volume rose. Lao Jong's breath was becoming strained and, even though his face was hidden, all there could tell he was in a trance. His arms began to twitch. He rose quickly to his feet, and his whole body and his head jerked in increasingly violent spasms. It was neither a dance nor a fit. Unseen deities were jostling for position inside his body. Lao Jong, the toothless farmer, was gone. Not one person there believed this specter in front of them was the man who had gone into the trance earlier.

Although he could see nothing, the shaman appeared to look around the room. His focus fell on Siri, who shrank back as everyone looked in his direction. His hopes of attending his first exorcism as an observer were soon gone. Lao Jong's body fell, not like a person, but like a tree crashing to the floor of a forest. It fell hard, face first, at Siri's feet.

Siri was sure Lao Jong had knocked himself out. His head was inches away, unmoving, unbreathing. Siri reached his hand forward to see if he could help. But in the speed of a breath, in one swift motion, the shaman rose to his feet. It was as if a film had been reversed. As if the tree had been *un*felled. The crowd gasped.

The new owners of Lao Jong's body leaned over the stunned doctor and brought the palms of the shaman's hands together in front of the hood. The deities spoke in their own voice, a voice that could never have belonged to Lao Jong.

"Yeh Ming. Tell us where the evil spirit *Phibob* is lurking. Whose body has he chosen? Who is the host?"

Siri was overwhelmed. This was a grave responsibility. Why him? Every eye was fixed on him, an actor who'd forgotten his lines. He gazed around the room and through the open windows. He looked at every face, every man, woman, and child, hoping there'd be a sign, an arrow or something, a flashing light. But he saw nothing and conceded defeat. "How the hell should I know?"

Even though the shaman's body had come no closer, Lao Jong's gnarled hand somehow shot forward and grabbed Siri's wrist. A sliver of pain shot through his arms and down his legs. It was as if his nerves were being over-stimulated. Then that energy traveled up through his body and settled at his neck. The amulet, which had been so cool against his skin, began to burn like a white-hot ember. He opened his mouth to scream, but no sound came out. He yanked at the leather to take it off, but the thong held. Worse, the amulet burned. It burned through skin, through muscle, to the bone. There was the sizzle of flesh. He tried to wrestle the thong over his head now, but the leather constricted, tighter and tighter, like a garrote. He couldn't breathe and he knew he was going to die. He was going to die an agonizing death. He was choking, but nobody came to help him. Nobody came to pull the burning amulet from his skin. He could understand none of it. Kumsing sat beside him as if nothing were happening. Couldn't he see the flames? Smell the burning flesh? He was writhing with pain, kicking his legs, yanking at the thong. Then in his death throes he saw her. She sat beneath the window smiling serenely like an angel.

Kumsing saw none of this. He only saw Siri gaze calmly around the room, close his eyes, and breathe deeply. Then Siri re-opened his eyes and looked directly at an old lady beneath the window at the farthest point from the altar.

Siri knew now who was killing him. The amulet had been a screen to stop him seeing *Phibob*. In his dream, she'd collected together the spirits of the jungle and released the plague of insects. It was *her*. Auntie Suab was hosting the malevolent spirits. *Phibob* was in her. He looked at her through the slits that were left of his eyes and she smiled. And the smile was red, not with betel, but with the blood of revenge. Suddenly he could see them, the unsettled souls of the troubled dead. They sat inside her. And with the last of his strength he raised his hand and pointed at the old lady under the window. And although his hearing was draining away along with his life, he heard her speak. He'd never heard such a sound. The voice that came from her mouth contained the voices of many, gruff, angry voices, voices of generations of lost souls. They belonged to the spirits of men and women who had suffered violence and indignation, unsettled ghosts denied a resting place. They all spoke from the mouth of the tiniest, most gentle lady in the village: "Fuck you, Yeh Ming. You'll be cursed for this. Believe us. You will be cursed."

Fire spread through Siri's chest and over his skin, the garrote cut through his neck, he kicked and grunted the finale to his death knell, and he was gone.

Kumsing watched as Siri stared at the old lady. The doctor sat cross-legged, his hands in his lap, more serene than ever. She smiled back at him, a little nervously. Then the doctor lifted his hand and pointed at her.

"*Phibob*," he said, calmly. "*Phibob* is in her." Then, as if he were suddenly tired, he keeled over sideways and collapsed.

That was the end of the ceremony as far as Siri knew. When he woke up, the sun shining through the unshuttered window was like warm balm against his face. He reached instinctively to his neck, but there was no dressing, no contusion, no injury at all. The amulet was gone.

"Spiritual wounds don't leave scars, Yeh Ming."

Siri looked to the end of the straw mattress to see Auntie Suab spooning soup from a large black pot into a bowl. His face must have shown fear. She smiled. "Don't worry, they're gone. You missed quite a show last night. I missed a lot of it myself, although I was apparently the star."

"I'm sorry for ratting on you."

"It had to be done." She brought the soup over to him and helped him sit up against the beam of the hut. He felt weak. She handed him the bowl and a spoon. He looked at the soup with suspicion.

"Nothing poisonous, Yeh Ming. You need some nourishment. You were as sick as a dog last night."

"I was?"

"At least you waited till they got you outside."

"I'm polite that way. What happened?"

She sat cross-legged on the floor as he ate. "I'm afraid Lao Jong was a bit beyond his depth. He's actually more of a fixing-of-stomachache, saving-of-vegetable-garden type of medium. He can deal with little troubles like that very well. But what we had last night was hell and brimstone. He'd never experienced anything like that before. Fortunately, you had."

A sudden dark flash came across Siri's mind. He saw himself

with his hands around Auntie Suab's throat during the exorcism. He shrugged it from his mind.

"Me? What good was I? I was unconscious."

"This body was. But Yeh Ming was with us. You acted as a mentor for Lao Jong. Kept everyone calm. Between the two of you, you were able to chase the *Phibob* from my body. [Siri again saw himself with his hands wrapped tightly around the old lady's throat, but this time there were sounds: the gong, screaming.] We made certain they couldn't possess anyone from the village, not even your soldier friend. He was crying like a baby at the end."

"Where did they go, the *Phibob*?"

"Back to the trees. They don't use hosts very often. They're more at home in the jungle."

"Why did they pick you?"

"The amulets, I suppose. I pick up a lot of bad karma from my clients. I handle a lot of cursed talismans. Malevolent spirits often target women."

"And you didn't know they were in you?"

"The host never knows. Their influence works on your subconscious. This, for example." She held up the black prism in front of his eyes. "I had no idea it had been tampered with."

As it swung back and forth, the images of the previous night became more vivid. He could smell the beeswax from the lamps. Suab was fighting him off with incredible, unearthly strength. Nobody came to help. Lao Jong lay unconscious on the ground, blood seeping from the corner of his mouth.

Auntie Suab looked at him. "What's wrong?"

"I . . . I'm getting visions of last night. They're so real."

"That'll continue for a while, I'm afraid. It's only to be expected after what you went through. That's one more reason why you need to put this back on." She slid across the floor toward him and held out the amulet.

"Put it on? But it was the amulet that stopped me seeing the *Phibob* in the first place."

"It stopped you seeing them while they were in the host. Now that they're gone from me, there's no danger. The amulet's charm has been reversed. The prism will protect you from their revenge. Are you listening?"

Siri was shaking his head. The quiet of the morning was invaded by the sounds of last night's ceremony: The villagers were chanting his name. A woman was crying; it was Lao Jong's wife lying over his body.

The morning was losing its warmth. The sun through the window had fallen behind a cloud.

"It's so real."

"Put this on, Yeh Ming. Put this on and it will all go away."

"I can't. For some reason I know I shouldn't. There's something wrong here."

"You must trust me." She was losing her patience with him. Her voice became deeper.

"How do you know they talked of revenge?" The tiniest drip of blood appeared at the corner of her mouth, and Siri understood. The night was not intruding into the morning; the morning was intruding into the night. He wasn't imagining he was strangling Suab. He actually was. That was the reality. The soft bed, the kind Suab, and the soup, was an image forced into his head by *Phibob*.

The malevolent spirits were lulling him, coaxing him to put on the amulet to weaken him. It was their only hope. He had Suab by the neck and he was casting the spirits from her. They couldn't withstand his power. They'd killed the medium, but Yeh Ming was too strong. He removed one hand from Suab's neck and with inhuman ferocity slapped her across the face.

"Be gone, *Phibob*. Be gone."

And gone they were, in a rush of static that sucked the air from the room. Suab's body became limp, and Yeh Ming let it drop. He looked around at the silent villagers, who held their palms together and cast their tear-filled eyes downward. His work was done. Slowly he crumpled to the ground and slept.

When he awoke he heard the sound of a spoon clanking against a pot but didn't dare look. He heard the sound of soup pouring into a bowl and tried not to listen.

"He's awake."

It was a man's voice and it was answered by the grunt of another. Siri looked up to see some of the elders sitting in a huddle at the far side of the hut. They got to their feet and hurried across the room. They seemed pleased to see him. The young girl he'd met before was dishing up soup for everyone. It smelled good.

Siri said nothing to the men. He watched them. He looked for abnormalities, anything out of place, sudden changes in the light. Tshaj spoke first.

"How are you feeling, Yeh Ming?" The voice seemed legitimate, but Siri wasn't about to make the same mistake twice.

"Who are you?"

The men looked at each other, confused. "I'm Tshaj. What's wrong?"

"What year is this?"

"1976."

"The date?" Siri figured a malevolent spirit wouldn't have an up-to-date calendar.

The elders looked at one another again. Unfortunately, dates weren't something they needed to concern themselves with either. One of them took a stab at it.

"November?"

"What day?"

"Monday."

"No. That isn't possible. What happened to Friday and Saturday and Sunday?"

"You slept through them."

"You've been out like a clod of earth since . . . that night."

It wasn't unlikely. He felt leaden and uncommonly hungry. The smell of the soup was bringing on rumbling in his insides. But he still wasn't absolutely at peace with what he was seeing.

"Where's Lao Jong?"

Tshaj looked down at his hands. "He's gone."

"Gone, dead? From the exorcism?"

The men nodded solemnly.

"He wasn't in physical condition to tolerate all that turmoil he was hosting. He'd never really done it before, not to that degree. He had a bad heart already, and the *Phibob* could tell. I can't think what they made him see that shocked him so. Not sure I'd want to know."

"I can imagine."

"Lucky for us, Yeh Ming was open to the deities. There was the devil of a battle."

"I think I met that devil. What happened to the *Phibob*?"

"Back to the forest."

"Just like that? They just happily scurried back to the forest with their tails between their legs?"

"There'll be nothing happy about it. There's still a lot of mischief to be had in the jungle. But they'll think twice about possessing any of us, now that we're protected. Yeh Ming left us a blessing and put a spell on our village."

"Nice of him." Siri decided this was reality, if only because his stomach was bleating like a tethered goat from the aroma of the soup. Recovering from seventy-two hours of sleep is no easy matter, and he needed help from the elders to sit up. They were flesh and blood, but mostly bone. The blushing girl spooned soup into his mouth. He could have done it him-self, but he rather liked the service.

"What about the captain?" he asked between slurps.

"He was blessed too. It seemed to make him very confident. He decided to protect his men as well. Auntie Suab's doing a roaring trade in amulets for the army. She can't make them fast enough."

Siri stopped eating. "Auntie Suab? Is she all right?"

"She's fine. She knows nothing about that night. The host can feel nothing. Once you exposed her, she was unconscious and the *Phibob* took over."

"But I was . . . wasn't I choking her to death?"

"No. You were attacking the *Phibob*. They weren't your hands and it wasn't Suab's throat."

"Thank goodness for that. Feed me, my sweetness."

The girl blushed and spooned more soup into his mouth.

Once he had shaken the sleep from his body, and the food had re-stoked his energy, Siri felt better than he had for many years. Perhaps he felt better than he ever had. Something was stirring inside him that made him think of youth, of his romance with Boua. It was a marvelous feeling.

An hour after waking, he was walking around Meyu Bo receiving small gifts and congratulations and saying his good-byes. At Suab's hut he apologized again, but it was certain she neither remembered nor felt a thing. She had no idea what he was talking about when he mentioned the trick she'd played. She handed him a small leather pouch, which he accepted cautiously.

"This isn't a black prism?"

"No, Yeh Ming. That was destroyed. Smashed to a thousand pieces and scattered over the forestry site. Take a look." He pulled the drawstring and found a white talisman inside, smaller than the prism but every bit as ancient. It hung on a string of plaited white hair. "This is the converse of the black prism. Where there's evil, you'll see it. No spirit can blind you, if you have this.

"I hope the *Phibob* is finished with you, but it's a wicked spirit, an amalgam of many malevolent souls. The exorcism probably showed him who's boss, but I want you to be prepared for revenge. If he chooses to follow up on the curse, you'll need this. Promise me you'll carry it with you always."

A feeling of déjà vu came over him, although it seemed unreasonable. Auntie Suab wasn't *Phibob*. She was offering him her help. It was just that, if she had no recollection of the possession, how did she know about the curse? He dismissed the thought.

He thanked her for the amulet but had no intention of carrying it with him. He wished her well with her amulet sales, and hoped they would bring in enough revenue for the village to reverse its slide into poverty. There were an awful lot of soldiers, and superstition spread faster than a forest fire.

Later that afternoon, Kumsing escorted Siri to the airstrip. The captain did indeed seem to be a new man. His nervous tic was gone, and he was wearing his uniform with resolute defiance. His own amulet peeked out from between the straining buttons.

They watched the Yak approach from the horizon, like a bee full of pollen. Siri and Kumsing walked toward it with their arms around each other's shoulders like survivors of a great ordeal.

"You don't have to hurry back. You could stay and rest up for a day or two," Kumsing said.

"I think three days of sleep's enough rest. And who knows when our charming Soviet friends will be back this way again? I have to take the opportunity while it's here."

"Siri, about the reports . . ."

Siri laughed. "If your bosses are anything like mine, I think the last week will have been very mundane. I took a couple of days to do the autopsies. Then I came down with a mild bout of . . ."

"Malaria."

"Malaria, that'll do, and I had to rest up until it passed. I don't recall anything about any Hmong, do you?"

"Not a thing." They shook hands. "Siri, how do you feel?"

"About what?"

"This whole bloody circus. I know I can never be normal again after all that's happened, and I was just an observer. You must be—I don't know—confused?"

"How could I not be? I'm a man of science and I have not one sensible explanation for what I went through. And yet it happened. You saw it. I felt it. How can I ever go back to being Dr. Siri, the downtrodden, after that?"

"I admire you."

"Because?"

"Just think how interesting the world will be from now on."

"I'm seventy-two, boy. I was planning on gradually *losing* interest in the world, not acquiring it. What I'm hoping is that this will all go away once I leave Khamuan. Frankly, the thought of taking Yeh Ming back to Vientiane frightens the life out of me."

Their conversation was drowned by the sound of the airplane bouncing along the strip with its motors roaring. Once it was almost stopped, the Yak opened its door, coughed out one passenger, and sucked in Siri and two forestry specialists. It pivoted, accelerated, and was airborne again all in the space of ten minutes.

Through one small porthole, Siri could see the captain walking back to the truck. A crow with a brown crest, unmoved by the noisy aircraft, sat on a log not five meters from it. The driver ran at the bird, expecting it to fly off, but it sat defiantly and the driver gave up. When the truck drove off, the crow followed.

The shirtsleeved forester was very helpful in pointing out the project site to Siri as they passed over it. The doctor was overwhelmed by its scope. Hectare upon hectare of prime jungle had been shaven bald. The devastation extended in each direction as far as his eye could see. He pressed his nose up to the scratched glass and shook his head slowly.

"Shit." He noticed how his hand had involuntarily reached

into his pocket and was holding the leather pouch. He mumbled an apology to the *Phibob* and the other displaced souls. "I'm sorry, I didn't realize."

"What was that?" The forester leaned over to hear him better.

"Nothing, just a little prayer."

"Afraid of flying, are you?"

"Afraid of going back down to the ground, more like. Listen, comrade. You wouldn't happen to know exactly where this timber goes to in Taiwan, would you?"

A Fear of Landing

Siri's fear of landing was justified in this case. The Yak didn't have any problems outside of its bad manners. But as soon as it set him down at Wattay, all the suspicion and apprehension he'd left behind awaited him. The invincible Khamuan warrior had apparently missed the flight.

He nervously eyed the visitor's balcony at the old terminal. Every one of the onlookers could have been holding a gun. The officer who checked his travel papers seemed to stare at him longer than he needed to. When the *samlor* driver mistakenly took a wrong turn on the way home, Siri interrogated him till he was almost in tears. He got off a block from his house and walked the rest of the way, being careful to pause at the corner of the lane and scan the houses opposite his own.

By the time he reached his front path, all his instincts were honed. He was prepared for every eventuality—that is, apart from the eventuality that actually eventuated. To his utter amazement, Saloop looked up at him from the front step, smiled, and waddled toward him. The dog's tail was flapping away like the national flag in a monsoon. It nuzzled up to his legs and craned its neck as if expecting affection in return.

The pink sky signaled the end of the day, and Miss Vong walked over to her curtains to light her lamp and close the shutters. Never could she have expected to witness the sight of Siri patting Saloop's stomach as the animal lay on its back bicycling the air. She stood with her mouth wide open.

Siri looked up and laughed. "Evening, Miss Vong." And under his breath: "Don't *you* get any ideas now."

Still flabbergasted by his new relationship with Saloop, he stopped off in the downstairs bathroom and got some water boiling for a hot bath. He deserved that much.

He could tell someone had been in his room. He could also guess who. There was an unmarked envelope on his desk. Its deliverer, unquestionably some spinster from the Department of Education, had taken advantage of her excuse to enter his room by dusting, sweeping, washing up, and disorganizing his books into neat regiments. It was time, he decided, to invest in a padlock. Some things were worse than crime.

He went down for a leisurely bath and soaked his hair in the left-over rice water they all used as shampoo. He inspected his well-worn body for evidence of the battle he'd just fought, but, if anything, he looked better now than he had when he left. Clean and refreshed, he returned to his room, wrapped himself in a dry loincloth, and waited for the pot to boil for coffee. He carried the oil lamp across to the coffee table and blew the steam from his cup. Not until then was he ready for his letter. He checked the seal of the flap. It seemed untouched, no evidence of steaming or soaking. He slit it open with an old scalpel and pulled out the two sheets it contained.

Turning first to the signature, he saw it was penned by "a fellow crime fighter," an indication that Phosy also feared it might be tampered with.

It began with a jolt.

My dear Maigret,

The hairdresser's dead. My first suspicion upon hearing that was probably the same as your own. But comK was away at the time and this had all the hallmarks of a suicide. I was in the station when the case came in. The officer who'd gone to her apartment found the body, together with a suicide note. She'd slashed her wrists with one of the cut-throats from the salon.

Her arms were in a bowl of water that I assume had been warm at the time of the suicide. This is a way to stop the blood from clotting. She was paper-white, so it was quite obvious she'd bled to death. It's unfortunate you were away, as the body would naturally have gone to you. As it was, the temple was eager to get her in the ground for all those religious reasons I'm sure you understand better than me.

The note confessed that she'd been desperately in love with comK, that she was jealous of the wife but couldn't see him leaving her. She decided to do away with the competition. Access wasn't a problem. One little detail I'd forgotten to check (sorry, I have been growing vegetables for a year) was that the salon she worked at was the same one where Mrs. N had her hair done. I guess it wouldn't have been so difficult for her to add the Cy. to the headache pills while she was under the toaster or whatever it is women do in those places.

I interviewed comK. He appeared to be distraught. I got the feeling he really had a soft spot for the girl. I've got one or two thoughts about all this. I haven't submitted a report on anything other than finding the suicide victim. I'll get your views when I'm back from the north (seminar). 1. comK is off the hook as far as I can see. 2. The murderer has already been tried and sentenced by her own conscience. 3. I wonder whether it's to anyone's advantage to make any of this other stuff public.

But of course I'm just a cop. What do I know? If you disagree, I'll be happy to reconsider. Hope your holiday went well. Look forward to hearing the stories. Best wishes.

A fellow crime fighter.

The coffee was cold.

"Well, I suppose that's that." He reheated the water and

spooned the last of his Hanoi coffee grains into the filter. "All neatly tied up and buried." He took his fresh coffee to the desk, but left the lamp on the coffee table. He blew away the steam and looked out at the moonlit temple grounds.

Saffron robes swayed gently on the washing lines. An elderly monk ladled water from a large earthenware jar onto the head of a young novice. A rusting Renault, now a garden ornament, wore two sleeping temple cats as hood ornaments. Everything was at peace.

"All neatly tied up and buried."

Time to Kill

Siri went to bed late, woke up early, and had no dreams at all. As he was leaving the house, he used his old chisel to gouge out the two shells from their holes in the front door. It left two ugly scars that he knew Miss Vong would complain about for a month. Saloop sat at his feet as he worked and looked up at him faithfully.

Eager to see the results of Nguyen Hong's investigation, Siri was at the morgue by six, too early even for roadside noodles. If he'd expected to find something at the morgue, he was disappointed. His desk was empty of messages, notes, or completed reports. Hok and Tran had vacated the freezer, which stood gaping and unplugged. The last notes in Dtui's exercise book were about his autopsy of Tran 1, not surprising as she couldn't possibly have taken notes from the Vietnamese coroner.

There was little point in being there at all. He had a lot of time on his hands, so he penciled a note and walked it down to the offices behind the Parliament building. Joggers and cyclists still owned four-lane Lan Xang Avenue at that hour. A small group of tai chi uncles did combat with invisible slow-motion enemies in the shadow of the great Anusawari Arch.

Parliament was still in bed, but the guard promised to hand the note to Comrade Civilai when he got in. The noodle man was setting up when Siri got back to the hospital. He was given the first batch of noodles, in broth that had been freshly made, but it still tasted the same as ever: stale.

He ate slowly and dawdled his way into the hospital grounds, but he still had half an hour to kill. So he strolled around to the back of the morgue to the *khon khouay* office. He wasn't at all surprised to see Comrade Ketkaew sitting at his metal desk, writing some urgent exposé of this or that traitor.

"Morning, Comrade Ketkaew." The man looked shocked to see him. The small earphone on a wire that he had been wearing vanished into his desk drawer.

"I hope you aren't secretly listening to Thai radio."

Siri walked in and sat on the spare chair the chicken counter reserved for interrogations. Ketkaew nodded but didn't bother to speak. He eyed Siri suspiciously.

"I hope your wife gives you a good breakfast to build up your strength, working as hard as you do."

"I cook for myself," Ketkaew shouted, even though Siri was not a foot from him.

"Don't tell me you aren't married."

"Who has time for all that? In case you hadn't noticed, I have a very responsible job. Now, what is it you . . . ?"

"That's very interesting."

"What is?"

"That a good-looking chap like you doesn't have a wife."

"Hey, listen. I like women, you know. I'm not . . ."

"Of course you do. And it's quite clear women like you, too."

"I could have my pick."

"Naturally. Responsible job and all."

"Anyone I want, really. If I could be bothered."

"Exactly. That's just what I told her."

"Her?"

"That's why she didn't think she had a chance, not with all the competition, and you having so little time." He stood to leave. "I'll pass on the message."

"You. Is this, er, someone I might know?"

"Probably not. 'Bye."

"I know a lot of people, you know. What's her name?"

"Vong."

"Vong what? I've got several Vongs in my district. Where does she work?" Siri noticed a pearl of saliva at the corner of the man's mouth.

"Department of Education. Right in the middle of your domain of responsibility, if I'm not mistaken. She was here the other day, noticed you diligently performing your revolutionary duties, and I swear I saw the poor lady blush. She asked me about you."

Ten minutes later, Siri was back in his office with a big naughty smile on his chops.

"Oh, to be a lizard on the wall of Vong's office when the chicken counter comes a-wooing."

Eight o'clock arrived and he stood under the MORGUE sign, waiting to welcome his staff. He'd missed them. At 8:15 he was still standing there; no sign of Dtui or Mr. Geung. He went back inside to check the calendar, but there was no mention of a national holiday. He paced anxiously up and down in the carpark. He wasn't worried about their being late. He was more concerned about their being dead. The shells in his pocket rattled together as he walked.

At 9:30, Siri was sitting outside the office of Suk, the hospital director. Suk had ignored Siri on the way to a staff meeting, then ignored him again on his way back. Right now there was a North Korean pharmaceutical company rep in with him. Communism matched up some strange bedfellows.

When the Korean left, Siri slipped onto the warmed seat he'd vacated.

"Well, Dr. Siri. You finally ran out of holiday money."

"It was a case. I was sent by the Justice Department."

"For an autopsy that took a week."

"For two autopsies that took two days. The rest of the time, I was getting over malaria."

Before becoming a paper-shuffler, the director had been a doctor. He looked Siri up and down for some sign of a man who'd just gotten over a disease that killed twelve thousand Lao a year.

"I'm delighted you survived."

"Thanks. Where is my staff?"

"They were reassigned."

Siri felt a tremendous relief. "They can't be reassigned without my agreement."

"Really? Well, as you weren't here, nobody objected. We're very understaffed, as you know. I wasn't about to let a qualified nurse sit around reading comic books on the off chance you might come back."

"Where is she?"

"Urology."

Siri chuckled. "That'll teach her. What about Geung?"

"He's digging a sewage trench."

"He's an experienced morgue technician."

"His absence of written qualifications makes him a sewage trench digger."

"I want them back."

"You have nothing for them to do."

"I'll have a body by 1:30."

"How can you be so sure? You planning on killing someone yourself?" Suk laughed at his own wit until he noticed the macabre way Siri was eyeing him.

"Hello, Doctor."

"How you doing? You got my nurse, Dtui, in here?"

"Sure do. She's out back. Go on through."

An elderly lady was up on a couch naked from the waist down. Dtui in plastic gloves crouched between her legs. She looked up and seemed truly delighted to see Siri.

"Doc? Thank God. Rescue me. Take me back to the morgue. If I have to insert my fingers in one more grumpy old lady, I'll scream."

The lady tried to cover herself up.

"It's okay. I'm a doctor."

"Actually, he's a coroner. But live ones, dead ones, they're pretty much the same to him."

It was too much for the lady, who wrapped her *phasin* around herself and fled.

"I can see why you prefer to work with corpses. But fear not, nurse Dtui. You'll both be back in the morgue this afternoon. Anything unusual happen while I was away?"

"Nothing much. Your Vietnamese mate's gone back to Hanoi."

"Did he say anything?"

"Probably. But we had no idea what it was."

"Did he leave anything for me?"

"His report and a letter or something."

"Good."

"Given there's a lot of secret stuff I don't know about, I hid 'em."

"Good girl. Where are they?"

"In the hospital library. Under 'V'. You know nobody ever goes up there."

He decided to leave the Vietnamese report where it was. He was certain somebody would like to get their hands on it. He spent a few minutes breaking the law back in his office, then set off on Dtui's bicycle toward Dongmieng.

The temple at Sri Bounheuan was just as well cared for as Hay Sok behind his house, but the atmosphere there was more frenetic. The Departments of Culture and Education had set up a pilot literacy project. All the monks, regardless of educational backgrounds, had been recruited to teach.

The current philosophy was that Buddha was a communist.

He'd given up his status and wealth as a protest against capitalism, and had striven to break down class barriers. As a reflection of these socio-politico-economic roots, monks were being yoked to blackboards up and down the country.

The number of liberated Lao citizens attending school had risen 75 percent since the Pathet Lao takeover. Lao radio never let anyone forget that. It didn't mention what they did in the schools they attended, or the near-absence of qualified teachers. And it didn't say that the burden of this new education system fell broadly on the shoulders of the monkhood.

They'd built rows of banana-leaf classrooms and filled them with logs split down the center for benches. The students ranged from five-year-old orphans to sixty-five-year-old grandmothers. They didn't have any books or pencils, and the blackboards were the backs of old Royalist billboards. They may not have been learning a lot, but they all seemed to be having a good time.

The abbot was up a crooked bamboo ladder painting a stupa. His robe was tied up between his legs like an orange diaper. He was turning the dirty grey tope into a light blue birthday cake.

"Shouldn't that be white?" Siri asked.

For some reason, the only paint to be had for the previous few months had been swimming-pool blue, a color that was slowly becoming synonymous with the new regime. The airport already blended nicely with the sky. Civilai argued it was the committee's long-term plan to paint everything Wattay blue so astronauts would be able to recognize Laos from space.

"I don't care if it's black, as long as we can keep the elements off it for another year." The abbot hooked the paint can over a cement elephant's trunk and came down. He looked over the top edge of his glasses at his visitor. "I seem to remember you."

"So you should, Abbot. We were in Pakse together about two hundred years ago."

"Well, I'll be . . . Siri, isn't it?" Siri smiled and started to make an obeisance, but the old abbot grabbed his hand and pumped away at it. "You don't look any different."

"Really? You mean I was a wrinkled old codger with a stoop, even then?"

"Neither of us was really sure what we were then. You had to decide whether to follow your pretty wife to Vietnam, if I recall. I had a choice between riding a pushbike for the national team in the Asia Games, or following the love of my life to Australia."

"Which one did you go for, in the end?"

"Neither. Look at me. I was so confused, I went on a retreat at Wat Sokpaluang and they never let me leave."

They laughed.

"How on earth did you find me?"

"Oh, I heard a while ago you were here. One of the other teachers from the youth camp told me."

"And how's that pretty wife, Siri?"

"I'm afraid she died a few years back."

"Ah. I'm not surprised. It can be tough for a woman in the jungle."

"It's even tougher if someone throws a grenade at you."

"You aren't wrong. Still, no shame in being brought down in battle."

"She wasn't in battle. She was in bed. She was sleeping. I was off on some campaign. It seems someone tossed a grenade into her tent. We never found out who."

Siri was surprised at how easy it was to talk about. He'd kept this story inside himself for eleven years; now here he was blurting it out to a monk he hardly knew. The Catholics had it right. It was very therapeutic to share a burden with a man of the cloth. Except the Catholics probably handled it more delicately than the Lao.

"I bet it was meant for you."

They walked to a bench and shared memories from their year at the youth camp. But Siri had to get to the point.

"A few days ago, they brought you a girl who'd slashed her wrists."

"Yes, they did. How did you know that?"

"I'm currently the state coroner."

"My! Congratulations."

"And I'm afraid I need to dig her up again."

"Oh, but you can't."

Siri pulled a sheet of paper from his shirt pocket that he'd written, stamped, and signed on Judge Haeng's behalf. "I have here a warrant signed by . . ."

"No. I don't mean I doubt your right to do it. What I mean is you can't dig her up, because we haven't buried her yet."

"It's been four days."

"I know. Normally we'd have her in the ground right away. But this was a bit difficult."

"How?"

"She has a sister."

"She has?"

"They came down from the north together. She refused to let her sister be buried here. She's trying to get the money together to take her body back to the family in Sam Neua."

"Where is she?"

"The sister?"

"Both of them."

"The body is in an old kiln we have here. We used to make pots. It's dry and quite airtight. With all the kids here I couldn't have her lying around."

"I understand. What about the sister?"

"She's living with a fellow who fixes bicycles, just down from the Thai Embassy."

Siri wheeled Dtui's bicycle under the straw canopy of the repair shop. It seemed to be deserted. He coughed and heard a rustling from out back. A taut-bodied young man wearing nothing but soccer shorts came out through a gap in the wall.

"Hello, boss. What's wrong?"

"Can you fix the brakes? They only work when you're going uphill."

"No trouble." He flipped the heavy bike over onto its handlebars as if it were made of balsa wood.

"Is there somewhere I can take a pee?"

"Sure, boss. There's a latrine out back, if you don't mind the flies."

Siri walked through the gap, where he found a tall, slim girl in a *phasin*, shelling tamarind. There was a five-month swelling beneath the cloth of her skirt. He didn't bother with the latrine. He knelt down beside her; she didn't seem to care very much. Her mind was elsewhere.

"Hello. I'm Dr. Siri. I just came from Sri Bounheuan temple." Her eyes grew wide and in some way afraid. "That's your sister there?" She nodded slowly.

"I'm a coroner. Do you know what that is?"

"Yeah."

"I need your permission to look at your sister's body."

She emptied the seeds from one more tamarind pod before she responded. "Can you tell? If you look at her, can you tell if she killed herself?"

"I think I can. But I need to operate on her."

"You mean cut her open?"

"Yes. Is that all right?" She didn't seem to like the thought of her sister's body being defiled. "If it becomes my case, I can arrange for the body to be shipped back to Sam Neua."

"Free?"

"We'll pay."

"She won't be a mess, will she?"

"I can get the embalmer to make her look nice."

"She didn't, you know?"

"Kill herself?"

"Yeah. She didn't kill herself."

"How sure are you?"

"I know her."

"Do you know where Mahosot Hospital is?"

"Yeah."

"If you come and see me there this evening about six, I should have some answers for you. I'd like to talk to you, too."

She nodded again. "Thanks."

The morning had passed him by. He didn't even have time to put the bicycle back in the carpark. He pulled up alongside Auntie Lah's stand to get some lunch.

"You? Dr. Siri?" She lit up like a brand-new traffic light. She was so pleased to see him, she used the illegal royal "you," and bowed her head in a very polite *nop*.

"Now, Mrs. Lah, didn't they teach you anything at your political seminars? You don't want to let our chicken counter see you do that."

"Ah, Doctor. That little twerp doesn't scare me. Where've you been?"

"Khamuan."

"I made your sandwich every day last week."

"Oh, I'm sorry. I forgot to cancel. I'll pay you for them."

"Not to worry. I ate them myself. I was just worried you wouldn't be coming back. It's lovely to see you."

She fixed him a very special baguette and gave him the opportunity to look at her. She was a fine-looking woman. He couldn't imagine why old men would chase new-hatched chicks when there were pretty hens in the yard. Something in him stirred, and he wondered what it would be like to be with her. He hadn't been with a woman since he lost Boua.

"How's your husband?"

She didn't look up, but he noticed her blush. "Oh, he's fine. At least he doesn't give me so much trouble anymore."

"I see."

"Just have to dust the urn now and then."

Siri smiled, climbed back on the bike, and ferried his lunch down to the river. She stood, watching him go.

Civilai was sitting alone on the log. Crazy Rajid was lying naked on the bank a few meters from him.

"Am I disturbing anything?"

"No, you're right on time. I was just starting to get envious."

"He certainly has something to be envious of. Nothing compared to me, of course." He sat down beside his friend.

"Really? I assumed it must have dropped off from lack of use by now."

"No, still there. I felt a little bit of activity just now, to tell the truth."

"Not one of the bodies? Don't tell me you've stooped so low."

"You know Mrs. Lah? The one who makes my sandwiches?"

"Her on the corner? She's old enough to be your . . . daughter. Nice pair of hooters, though. I'd give her a run around the paddock."

"Dream on, you old fogy."

"How was Khamuan?"

"Interesting. Cut up two bodies that died of unknown causes, got malaria, and became fluent in Hmong."

"Of course you did. Let's hear it then."

"You don't speak Hmong."

"Probably more than you. If you want to talk about chasing girls round paddocks, I've done a few laps with those lasses. Come on."

Siri opened his mouth to speak but nothing came to his mind. He thought of a simple Lao sentence but he couldn't even translate that. The language he'd been speaking naturally a day before had vanished.

"That's odd. I've forgotten it."

"Ah, yes. Languages are like that. Here one minute, gone the next. I was fluent in Japanese last Thursday."

"No. I really could speak it." Civilai grinned and chewed on his roll, and Siri knew it would be useless to argue the point.

"Do you know what the army is doing up there?"

"Crop replacement, isn't it?"

"Yeah. Replacing trees with fresh air. The province will be a parade ground if nobody stops them. Is there anything you can do about it?"

"Who do you suggest we send in to stop them? Prince Boun Oum on his elephant? No. The generals fought for the revolution for decades. This is the little pat on the back they're giving themselves."

"I must have missed that page in the manifesto. I thought corruption was the *reason* for the fight, not the reward. How much is the military giving you lot for forestry rights?"

"Is this what you called me here urgently to badger me about?"

"No. Well, partly. But I was wondering how diplomatic relations are going with Vietnam."

"Fine."

"Good."

"Except there aren't any."

"What happened?"

"Hanoi recalled the ambassador and most of the diplomats. All their aid projects are on hold. We brought back our fellow from Hanoi to show them we could be every bit as tough as they could. Now, nobody's talking."

"Damn. Not all over this torture accusation?"

"They aren't satisfied. You didn't come up with anything to suggest we didn't work their men over?"

While Crazy Rajid waded into the water and started swimming across to Thailand, Siri went over the details of the case. He told of the visit to Nam Ngum even though he was sure his older brother had seen the district chief's report already. But then he added something he was sure Civilai wouldn't have read.

"Somebody tried to kill me."

"I beg your pardon?"

"The day we got back from the reservoir. Nguyen Hong and I decided there were still too many questions unanswered." He produced the two deformed shells from his pocket. "I got home late. I bent down at the front door, and these came flying into the wood over my shoulder."

Civilai took them from him. "Siri. You . . . you don't think this has to do with the *Vietnamese*?"

"It was a bit of a coincidence otherwise."

"But why? Did you find something that could incriminate anyone?"

"No. But I bet you the rest of your roll, somebody thought we did."

"Whew."

"My problem is, I don't know which side it was."

"Oh, come on. You don't think our people would try to do away with you."

Siri laughed. "You're quite naïve for a genius, aren't you, brother? Of course they would. If I had evidence *we* had 'interrogated' those boys, we'd have a lot more than just diplomatic détente; there'd be a damned war."

"All right. For the first time in fifty years, you have my undivided attention. What do you want me to do?"

"Do you know what that Vietnamese delegation came here for?"

"No."

"Civilai?"

"No, really, I don't."

"Can you find out?"

"I can try."

"Good. I'll go through Nguyen Hong's report and see if I can contact him in Hanoi somehow. We still have a lot of unfinished business."

"Have you told your judge all this?"

"No. You know, I'm starting to think what a coincidence it was that the Justice Department would send me away in the middle of this investigation."

"You have to start trusting people. You need allies."

"You're them, Comrade."

"Oh, the pressure."

"Do the words 'Black Boar' mean anything to you?"

"Not apart from the obvious."

"Can you ask around? Something to do with the delegation. Perhaps the war. Vietnam."

"Where did you get that?"

"From . . . I'm afraid I can't disclose my sources."

"Anything else?"

"There was something, but I can't rem—oh, right. You speak French pretty well, don't you?"

"Like Napoleon."

"Dead?"

"Elegantly. Don't tell me your French went the way of your Hmong."

"Shut up. What does *precipitation* mean?"

"Well, it could be when you separate a solid from a solution in chemistry."

"Or?"

"Falling from a height."

"Falling from a height? Of course. Of course! They weren't waterskiing at all. *Felicitations, mon brave empereur.*" He kissed Civilai on both cheeks and saluted him.

The Hairdresser's Bruise

Siri got back from lunch at 1:30. His arrival coincided with several unheard-of examples of Lao punctuality.

As Dtui reached the door of the morgue from one direction, three monks with cloths around their noses, carrying a rolled coconut mat, arrived from the other. Geung walked out of the office at exactly the same time. He was in a terrible state.

"Doctor S . . . S . . . S . . ." He was too flustered to get beyond that. Siri massaged his shoulders and focused him on his breathing while Dtui ushered the monks into the examination room.

"Mr. Geung. What's wrong?"

"Your o . . . o . . . office is . . . is broken." He grabbed Siri's hand and led him to the office door. Sure enough, the room had been turned over pretty thoroughly. Dtui, from a very polite distance, was seeing off the monks.

"Dtui. Could you come here, please?"

She stood between the two men and looked at the mess. "Ooh."

"This happened in the last three hours. How's the examination room?"

"Normal, and the storeroom."

"So, they were obviously after something in here."

"Oh, no. My comics!"

"Listen, Dtui, Geung, this isn't a joke. This is all part of the danger I told you about before I left. This is why we all have to be very careful from now on. Do you both understand?"

"I understand. I understand," Geung said, very seriously.

Dtui nodded her head. "Yes, Doctor."

"That's good. I'm afraid the only officer I trust is away right now, but we'll have to tell the police about this. Before we do, I want us to go in there and get an idea what's missing, if anything. We'll try not to disturb too much."

Only one thing was gone: Dtui's notebooks had been taken from her desk. All the notes, from every autopsy they'd done together, were missing. While they searched through the debris, Siri told them everything he knew about the Vietnam case, including the attempt on his life.

They came to the same conclusion, that whoever had ransacked the office had been looking for Nguyen Hong's report.

"Dtui, hiding it was inspired thinking. Well done."

"W . . . well done, Dtui," added Geung.

"Give me a raise."

"From now on, you two have nothing to do with the Vietnam case at all. I'll take the file home and go through it. Wait, what about the photos? Did they get the autopsy photos?"

Dtui looked skyward. "No, they didn't."

"How can you be so sure?"

"Well, because they're in Sayabouri."

"Sayabouri? What are they doing in Sayabouri?"

"Well, you remember how it was Sister Bounlan's wedding and we used the end of one film and the beginning of the next for the ceremony?"

"Don't tell me."

"She sent them all home to her family. They were in the same packet. Someone was leaving for Sayabouri and she wanted them to take the pictures. She came and picked it up from my desk when I was out. She didn't have time to check."

"I can imagine how much granny enjoyed that."

"She didn't. They were all as sick as dogs. They put the packet in the post the next day. Should be here by now."

"You see? Even when you mess up, it's perfect."

"It is?"

"Certainly. If our visitors here wanted the notes so badly, I'm quite sure they'd have loved those pictures too. Maybe the pictures can tell us what these people are so afraid of us finding out.

"Mr. Geung?"

"Yes, Doc . . . tor Comrade?"

"Dtui and I will get ready to look at our new guest. Would you be so kind as to go and tell Mr. Ketkaew and the hospital administrators about what happened here?"

"Yes, I would."

Siri and his team were in the examination room. Two uniformed officers were sifting through the wreckage in his office. They worked with the unrequested and unwantedly loud assistance of Mr. Ketkaew. The officers had white hospital masks to keep out the smell from the next room. Ketkaew had a small bottle of smelling balm he snorted every few seconds. He was feeling bad; a major crime had taken place barely ten meters from where he sat working.

Neither team felt obliged to interfere with the other. When the police were finished, they left without saying goodbye.

"You don't suppose they're reading my fan magazines in there, do you?"

"Dtui, will you please concentrate?"

"Sorry." Mr. Geung giggled as he weighed the heart on the butcher scales suspended from the ceiling.

"Right. What unusual signs have we seen so far?"

Dtui closed her notebook and answered from memory. "One. There's only one deep slash on each wrist."

"And that's odd because . . . ?"

"Because wrist-slashers usually take two or three attempts to build up the courage to cut deep enough."

"Good. Two?"

"Two. Hypostasis on the back of the victim suggests she was in a supine position after she died."

"So?"

"So, she couldn't have arranged herself leaning forward, with her arms in a bowl of water, without help."

"Three?"

"Three. Face pale, body dark blue."

"Indication of . . . ?"

"Of asphyxia."

"Wonderful. I think I'll retire."

"Before you go, tell me just how sure we are that she didn't kill herself."

"I'd say we're 92 percent sure. But just in case we need a few more percentage points, let's take a little look in here." He'd peeled back the epidermis from the neck and was cutting down through the muscle. He held open the folds and showed Dtui the larynx.

"Hmm. Hemorrhage."

"And up here, my dear assistant, we have some hidden signs. Bruises that had vanished from her skin are still lurking beneath." Discoloration of the tissue structures showed distinctive prints of what could very likely have been hands. "Conclusion?"

"The poor bitch got herself strangled."

"Ha." Mr. Geung snorted. "Poor bitch."

"That's enough, you two. Show some respect for the dead."

"What do we do now?"

"We write this all up so clearly that even a judge can understand it. Then we keep our mouths tightly shut, and wait for Inspector Phosy to come back tomorrow. Dtui, dearest, we'll need a third copy of this, for security. Can you get one more layer of carbon through that typewriter?"

"The words might be a bit flatter, but I think so."

"Good. We'll put this nice lady back together and send her to Mrs. Nan, the embalmer. I'll start clearing up the office. We have a guest this evening."

At 6:15, Siri was alone at his desk. He'd stopped earlier at the little room they called a library and taken out the Vietnamese file. It was in his shoulder bag now, on top of the old green cabinet. As the sky darkened, he felt suddenly vulnerable again. He had the walk home ahead of him, and he'd be carrying evidence someone was willing to kill for.

Before vegetable-and-fruit duty, Geung had ridden over to the market and bought the biggest padlock they had, and two sets of hasps. The salesman told Geung people had stopped buying them, but those people obviously weren't getting shot at.

His reverie was disturbed by the flap of rubber sandals on the concrete step. The pregnant sister entered nervously. Siri rose to escort her in.

"Thank you for coming. Your husband didn't come with you?"

"He's playing cards." Siri wondered about his priorities. "And he ain't my husband."

"Is this his?" Siri pointed to her round belly. It poked out like a knot in the bark of a tall young tree. She nodded without enthusiasm.

"Sit down, will you? Drink?"

"No."

Siri pulled his chair around to her side of the desk and spoke quietly. "When we were talking this afternoon, what made you say Mai didn't kill herself?"

"Because she . . . she didn't care."

"About what?"

"About anything. Nothing worried her. It was all a big game."

"What was?"

"Life, work, love. Everything."

"Did she come to Vientiane for love?"

"She come looking for it."

"You don't think she might have followed someone down here? Someone she was having an affair with in Sam Neua, for example?"

"No."

"You sure?"

"Yeah, I'm sure. We talked about everything. She come to Vientiane 'cause I was here. She come to find herself a rich husband. She was pretty enough." Her eyes had reddened and Siri could see the ceiling lightbulb reflect in the tears waiting there. "She wasn't short of fans. It was one of them set her up in the room. She wasn't whoring, don't get me wrong. It was all strict romance."

"Do you know who he was?"

"The room? Just one of the horny bastards that was after her."

"Did she talk about him?"

"She talked about all of them."

"Was there someone special? An older man? Someone important."

"There was some ancient old codger . . . no offense. He was chasing after her."

"Did you ever meet him?"

"No. My man doesn't let me go out. This is different tonight, 'cause this is a hospital. I told him I was having the baby checked out. He dropped me off. But with Mai, I only ever got to talk with her when she come over to see me. I didn't meet any of her fellows."

"Does your man know you're taking her back to Sam Neua?"

"No."

"You coming back?"

She smiled. "You know a lot, don't you? No, I ain't coming back. He ain't what I'd want for my baby's father."

"That's very brave of you."

"It's in the blood. We was both really stubborn, me and Mai. You've looked already, haven't you?"

"Yes. I've looked."

"She didn't, did she?"

"No."

She sighed with relief, and the sigh unlocked tears. They rolled down her cheeks, and sobs heaved in her chest. Siri ripped some tissue from the roll on his desk, and she blew her nose.

"Thank you. What happened?" she asked.

"Someone strangled her. Then they set it up to look like suicide."

"I knew she wouldn't." She seemed somehow relieved. It was as if she could cope with the idea that her sister had been murdered far better than if she'd killed herself.

"She's with an embalmer I know. She'll make your sister look presentable for your family, and I'll arrange for the body to be shipped up north." He started to write down Mrs. Nan's address, then stopped. "Can you read?"

She shook her head. "No, sir."

"Okay. I'll get Nan to come to your shop. When everything's ready, she'll find a way to let you know."

She took both of his hands in hers, which was the most generous thank-you she could give. She didn't mention revenge or ask about justice, perhaps because she'd never known any herself. But Siri wanted her to believe in it.

"I'm going to find the man who killed your sister. I promise you and your family. Can you remember anything about her men that would help me identify them?"

"I can't think right now."

"I understand. If anything comes to you, you know where I am. But, in the meantime, you aren't to say a word to anyone about murder. Not *anyone*."

"Don't worry." She ripped off more tissue and wiped her face. "How do I look?"

"Beautiful. Really beautiful."

She smiled, unconvinced but happier, and walked from the office. Siri collapsed back into his chair. Encounters with the living always drained him more than those with the dead. And women most of all. Give him a dead man over a live woman any day.

There hadn't been a day of his marriage that he hadn't loved Boua. But the last three years of her life had stretched that love to its limit. She'd always been stronger than he in many ways. The few arguments he didn't lose because he deserved to, he lost because it was wise to do so. As she got older, her fuse got shorter.

She couldn't contain her frustration over the tortoise pace of her revolution. It was as if she'd opened the chest where all her girlhood dreams were kept, dreams of a world full of fairness and logic and happiness. And all she found in there were the shriveled remains. Once she started to believe her army had neither the commitment nor the unselfishness to form an administration solely for the people, she changed.

She didn't seem to notice it herself, but she began to punish Siri for her disappointments. He never raised his voice to her, or defended himself in public when she belittled him. He was a doctor and she was a woman with an infirmity. There were no drugs to calm her anger, so he had to use the most natural therapy he could find: compassion.

During her last year, he'd accepted more missions away from their camp. It was a deliberate ploy to spend time apart from her. Perhaps his being near her was a catalyst to her anger. Two days before her killing, he'd gone to Nam Xam to help set up a field hospital. There'd been no exchange of niceties between doctor and wife. There was no kiss goodbye; not even a token "I love you." He just told her he was going, and she nodded.

The one person he'd always searched for in his dreams had never come. Boua died believing he didn't love her. She died hating him. He wanted a chance, just the briefest contact: enough time to put everything right with her. But she didn't ever come.

The cicadas drowned out his thoughts, and he used the tissue to dry his own damp face.

He took his shoulder bag with the Vietnamese file inside, turned out the lights, and locked the door. He said "good evening" to a flock of nurses arriving for their shift, and walked boldly through the gates of the hospital. It wasn't until he reached the dark riverbank that he remembered how perilous this journey might be.

He turned around, passed the hospital again, and walked toward home along comparatively bright Samsenthai Avenue. But even here the yellowish lamps turned every doorway into a lurker's cave. Every person he passed, he watched from the corner of his eye. When he was beyond them, he strained his ears to listen for their footsteps doubling back.

He reached his block from the opposite direction from the one he was accustomed to, and had to cut through the temple grounds. He could see the monks in their chambers doing their final chores by candlelight. He stood in the shadows of a small *champa* tree and looked up at his window. It gaped back at him blackly. No movement inside. Or, perhaps? No, just the gentle wave of the curtain in the breeze.

He didn't hear the man approach.

"Something wrong there, brother?"

Siri jumped out of his skin. The silent monk had sneaked up behind him, with his rake poised to defend himself. Siri caught his breath and smiled at his own foolishness.

"No. Just enjoying the peace. That's my room up there."

"Oh, sorry."

"Good night." He walked off.

"Good night, Yeh Ming."

Siri turned, but the monk was already on his way back across the yard.

It took Siri half an hour to attach the hasps with his old tools. The little girl from downstairs came up to watch him, and to escape bed. She was six, and precocious in the nicest sense of the word.

"But why?"

He didn't want to frighten her with tales of burglars, so he ventured off into the type of epic lie that always comes back to catch you.

"Because I'm very handsome." He told her he was bolting the door because so many women wanted to marry him, they disturbed him day and night.

"No you aren't. You're old."

"Aha. To somebody who's six, I may look old; but to an older lady, somebody over ten, for example, I'm terribly handsome."

"Manoly?" The mother had noticed she'd lost this one.

"Shh. Don't tell."

"She's up here, Mrs. Som."

"Ooh, you meanie. I wouldn't marry you."

Once he was locked in his room and the desk was against the wall, away from the open window, he felt secure. Not safe, exactly, but secure. He washed his hands and face at the basin, and started to make coffee. There was a new package of beans, unopened on the shelf. The padlock hadn't come a moment too soon. Miss Vong was slowly moving herself in.

He pulled the Vietnamese report from its temporary hiding place under the floorboards and sat at the desk. Nguyen Hong's handwriting was neat, but Siri still needed to refer to his Vietnamese dictionary a few dozen times. There wasn't really anything new in the report. Like the earlier Tran, Hok had been tortured with the same electric current applied to the nipples and genitalia.

But it was in his personal notes at the end that the Vietnamese turned Siri's thinking around completely.

"Just from my observation, it appears that the current used is somewhat excessive for the purpose of torture. The men would likely have become unconscious before they could offer up any secrets, which seems to defeat the object. It could very well have been enough to kill them. This applies to the other two, also.

"In two of the victims, our Tran and Hok, there seems to be little positive vital reaction. Odd as this may seem, the suggestion is that the electricity may have been applied postmortem. But at the moment, this is completely conjecture on my part."

"Postmortem?" Siri drained the last of his coffee and went to make another. He knew that "vital reaction" was a reddening of the skin beyond the burn marks where the body begins to repair the damage. If there were none, the body hadn't been doing its job. "Postmortem, eh? If that were the case, it would lead us completely away from the idea of the Lao torturing Vietnamese, and more into the realm of someone setting it up to look as if we had done so. Now, if we could only prove that, somebody's hard work would be completely wasted. I can see that being reason enough to kill me."

He returned to the desk, ducking low as he passed the window. He missed the natural breeze that skimmed off the jasmine bushes, but he would have missed his life more. He read the final paragraph.

"I think I may have identified a cause of death. (See photo A.) It was so well concealed, we needn't be ashamed we missed it earlier. But it isn't something I can confirm without more research. I have to leave with the embassy entourage tomorrow. I'll try to get transport down to Ho Chi Minh City as soon as I can. I may find my answer down there. I'll try to call you at the hospital when I get back. Have faith, my friend."

There was a Polaroid snapshot stapled to the back of the file. It was a groin shot of the second Tran. The epidermis around the inner thigh had been peeled back. Apart from the charring from electricity, there appeared to be a very distinct circular bruise about the size of an American dime. Nguyen Hong had marked it with an "A." On the back, he had written: "Once we confirmed all three bodies were ours, your people released them to us. This instant photo is the best I can do to show you what I mean. I couldn't find your autopsy photos. Check them and you should see they all have the same mark. Could be important."

Siri laughed to himself. Perhaps he could phone Sister Bounlan's granny and ask her if she had noticed anything odd in the wedding photos. Although there wasn't yet anything that could be called evidence in the report, there was a speck of hope. It might slow down the warmongers on either side who hadn't had enough of killing.

He took out a pad of paper and a pencil and began to draw up an alternative scenario based on conjecture and half-truths. Two hours later, he'd convinced himself that he was on the right track. There were still several gaps in logic that he needed to fill in before he could show it to anyone. But the sooner he shared, the less likely he was to be shot. He needed a little help. If they weren't busy, he wouldn't mind a visit from Tran, Tran, and Hok in his dreams that night.

Succubus Terminal

The Vietnamese couldn't make it, but Siri certainly wasn't left alone. Before going to sleep, he lay back on his thin mattress and took the white amulet from its pouch. He looked at the worn characters that had been rubbed for luck so many times, he wondered if there could be any left in it.

He wondered how the monk here at his local temple could know who he was. He wondered whether the *Phibob* had forgiven him, or given him a thought since Khamuan. And with all that wonder in his mind, he fell asleep.

It could have been minutes later, possibly hours, when he opened his eyes to see the oil lamp still burning beside him. He was annoyed that he hadn't put it out. Lamp oil was still available on coupons at the hospital co-op, but it wouldn't be for much longer. Soon he'd have to use cooking oil and stink the place up.

He pulled back the mosquito net and lifted the glass bowl. But before he blew out the light, he had an odd feeling that his room was different. He looked slowly from wall to wall. He knew something was wrong, but he couldn't tell what it was. He puffed at the little flame and the room fell into moonless blackness.

He looked around at the darkness one more time, then retreated under the mesh tent. He lay his head on the small pillow. Still the feeling lingered. Then suddenly it came to him. It wasn't a difference you could see; it was a smell. The scent of cheap perfume pervaded his room, and was becoming more potent.

The moon fought free of its cloud for a second and sent a glow through the window. At the very same moment, a tiny sigh like the breath of some small animal puffed past his left ear. He turned his head in surprise and, to his amazement, there was the sleeping face of Mai beside his own.

He retreated as far as the mesh allowed and held his breath. She lay breathing almost silently as she slept, a smile on her young face. Her perfect naked body stretched downward on the mattress beside him. Before the moonlight left them again, he noticed the deep slits at her wrists, the blood congealed and glinting red.

Then it was black again. He focused on her breathing. Not seeing her, but knowing she lay there, was even more erotic. He knew how inappropriate his feelings were, and wondered if this were penance for his immoral thoughts earlier in the day.

He had no idea what to do. Should he wake her? What was she doing sleeping here? If she'd come to him, presumably she had something to say. So why didn't she say it? Perhaps the journey had tired her out. So he lay, shuddering with agitation, while she slept in peace.

Perhaps this was the message. Was she telling him she could be at peace now? Did she want to thank him for . . . ?

There was a knock at the door, a tap as if someone were trying not to wake the neighbors. Siri jumped, like an unfaithful husband caught in the embrace of his naked lover, his naked, dead lover. He cursed whoever it was. All the ridiculous thoughts of half-sleep ran through his head as he prepared to answer the door: how could he hide her? what excuses could he give?

Then a man's voice, a whispered shout, called out: "Mai, Mai, it's me."

Damn. This was part of it. It was all part of the show.

Psychics, he decided, would never have need of other entertainment. She stirred beside him. Her perfume floated over him when she moved. Then he heard her drowsy voice.

"I'm sleeping. What time is it?"

"Three. I just got back."

She sighed again, this time with pleasure. "Go away."

Siri lay back spellbound, like an audience listening to a radio melodrama.

"Nah, don't be like that. I've got something for you."

Siri heard her pull back the net and pad barefoot across the floor toward the door. "Does it have four wheels?" she giggled.

"Better than that. Don't be cruel. Let me in. I'm dying for you."

"What could be better than a car?"

"Didn't you ask me to bring you something from Viengsai?"

She squealed. "Rubies? You didn't! Did you bring me rubies?"

There was the sound of a latch hurriedly shifting. As the door opened, a dim light bathed her. She stood naked in the doorway, magnificently unashamed. The suitor remained hidden in the hall. She giggled again and reached out to him. But the strong left hand of a man grasped her wrist and yanked her outside. The door closed behind her, and darkness returned.

Siri, still breathing heavily, still shaking, scrambled from his bed and hurried to the door. He could hear the muffled sound of a woman choking beyond it. He found the handle and pulled it, but the door wouldn't open. It was held fast by a large steel padlock.

At six, Siri woke confused. He lay still for some time before a crustiness at his groin brought all the memories of the night back to him. Slightly ashamed, he went down to the bathroom and sluiced himself with cool water. It was fifty-six years since such a thing had last happened to him, and he didn't feel any less guilty this time.

Death by Intercourse

"Good morning, Siri." Professor Mon was the director of the Lycée Vientiane. He was also Teacher Oum's father. He was standing uneasily in the vestibule. He didn't want to go into the morgue examination room, so Siri came out to meet him.

"Mon, how are you doing?" They shook hands.

"Fairly well, I suppose. I have a letter here addressed to you and Oum." He handed a grey envelope to Siri. The stamp was from the USS.R. "I think it's about the chemicals you asked for."

"It's unopened."

"There's no one to open it."

"Oum?"

"You obviously haven't heard. They picked her up just after you left. They took her for re-education up in Viengsai."

"Teacher Oum? What the hell for?"

"They said she'd picked up some radical ideas in Australia. They said her attitude was detrimental to the struggle against individualist thinking."

"That's ridiculous. What about the baby?"

"Her mother and I."

"Look, Mon. This is absurd. I'll talk to some people. I mean, she's virtually my assistant. She's the only chemist I've got access to. I'm sure for that reason alone . . ."

"If you could. We are quite anxious."

"Don't worry, friend. We'll get her back."

When Mon had left, Siri stood in the vestibule fitting one more piece into his scenario jigsaw. Not a coincidence, this. Not at all. It was so frustrating not being able to contact Nguyen Hong.

An unfortunate old gentleman chose that morning to pass away in the hospital operating room, and was sent to the morgue for an immediate autopsy. Siri was asked to confirm that there'd been no malpractice. It was ten, and he had to meet Civilai at twelve. He didn't like to leave a job in the middle, but this job was going to take a long time. So they made preliminary notes and put the body in the freezer until after lunch. Suk, the director, was furious, but Siri didn't care much.

He was seated on the log by the river some ten minutes before Civilai arrived.

"Where's our other member?" Civilai asked.

"I think he must have drowned the other day."

"Or the fascists got him. I bet they can't make him talk. Can you believe those Thai tin soldiers? They take over the country by force, then issue a statement that we're an unlawful governing power. What balls they have!"

"What have you got for me?"

"Oh, *sit down, Civilai. Relax. How are you, Civilai?*" his brother prompted.

"Civilai."

"All right. I suppose your life is in danger," Civilai conceded. "You'd be proud of me. I've been a good spy. But I've had to share this with a few people to get the information."

"That's not a problem. I think it's time to share what we've got with everyone you trust. The more people who know . . ."

". . . the less likely you are to get your brain splattered all over your front door."

"They've sent Teacher Oum to Viengsai."

"The chemist girl? H'mm."

"Somebody's covering up."

"I'll see if I can find out who gave that order."

Siri pulled four sheets of paper from his pocket and unfolded them. Neither man had thought about eating his lunch. "I've been putting all the bits and pieces together. I've come up with a hypothesis."

Civilai looked at the untidy notes. "Brother, I'd have to be an Egyptologist to understand that garbled mess. Let's start off with what I've found out and see how it fits your theory.

"The Vietnamese delegation was here at the invitation of the Security Section chief. They were coming to identify a suspected traitor. It was all supposed to be very hush-hush. One of your Vietnamese had been involved in a covert operation in the south. There was an ambush and all the Vietnamese were killed, except for him. He'd been shot up pretty badly and everyone assumed he was dead."

"That's Hok, the last fellow we found at the dam. He had a hole in him as wide as the Pha Ban cave."

"Well, he must have done a very good job of playing possum, because when the Hmong commanders came down to inspect the damage, they had no idea he could see them. According to your Hok, there was an elderly man there in plain clothes, acting as a sort of adviser. But Hok had seen him once, about two weeks before, in an LPRA uniform."

"Hok had a hell of a wound. How sure could he have been that it was the same man?"

"He was positive. He'd seen him around at the Operations Headquarters up at the border. They'd spoken a couple of times. He was there the day they planned the mission that turned into a disaster. The VC found the aftermath of that massacre, and Hok, who was barely alive. They flew him back to Hanoi.

"As soon as he recovered enough to be angry, he was telling everyone about the adviser. He must have convinced people in high places, because they took our ambassador to see him. He contacted us, and we invited Hok to come over and help us identify the man."

"Couldn't they just send pictures?"

"What pictures? The regimental yearbook? How many pictures have you had taken over the last twenty years, Siri? Anti-government rebels don't pose in uniform as evidence for possible treason hearings."

"All right, all right. So, as soon as Hok was well enough to travel, they sent him here."

"With a Vietnamese colonel and a driver. They had top-level clearance."

"Well, that makes it even less likely we'd torture them, doesn't it?"

"Not necessarily. A Lao officer advising the Hmong! That doesn't look good for us. The Vietnamese were already suspicious before this happened. And there was all the secrecy on this side. Not many knew about it, only the Security Section, a few top Party people, not including me, the prime minister, the president. The idea was not to alert the guy we were on to him."

"So, he's still out there somewhere, and now there's no one to identify him. Did we get any information at all?"

"His rank. He was a major."

"Can't we find out which of our majors were hanging around at the Operations Center when Hok was there?"

"We're working on that. But it's a large center and people come and go all the time. It's not like we have an efficient records system of placements and troop movements."

"Anything on the Black Boar?"

"God, you're so demanding. You'd better remember me in your will for all the help I'm giving you."

"You'll be gone before me, pal."

"I don't see anyone shooting at me."

"There will be, after today. I bet there's someone with a long-range rifle up on a rooftop right now with you in his sights."

There was the crack of a branch from the tree above their heads. Both men moved faster than they had for many years. They were twenty meters farther along the riverbank before Siri looked back. He stopped and caught his breath.

"Rajid. What the hell are you doing up there?" Civilai turned back to see the crazy Indian high in the tree, mouthing one of his silent laughs. He'd had his thrill for the day.

"I bet he's a spy. He's probably fluent in six languages." They put their arms around each other's shoulders and laughed as they walked back to the log. They unwrapped their sandwiches and ate for a while until their nerves had settled. Siri spoke.

"Now, Black Boar?"

"According to my sources, Black Boar was the code name of an American Marine special operations unit. They did a lot of nasty stuff inside Vietnam during the war. They were out of uniform and nobody officially claimed them, but word was they were attached to the CIA."

"Wasn't everyone?"

"They did a lot of damage. Why did you want to know about them?"

"What if they've moved over here?"

"Doing what?"

"Same kind of thing. Causing trouble."

"You think this torture mystery might have something to do with them? I can't imagine a bunch of Americans living here without anyone reporting them."

"Why not? There are still a lot of Hmong villages to hide in. Goodness knows, the Yanks would love to see our regime collapse."

"Okay. Show me everything you've got so far. I'll tell you how silly it all sounds, then I'll go and pass it on to the Security Section." He looked up at Rajid hanging still from a branch like a bat. "And keep your voice down."

* * *

The autopsy that afternoon took longer than Siri had expected because he was diverted by the fact that the elderly gentleman had a six-inch nail in his intestine. They photographed it and Siri spent a couple of hours working out how it could have killed him. In the end, it turned out it hadn't. It had been in there for a considerable time, and how it got there would have to remain a mystery. He already had enough of those to solve.

The cause of death, it turned out, was sexual intercourse. The man was scheduled for an appendectomy. Due to the shortage of nursing staff, friends and relatives were invited to sleep with patients overnight and look after them. This usually only involved curling up on the floor, but this particular gentleman had recently found himself a very young wife. Her close proximity on the eve of his big operation led to a spontaneous burst of sexual activity. He complained to her almost immediately of a splitting headache, but he endured it till time came to enter the operating room. As he'd been sedated beforehand, he was unable to alert doctors to his incredible pain, and just as they were about to cut into his stomach, he died of a ruptured cerebral aneurysm. His brain had popped. If Siri hadn't wasted so much time on the intestine and had moved onto the brain, he would have found it right away. But it was obvious to his devoted staff that Dr. Siri's mind was on other, more important things.

"Anyway, let this be a lesson to you, Dtui. Sex can kill you."

"I should be so lucky."

Mr. Geung snorted.

While they were clearing up, the mail arrived. It included a package from Sayabouri with two rolls of autopsy photos in it. When Dtui went up to type the report, she took them up to the library to file under "P." But she was back, breathless, five minutes later.

"Doc, there's an urgent call from Vietnam."

Watching Siri and Dtui "run" to the administration block

would have saddened even the most benevolent of athletic coaches. Siri thought about the man in the freezer as he ran up the steps, his head pounding. He wheezed into the phone mouthpiece, unable to catch his breath or hold his heart still.

"Siri? Dr. Siri? Is that you?" Siri nodded his head. "Siri?"

"Nguyen?"

"Good God. What's wrong?"

"Ex . . . ercise. You . . . talk."

"What? All right. I believe this is what happened. I believe the men didn't die as a result of the torture. Two of them, I'm quite sure, died of air embolism."

"Of what?" He didn't know the term in Vietnamese.

"They had air injected into their veins."

"We didn't see any evidence of that."

"That's just it. After seventy-two hours, most of the indications are gone. There's a slight chance you'd notice something on an X-ray, but we didn't have one at our disposal. Plus we weren't really looking for it. It's going to be very difficult to prove. I may have found puncture marks in one of the veins, but they're all very badly deteriorated.

"All three men have that same round bruise under the burning. I believe it's the mark from the nozzle of some kind of pump, or a very large syringe. They would have had to punch it in to penetrate the muscle. Even then, it demanded a great deal of skill. I'm thinking they used the excessive electrical burns to cover up the marks."

"So why do you say only two died from this air embolism?"

"Tran, the driver. He certainly died from the internal bleeding we found around the aorta. Perhaps because he was fatter than the others, they had trouble locating a vein. I still don't know what caused the bleeding."

"I might know. Look into the possibility that he fell from a height, perhaps from an aeroplane."

"Do you know something?"

"Just guessing right now, but I've got a friend checking reports of unauthorized air traffic three or four weeks ago around the reservoir. And listen, do you know where you can find Tran's wife? Tran the colonel?"

"His wife? I can find out."

"Try to talk to her. Ask her about her husband's tattoos."

"What specifically?"

"Get her to describe them. Maybe you could show her the photos. Ask her if there's anything different about them. Whether they've been altered in any way. I imagine he—"

The line was cut. That wasn't such an unusual thing in those days, but in the current atmosphere of suspicion, he was ready to assume the worst. He waited another half hour, but Nguyen Hong didn't call back.

He walked slowly back to the morgue, weighing the new information against his hypothesis. In his office, he found Inspector Phosy waiting for him.

"You look exhausted," the inspector told him.

"Hello, Phosy." They shook hands. "I'm afraid the last few days have started to catch up with me. It's hard to get my mind around everything. You just get back?"

"No, I got in early this morning. Went home and caught up on some sleep."

"Seminar?"

"They like to keep reminding me how lucky I am to be in the socialist system. But it wasn't so bad. Did you get my note?"

"Your note? Oh, goodness, yes. That seems so long ago. We have a lot to talk about."

"Good."

"You thirsty?"

"Always."

The Disappearing Room

Phosy bought a full bottle of Saeng Thip rum from the delighted bar mama, and commissioned a whole bucket of her magic ice. They sat at a table, away from anyone else.

"Did you win the lottery?"

"What's the point of earning this huge policeman's salary if you can't go out and spend it every now and then?"

"No. That doesn't work. Our salaries are posted by our departments. Everyone knows how much you earn."

"Darn. Well, in that case, I did a bit of shady business up north."

"That's more like it."

Mama fixed them generous drinks, and they told her they could take care of themselves from then on. She left them to their secrets. A fisherman in a huge hat was knee-deep in the water casting and re-casting his weighted net. They watched him untangle the small fish from the mesh and put them in a plastic bag tied around his neck.

"So, what's the big news you have to tell me?"

Those were the last words Phosy spoke for half an hour. He could only sit in silence, sipping his drink as he listened to Siri's tales. First was the account of the assassination attempt, then the whole trail that uncovered the truth about Mai's murder. At the end of it, Siri reached into his bag and handed the policeman his autopsy report and recommendations.

He sat back on his rickety chair and took his second sip of a drink whose ice had melted long before. Phosy looked down at the file and up at the smiling doctor.

"How'd I do?" Siri asked.

"That really was astounding."

"Thank you."

"I really had no idea you were . . ."

". . . a brilliant detective?"

"Exactly. I raise my hat to you." He lifted his imaginary hat. "Really. I'm very impressed."

"You don't look very happy."

"I don't? Perhaps that has something to do with the fact that I'd hoped this whole thing was over with, not just beginning. Were you able to estimate a time of death?"

"No. Impossible. I didn't see her until three days after she died."

"All right." He finished his drink and poured another. "The game's back on. Have you given Judge Haeng the original?"

"No. I've been waiting for you to get back and tell me what to do."

"Good. Don't do anything. I'll ask at the girl's apartment building and see who's been hanging around there."

"Do you suppose Comrade Kham got someone to set it all up for him and left Vientiane to establish an alibi?"

"It's possible. But what do you say you leave a little bit of policing for me? Don't forget, we still don't have an iota of evidence that he's in any way connected to either murder. The only way we could possibly implicate him would be by finding Mai's killer and getting him to talk. Who else knows about this?"

"My staff, me, and you so far."

"You haven't told anyone else?"

"No. Well, the sister. She's taking the body back to Sam Neua. But she's just glad Mai didn't kill herself. She isn't going to say anything to anyone."

"We can't be sure. If she mentions it to anyone up there, it could get back to Kham. His people are all from Sam Neua. To tell the truth, we can't be sure of anything. We're back to the beginning. First thing we have to do is put the original report and the photos of the autopsy somewhere safe. Are they at your office?"

"No, they're in the hospital library."

"*Where?*"

"Nobody ever goes there. Since they burned all the foreign books, there's only crap up there. It was Dtui's idea."

"Is the library open now?"

"No. The building doesn't open till eight tomorrow."

"Okay, I'll come by then. Now, in the meantime, how are we going to keep you alive?"

Siri pulled a crumpled shell from his pocket and put it on the table. Phosy whistled.

"You know anything about bullets?" Siri asked.

"I know it's from a rifle, but I'm no expert. There's someone at the office I can show it to. Where's the other one?"

"The other one?"

"You said there were two shots, didn't you?"

"Oh. That's gone to the Security Section. I mean, the army should have ballistics experts."

"Good plan. I'll take this anyway and see what I can find."

They drank for a couple of hours and talked about things outside of crime and politics. Phosy insisted on taking Siri home. When they pulled up in front of the house, the policeman kept his light on. It lit the lane ahead, making all the dips in the dirt look like black pits. The eyes of cats blinked under bushes. But they spotted no assassins.

"Want me to go inside and see if anyone's lurking in the hallway?"

"No. I think I've shared this with so many people, there's no longer a point in killing me. If they did, they'd have to wipe out half the Security Section as well. I think my chances of making newspaper headlines are over. Besides"—he lowered his voice— "if any man were foolish enough to lurk in our hallway, I wouldn't give him a chance against *her*."

The downstairs curtain shimmied.

"All right. I'll see you in the morning then." They shook hands.

"Thanks. Good night."

The bike growled away, leaving Siri in the lane in the dark. Despite his brave words, it was still an eerie spot. Around him there were a few yellow lamps, some candles in neighbors' windows. There didn't seem to be insect noises anymore at night. People wondered whether the bugs had all escaped across the river, too. The sound of Saloop panting was an oddly comforting one. The animal loped along the lane toward Siri, stopped several meters away, and turned back.

Siri knelt to greet him, but he didn't approach. The dog again ran toward the doctor, then turned back. Siri recalled some black-and-white movies he and Boua had watched together in Paris. There was a dog, a collie or some such type, that used to save children from burning houses and catch criminals. He'd seen this act before, albeit from a more handsome dog, in better shape: Saloop wanted him to follow.

"I'm tired. I'm not in the mood to play tonight."

But the dog continued to run round in circles, egging him on to follow. When he started to bark, Siri set off after him. He'd ruined enough silent nights for the neighbors over the past year. "All right. But this better be good."

Saloop immediately came to heel and walked proudly alongside Siri. They crossed the intersection and headed down to the river.

"So, tell me, dog. Does this mean I'm not possessed anymore, or did you just get over your fear of ghosts? Is there something else I should know about?" The dog didn't answer.

When they arrived at the river, instead of turning left or right, Saloop crossed the road and sat on the riverbank. Siri stood opposite, and the dog looked back over its shoulder at him.

"I don't believe it. *This* was the fuss? You wanted us to come down and watch the river together?" Saloop panted and Siri shook his head. With a chuckle, he crossed the empty road and selected a flat spot near his new friend. "Well, at least you make more sense than my usual river date."

Doctor and dog sat watching the Thai lights shimmer on the river. They looked at the small bats that flapped back and forth across the indigo sky. It wasn't exactly romantic, but it was very pleasant. It was the last real peace Siri would know for a while.

The explosion rattled the silence, and the ground trembled under him. He got to his feet and looked back the way they had come. An almost invisible cloud of dark gray smoke rose into the night sky about a block and a half away. He didn't have to wonder where it had come from. He knew.

He hurried back along the small lane that led from the river and over the wide cross-street. The area was already filling with householders in their nightwear who'd been jolted from their sleep by the blast. They seemed disoriented, as if they weren't sure whether they'd dreamed of an explosion.

Siri continued back along his own lane until he came to the house. It seemed impossible. It stood there still dark and silent, ostensibly untroubled by any disaster. But he knew that could only be an illusion. He knew something horrible lay beyond the front wall. He ran along the path and pushed open the heavy door. It opened more easily than ever because the rest of the house had shifted, so it now sat evenly in its frame. The damage done to the back of the house was unbelievable. Although pictures and ornaments had been shaken from the walls, the front two rooms up and down had only been rattled by the chaos. But when he looked up the staircase, he could see the sky. His room, and the roof above it, were gone. The room beneath his seemed warped somehow. Miss Vong was at its door trying to push it open. She was calling out to the children and to Mrs. Som. The woman's husband was away training in Europe, so she was there alone with her three girls.

Siri hurried over and helped Vong to open the door. The young couple from the upstairs front room could only look down at them helpless, as there was now no way for them to descend. Half the staircase, and the balcony, were gone. The door shifted enough to squeeze through, but it was dark as a grave inside. They could hear the whimpering of the youngest child, and coughing. Siri told Vong to go for a flashlight, and she ran back to her apartment.

He put his head into the room and called out:

"Mrs. Som? Manoly? Are you in here? Can you hear me?"

Manoly's voice came back to him. "Mommy's still asleep. I can't wake her up."

"How are your sisters?"

"They're frightened."

"It's all right. There's nothing to be frightened about. That was the last big bang. I'll tell you what to do. I want all three of you to follow my voice and walk carefully this way. Hold hands now. Manoly, you lead."

"What about Mommy?"

"I'll go and wake her up after you three are out." He sang a song to comfort them and give them a destination. All three were coughing by the time they reached the door. They had their pillows against their faces. The room was cloudy with dust.

"Good girls."

Vong arrived with the flashlight just as the girls emerged. "Oh, goodness. Thank heaven you're all okay." She shined the light toward the room, but Siri stood in front of it.

"Put that out for now." She did as she was told. "Take the girls into the street. I think they've swallowed a lot of dust.

Find them plenty of clean water to drink. Then get them down to the hospital as quickly as you can."

By now there was a small group of people gathered around the front door. They collected the girls and asked what they should do. Siri told them the building wasn't safe and said they should stay back. If anyone had a ladder, they could run it up the front of the house and bring down the couple upstairs through the window. But other than that, they should stay out.

Once he was alone, he turned the flashlight back on. He hadn't wanted to shine it into the room while the children were there to see, just in case. Before going inside, he unbuttoned his shirt and pulled up his undershirt to cover his mouth and nose.

The room was devastated. Large chunks of masonry had fallen. Although much of the ceiling was still in place, it had dropped toward one end of the room, and might cave in at any second. The dust was blinding.

At the point where the back wall had once stood, the ceiling was no more than a meter from the ground, and he had to get on his hands and knees to reach the place where the family had slept. The flashlight reflected from the dust like headlights on a fog bank. He could feel his lungs getting heavy.

"Dr. Siri?"

His heart leaped, and he swung the flashlight beam to his left from where the voice had come. "Mrs. Som?" He crawled across the debris until he could make out the shape of the girls' mother kneeling, facing the bedrolls where the children had slept below the open window. Despite the dust, she seemed very neat. She was dressed in her best *phasin* and her hair was pulled tightly back from her face into a bun. She turned her head to him and smiled. He smiled back to show his relief.

"You've been lucky. Come. We have to get out of here before this ceiling comes down completely." She didn't move.

"Dr. Siri. I'm worried about my girls."

"No. They're fine. Come now." He reached out a hand for her.

"I'm afraid they'll be lonely."

His hand dropped. He knew right away what she meant. He understood, and his stomach turned.

"Oh, no, Mrs.—"

"I was often cross with them. I shouted at them a lot. Perhaps they won't understand that was a mother's way to show how she feels. Can you be sure to tell them I love them?"

He lowered his head. "I'm so sorry."

The large crowd gathered at the front of the house gasped and muttered when Siri appeared at the front door. He'd carried Mrs. Som's crushed body as far as Vong's room and left it there. He didn't want the girls to see it or to raise their hopes she might be alive. He wheezed a few orders here and there to the neighbors, made sure the couple upstairs had been brought down, then collapsed inelegantly in the vegetable patch.

A Hospital Without Doctors

He awoke in one of the few private rooms available at the hospital. His eyes were so sore, it was like looking through greasy windows. The walls and ceiling were Wattay blue. There was one unshaded strip light on the ceiling. A Thai plowing calendar was the only decoration. It was a room devoid of therapy.

"Welcome back." Dtui was beside the bed, fussing around with several trays of roots and powders. The hospital budget could no longer stretch to foreign-made pharmaceuticals, and they had fallen back on natural remedies. In most cases, the patients could be thankful.

"What am I doing here?"

"Sleeping, mostly. You breathed in about a kilo of dust last night while you were being a hero. You passed out. They had to give you oxygen."

"Last night? Right. It's getting so I don't know what's real and what's a dream these days. I was hoping that was one of the imaginary disasters."

"No. Your house really blew up. It fell down completely after you got here."

"How are the little girls?"

"Sorry. Don't know. I just came to work this morning and they told me you were here. I didn't get a lot of information from your bodyguard."

"I have a bodyguard?" He coughed up phlegm into a cloth Dtui had waiting.

"Two at the moment. I believe they're from the Security Section. One's got a nice smile. He wants to talk to you when you come around. Have you come around?"

"I'm a bit weak, but we should get this over with."

"I'll tell him. I'll bring you some breakfast when he's done with you. I'll have to get it from outside. There was a fire in the kitchen last night. The food's so bad, it was probably started by the patients." She went over to the door.

"Oh, Dtui. Has Phosy been by the office yet?"

"The policeman? Not while I was there. Why?"

"He's coming to pick up the original of the report and the autopsy photos. You'll have to show him where they are."

"I'll tell Geung. He'll have to wait for the pictures, though: they aren't back from the photograph shop yet."

"And tell him," he started another coughing fit. "Tell him I'm in here."

"Yes, my leader."

The young man from the Security Section was very polite and very thorough. He'd already been briefed on the information Siri had given Civilai, but he wanted it all again, in Siri's own words.

Talking gave Siri problems, and he had to take gulps of oxygen from time to time. It was during one of these resuscitation sessions that Civilai arrived.

"Hey. Take it easy with that stuff. It costs money. You can't just pluck it out of the air, you know." The security lad saluted and fell back.

"Hello, older brother. I see you didn't get blown up, too, last night."

"Slept like a baby. May I ask why you weren't safely in your own bed when it was blasted to Jupiter?"

"I was down by the river."

"Aha. With some little kitty, I suppose."

"A dog."

"Well, never mind. At your age, you have to take what you can get."

"How are the little girls from downstairs?"

"Stunned. I think only the older one really understands. She's a smarty. We found a family to look after them till the father gets back. We're trying to get word to him. He's going to have his work cut out for him, looking after those three."

"Do you know what happened yet?"

"A mortar. Hand-held type. Damned big one. May have even been two. We assume they were thrown through the window. They're still searching the rubble. The only incriminating thing they've found so far is the remains of a transistor radio. Don't suppose you know anything about that?"

Siri coughed. "The bastard must have thrown it in with the mortar shells."

"That's what we suspected. I'm afraid there wasn't much left of your stuff."

"No problem. There was nothing there of any value. I've spent too many years owning only what I could carry. I may miss the books, I suppose. I assume nobody saw anything?"

"Not a thing. How you feeling?"

"Lucky."

"Too true. Somebody up there's watching over you. No question about that."

Civilai went off to a committee meeting and left the Security lad to finish his interview. It was very relaxed and friendly, interspersed with Siri coughing his guts up from time to time. Dtui kept the boy amused while they waited for the doctor to finish coughing.

The lad was in his early twenties, tall, with ears like ping pong paddles. But Siri had to admit, he did have a good smile.

"I think that's about all for now, Comrade Doctor. I'll get this all typed, and I'll be back late this afternoon with my boss. And Nurse Dtui, my dear [she blushed], you'd better keep your jokes to yourself when he's here. He doesn't appreciate jokes. He had his sense of humor shot off when he was fighting the French." She saluted. "And, Doctor, we'd like to know as soon as your Vietnamese coroner gets in touch again. We really need some solid evidence."

"They'll have to invent a telephone you can carry around with you if they want me to talk to him while I'm in this state. It would take me a week to get to the office."

"H'mm. I'll see what we can do about that. 'Bye, sir, and thanks. 'Bye, miss."

"Miss? What makes you think a pretty thing like me is a miss? What makes you think I'm not married to the Lao national football team's center forward?"

He smiled. "Married women don't blush."

He left the room. Siri gave Dtui a knowing look that she pretended not to see.

Siri was napping again when his second visitor arrived. He opened his eyes slowly and focused on the saffron smudge at the end of his bed. Gradually he recognized the monk from two evenings before.

"Yeh Ming, are you awake?"

When the blur had just about cleared from Siri's eyes, he noticed the bodyguard standing behind the monk with his pistol drawn.

Siri sat up. "It's okay. I know him." The guard nodded and left. "Why do you call me that? Who are you?" The monk smiled but didn't answer. "Why are you here?"

"Your bomb made a mess of our temple grounds. I had to clear it all up. Cleaning up is my burden."

"Well, I'm sorry."

"These things are sent to test us. Life on earth's just the entrance examination."

"I'm sure you'll pass."

"Thank you. While I was sweeping, I found something that belongs to you. You're going to need it."

From a yellow shoulder bag, the monk pulled out the white talisman. He walked to the bed and hung it over the knob that topped the headboard.

"How did you know it was mine?" Siri asked.

"I'm afraid the pouch was burned." While still holding the amulet, the monk closed his eyes and chanted a short mantra. He used the same language Siri had heard in Khamuan, at the exorcism. The doctor put his palms together and bowed his head.

Dtui walked in on this scene and immediately felt embarrassed at her intrusion. She, too, put her palms together and closed her eyes. When the monk was finished, he let go of the talisman and turned to leave. Dtui took a respectful step back. At the door, he looked at her. He stared with a quizzical expression that made her feel uncomfortable.

"Your mother will have a better year next year." He opened the door and walked out.

Dtui glared at Siri. "Why did you tell him about my mother?"

"Dtui . . . I didn't."

At two P.M., three young men from the telephone company arrived with the short end of a cable and an old phone. So far he'd seen soldiers, monks, politicians, and technicians, but not a sign of a doctor. The hospital was understaffed, so they probably hoped he could take care of himself.

By the time the phone technicians had left, Siri had an extension line from the clerk's office in administration. He lay staring at it. After ten very quiet minutes, it rang like a fire engine. He was alone in the room.

"Dtui . . . Dtui?" She didn't come, so he had no choice but to pick it up himself. He put his ear to it and listened . . . and listened.

"Dr. Siri?"

"Yes?"

"There's a call for you."

"Where?"

"Right here. Hang on."

There was a rude electrical burp before Civilai's voice came through the receiver.

"Siri? You there?"

"Ai?"

"How's your new phone?"

"Frightening. How did you know?"

"I know everything. How you feeling?"

"Like I don't have enough air in my lungs. I keep coughing up pieces of my house."

"Good, that should keep you out of trouble for a few days. Listen, I've given all the numbers you need to the clerk. I want to know right away when your Vietnamese friend calls back. There are some angry words being exchanged back and forth across the border. I don't have to tell you how important this has all become."

"Important enough to blow a fellow up."

"See? I knew I didn't have to tell you."

A short while later, the bodyguard came in with a large envelope. He put it on the top sheet and turned to walk away.

Siri chuckled. "Aren't you planning to tell me where this came from?"

"Can't, Comrade. Someone left it at the reception desk. A nurse brought it up. It's all right. I checked it for explosives."

It was from his friend at the air base, a list of reports of unauthorized flights over the Greater Vientiane District for October and November. He was astounded at how many of them there were. Laos boasted seven planes of its own, but if only half the reports could be believed, the country was a veritable aviary of unlawful air traffic.

The period he was most interested in was the end of October, and the date that caught his attention was the twenty-seventh.

The Department of Aviation had received two reports of the sound of a helicopter in the vicinity of Nam Ngum Reservoir. Given the type of customers availing themselves of its services, the correctional facility on the islands there was very sensitive to such sounds.

It was overcast at eleven P.M., and there had been no actual sighting. By the time the anti-aircraft unit at the dam had dusted off its weaponry, the sound had stopped. Radar at Wattay picked up a blip, but before they could send out anything to investigate, it had disappeared from the screen.

"I bet that was you, Black Boar," Siri whispered as he re-read the reports. He underlined the date.

The amulet suspended from the bedpost clinked. Siri looked up at the window to see whether there was a breeze, but the curtains hung flat. The fan wasn't switched on. But the talisman continued to flip back and forth, rattling noisily against the hollow metal bedpost. He leaned over and put his hand on it to keep it still, but as soon as he made contact with the cool stone, an image filled his mind and a feeling of dread flowed through his body.

Talking to Dead People

"I hope you don't mind this intrusion." The lad from the Security Section stood in the doorway behind his superior, an older, serious-looking man. He hadn't bothered to knock. He walked over to the guest chairs, sat on one, and crossed his legs. "I'm Major Ngakum Vong. I'm in charge of . . . are you all right? You look white as boiled rice."

Siri reached for the oxygen and took several deep breaths. The major obviously wasn't the type of man who liked to be kept waiting.

"Look, I'll come back when you're in a fit state to answer questions." He stood and watched as Siri removed the mask and coughed.

"No, Major. I'm all right."

"You certainly don't look it."

The talisman twitched like a living thing in Siri's hand. Once the major had regained his seat, he noticed the white plaited hair curling out from the doctor's fist. "What the hell's that?"

"This? Just a lucky charm someone gave me."

"Really? I thought you were a doctor. I hope you don't believe in such rot."

At almost the same time, the stool at the end of the bed decided three legs weren't enough to stand on. It toppled sideways and cluttered onto the concrete floor. The sound echoed around the room. The lad bent to pick it up, and Dtui came running in to see what had happened. The major turned to her.

"You. You can wait outside."

"Me?" She gave him her ironic eye.

"Major Ngakum, this is my morgue assistant," Siri told him. "She was a witness to the autopsies. She could be useful for filling in the gaps in my memory."

"All right. Stand over there, girl." She ran to the wall and stood to attention beside the lad. He pursed his lips to keep from smiling. "Perhaps if the circus is over, we can get down to business. This is a very serious matter, and I want it resolved before it becomes an international incident. Doctor, I've read your version of events. I must say you strike me as something of a storyteller."

"How do you mean?"

"Well, everything I've read here is conjecture, far-fetched. There's not a thing we could take to the Vietnamese as evidence that we didn't torture their people."

"Criminals have been convicted on less. There's enough circumstantial evidence there to at least—"

"One. We aren't convicting criminals. We're protecting the good name of our country. Two. Your circumstantial evidence is based on the word of an amateur coroner with . . . how many years experience?"

"Ten months."

"Ten months. And on the strength of this . . . fiction, you want me to launch a major operation to search for an alleged band of mercenaries. And where that information came from, I have no idea. You want me to interrupt bilateral talks on the say-so of a pathologist who hasn't even done so much as the equivalent of an apprenticeship. Honestly, Doctor."

"I see what you mean," Siri said.

Dtui grunted. She'd been expecting a fight.

Siri continued: "I must admit, if I looked at it all objectively, there really isn't much there."

"Exactly. So you're telling me you don't have anything else for me to go on."

"No. I'm sorry."

"H'mm. Don't think we don't appreciate everything you've tried to do. Goodness knows, we'd do anything to avoid aggression with Vietnam. It's just that your efforts have been, at the very least, naïve."

"I understand."

Dtui could no longer restrain her anger. "You *understand*?"

"Dtui, the major's right."

Ngakum stood and turned to her. "So, girl. Do you have anything to add to this?"

Siri shook his head in the background.

"I suppose not," she admitted.

"Then I suggest you stick to nursing, and stop trying to do my job." He walked to the door and waited for his corporal to open it. "Take my advice, both of you. In this new society, ambition will only get you in trouble." And he was gone. The lad ran after him.

Siri could find no breath. He fumbled for the mask. Dtui hurried over and turned the spindle on the oxygen tank. While Siri was fighting to force air into his lungs, Dtui took his pulse and calmed him with her voice.

"Easy, Doc. Take it easy. Breathe slowly." Siri desperately wanted to talk, but Dtui held down the mask and shook her head. Soon, Siri closed his eyes and allowed his metabolism to calm down. When his pulse was normal and his breathing regular, Dtui gently lifted the mask. "All right, now you can tell me. But if you insist on getting excited, I'm going to put the mask back on you."

"Dtui, listen. This is very important. I want you to go to the Assembly offices and find Civilai. Make sure . . . [he drew more oxygen from the mask], make sure nobody follows you."

"You know you've got a phone here?"

"No. Can't phone. Take your bike, and insist on seeing

220 COLIN COTTERILL

Civilai. Lie down across the driveway if you have to. Kick up a fuss. But get him out of whatever he's doing. Nothing he has on his agenda can be as important as what I have to say. Tell him to come back here with you right away. He is to talk to no one else."

"Wow. You gonna tell me, too?"

"Go. Now."

Siri needed pure oxygen for another fifteen minutes before he felt well enough and composed enough to pick up the telephone. He didn't have to dial. A male voice answered.

"Yes?"

"Who's that? Where's the hospital clerk?"

"I'm Second Lieutenant Deuan. I'm with the Security Section. We'll be manning this phone twenty-four hours. What can I do for you, Doctor?"

Siri rethought his plans. "Could you put me through to police headquarters, please?"

"Is this related to . . . ?"

"No, it's another case."

"Very well, sir."

He assumed the security man would be listening in and taking notes. But he felt an urgent need of Phosy's support. He wanted someone he could trust on his team. He knew he wouldn't be able to ask directly. He had to use some pretext to get him to come to his hospital room.

There were one or two engaged signals before a flustered desk sergeant answered.

"Central Police."

"Hello, this is Dr. Siri Paiboun from Mahosot Hospital. Could I speak to Inspector Phosy, please?"

"Who?"

"Inspector Phosy." There was silence.

"Just a minute."

Siri waited for a few minutes until a gruff-voiced man came to the phone.

"Hello. Doctor? I'm afraid the Inspector isn't here."

"Damn. Could you leave a message for him?"

"Well, I'm not sure when he'll be around again, but I'll try."

"Could you tell him to contact Dr. Siri at Mahosot, urgently. Room 2E."

"Okay. I'll put it up on the board, but I can't guarantee he'll see it."

"Can't you put it on his desk or something?"

"Desk?" The man laughed. "He doesn't have a desk. 'Bye, Doctor."

Siri was left holding a silent phone.

"Doesn't have a desk?"

He lay back on the uncomfortable pillow and looked up at the blue ceiling. Two lizards were either mating or fighting. It occurred to him that peacetime was far more violent and chaotic than war. He became drowsy and must have nodded off again, because he was awakened by Civilai bursting through the door. Dtui was behind him.

"This better be good, little brother. What's the point of putting in a phone if—"

"Come here and sit down. You too, Dtui. And keep your voices down."

They pulled chairs close to the bed. Neither of them had ever seen him more serious or his eyes less green. He pulled himself up on his pillow.

"I'm going to tell you both something that you'll find incredible. I find it incredible myself. You'll assume I'm on hallucinogens, or that I've finally toppled over the cliff into senility. But in fact I've never been more sane or clear-headed in my life.

"I'll save you the full-Technicolor version because you'd really send for the nut-wagon if I told you everything. I'll just tell you the details that are relevant to this case." He took some oxygen. "For many years, I've been able to see things."

"Oh, heavens. Not the—"

"Civilai. *No.* If our friendship means anything, I ask you to just listen to what I have to say. Please." Civilai shrugged and folded his arms. "I see the spirits of the deceased. I have no control over when they come, or how they communicate with me. But it's true. Over the past two weeks, these visitations have been getting more regular, and, I don't know . . . stronger, I suppose you could say. I receive messages in certain ways.

"Ai, you asked me how I knew about the Black Boar. I couldn't tell you then because I knew you'd mock me, like you always do. But I knew because the Vietnamese told me they were still here. I couldn't have guessed it, or made it up. They *told* me."

Civilai shuddered. "You're starting to give me goose bumps."

"I get them all the time. I had a dream once. The Vietnamese were protecting me. A child tried to break through them to get to me, but they beat and killed him. The dead child's face peeled away to show it was really the face of an old man. I saw the same old man in another dream in Khamuan. He embodied the evil spirits that were destroying the forest. Not long ago today, his image filled me with the most dreadful fear.

"And then he walked into the room."

Dtui breathed his name. "Major Ngakum. I knew something was wrong."

"Yes, Dtui. The major. I don't know why; I have no proof. But I truly believe Major Ngakum is the adviser to the resistance forces. I'm sure he's responsible for this whole affair with the Vietnamese. And he's probably the one who's been trying to do away with me."

Civilai stood up to stretch his old legs. "I don't know what to say." He walked over to the wall calendar and inspected the dates. It was a year old. "It's positively the most preposterous thing I've ever heard from you, and goodness knows I've heard you say some shit over the years. Major Ngakum has been fighting for the revolution for most of his life."

"Ai—"

"But I know you believe it. And because you believe it, and

you're the best friend I've got, that means I have to trust you. And for some unfathomable reason, I believe it too."

"Thank you."

"It is true," Dtui spoke up. She'd been sitting, shaking like a leaf, since he first started to speak. "I knew for a long time, but I didn't dare say. My mom noticed right away when you came to the house. She said you had the gift."

"It could be a curse, Dtui."

"Look, both of you." Civilai came back to sit between them. "Obviously we can't do anything on the say-so of some senile old fool who sees ghosts. I'll get some military people I trust to look at dates. See whether it's possible Major Ngakum could have been at Operation Headquarters when Hok was there. See where he was when the massacre of the Vietnamese troops took place. We'll take a look at his records and see if anything stands out. If it all matches, then we can go on to stage two."

"That's fair."

"And I want back every *kip* you've ever won off me gambling. If I'd known you had accomplices on the other side, I never would have taken the bets."

They all laughed until Siri fell into another coughing fit. When he calmed, he looked at his two friends and smiled.

"But tell me, Nurse Dtui," Civilai asked, "how safe do you think the great gypsy fortuneteller here feels, knowing the guards outside his door were assigned by a man he thinks is trying to kill him?"

"No worries, Uncle. Mr. Geung went home to get some bedrolls. Dr. Siri will have his own personal bodyguards tonight. I'll protect him."

Civilai laughed. "I don't get it, Siri. Seventy-two years old, and you still have young nurses sleeping with you. How do you do it?"

How to Miss the That Luang Festival

In fact, there wasn't a lot of sleep to be had that night. Siri was restless, and his coughing kept the bodyguards awake for most of it. But, at least, they all survived until morning.

His first visitor of the day arrived with two special baguettes wrapped in greaseproof paper.

"Lah?"

"Doctor. They just told me what happened. I came right away. How are you feeling?"

"All the better for seeing you."

"You sweetmouth, you." She handed him the rolls. "The boy outside went through both of them looking for missiles or such like. Then he decided they might be poisoned, so he tasted both of them. That's why they have teeth marks." She smiled.

"You're very kind." Something about the visit and his own tentative grasp on life encouraged him to be uncommonly honest. "You know, Mrs. Lah, I was thinking last night about what regrets I'd have had if that old house had fallen down on me. There weren't a lot. But one of them was you."

"Me?"

"Yes, I've procrastinated too long. If I don't die in the next week, I'd be most honored if you'd have dinner with me one evening."

The sixteen-year-old girl who still resided in Auntie Lah sent out a smile that lit up the whole room. She came over to him, leaned over the bed, and gave him a very warm kiss on the cheek.

"You bet." She almost skipped to the door. She turned the handle, then looked back at him. "But if you die in the next week, I'll kill you."

When she'd gone, Siri couldn't stop smiling. There was a groan from underneath the bed.

"I . . . I . . . I'd be most hon . . . honored if you'd have—"

"Keep it to yourself, Mr. Geung."

Geung snorted and laughed cheekily. It was six, and time for him to get up. Dtui had left already to see her ma.

Out in the streets, people were already preparing for the That Luang Festival. It was one of the few dates on the Lao Buddhist calendar that was guaranteed to spark excitement across generations and ethnic lines. The golden Grand Stupa had watched over its excited children on the thirteenth day of the twelfth moon for as long as anyone living could remember.

This was the first festival since the revolution, and it promised to be a little more restrained than usual. The new regime had banned certain excesses: the popular freak shows, for one. There'd be no five-legged goats or three-breasted women to entertain the crowds. Alcohol was forbidden, along with gambling, so there were unlikely to be any spontaneous shootings to write about in the papers the next day. The government also put the lid on displays of opulence and "extravagant religious outpourings." All of which might have made one wonder what could possibly be left to celebrate.

But the Lao have a remarkable talent for enjoyment, and, for many, the excuse to get their good clothes out of the chest and mingle, in an atmosphere charged with excitement, was enough to keep them awake for a week in anticipation.

The Lao Patriotic Front announced that this year would be an opportunity for Laos to display its economic and cultural achievements under the new regime. Skeptics like Siri wondered how small that display might be. Civilai suggested an Inflation Marquee where children blow up balloons with "the Lao *kip*" written on them. Siri joked that they could have a show of the Xiang Thong Temple puppets with their nasty right-wing mouths taped shut.

Whatever happened, the That Luang Festival would still be the cultural event of the year and Siri, with his dust-filled lungs, would miss it again. In fact, as he'd never lived in Vientiane before this year, he'd *never* seen the festival. He and Boua had dreamed of attending, after the revolution. It was one of her many deflated dreams.

At seven, Siri witnessed a sight more rare than a five-legged goat: a white-coated hospital doctor came into his room and showed him his X-rays.

"Dr. Siri."

"Dr. Veui. I was starting to wonder whether they'd put me in a room at the Lan Xang Hotel by mistake."

"Now, now. No sarcasm. You know we're very—"

"Short of staff. Yes, I know. But you'll be pleased I didn't pass away from neglect while you were off tending to real patients."

"Your nurse has been keeping me informed as to your progress. We did have a couple of emergencies yesterday that kept us busy. You heard about the fire?"

"Yes. Kitchen, wasn't it?"

"It started there, yes. We were lucky it didn't spread to the pharmacy. Lord knows we have precious few drugs as it is. We did lose our unimpressive collection of books, though."

"What do you mean?"

"Think of your geography, Siri. The kitchen's directly beneath the old library. It was gutted. Nothing but ash and memories."

While Dr. Veui ran his stethoscope around Siri's chest and back, the patient breathed as deeply as he could. But his mind was on the library. How did that piece fit into the puzzle?

Sometime about eight, he had his nicest visit of the day. Miss Vong poked her head around the door and smiled.

"Miss Vong. Come in, why don't you?"

She didn't. "Can't visit this trip, Dr. Siri. How are you?"

"Not bad."

"I have to rush. I'm supposed to be at work."

"You don't want to stop off at the *khon khouay* office first?"

"The *khon khouay* office? Whatever for?"

"I'm not supposed to say anything, but it can't do any harm. Mr. Ketkaew spotted you at the Department of Education the other day. He came back frisky as a river rat, telling us all about this stunning woman he'd seen. He asked me if I knew you. He was positively glowing. I'm no expert, but I'd say he's fallen for you."

"For me? Don't be silly." She couldn't keep the corners of her mouth down. "Anyway, I'm here with some fans of yours. Manoly and her sisters wanted to come see how you are."

"Oh, how wonderful! How are they?"

"I don't think they've really come to terms with what happened. They've been very quiet."

"Send them in."

Vong left, and the three little girls came in as a chain. Manoly was the lead link. Siri chose that moment for his first serious cough of the day, and the girls stood back by the wall watching him. When he was through, he smiled and called them over.

"Well, ladies. How nice of you to come to see me. Where are you staying?"

Manoly was the spokeswoman. "Auntie Souk's house. She's nice. She's outside. You want to see her?"

"No. I want to see *you*. I was worried about you all."

"Auntie Souk said you were very brave when you went in to look for Mommy."

"Manoly, do you know where your mommy is now?"

"Yes."

"Where?"

"In the temple."

"That's not your mommy."

"Yes, it is."

"No. In the temple is just the package your mommy was kept in." The smallest sister giggled at this. Manoly seemed angry.

"It's Mommy."

Siri reached out for her hand and put it against his face.

"This skin, this hair, all this outside stuff. It isn't me. It's just my package. It's like the wrapper around the sweet; it isn't the sweet itself. What we really are is all inside the package. All our feelings. All our good moods and bad moods. All our ideas, our cleverness, our love, that's what a person really is.

"It's called a spirit. Your mommy's spirit has left her package already. I met your mommy's spirit when I was in your room that night."

"Is that like a ghost?"

"No. A ghost is just something in make-believe stories. A spirit is really *her*. Some people can see it, but most people can't."

"Did you talk to her?"

"Yes, she was worried."

"Why?"

"She was worried you might not love her because she was cross with you sometimes. But she wanted me to tell you, being cross was part of loving you."

"Did she say that? Really?"

"Really. And she said she loves you all very much. She always will."

Manoly's eyes filled with tears and she smiled. It was probably a bit deep for the other two, so they just stood there.

The younger one changed the subject. "Uncle Siri. I can almost go to school. Watch." She reached her right arm over her head and tried to touch her left ear. It was the method they used in the countryside. If you could reach your ear, you were old enough to start school.

"Oh, you're so close, Nok. Too bad you don't have ears like a rabbit. You could start right away." She giggled and jumped up on his bed.

When Dtui got back from her mother's, she found all three of them lying there listening to a story about tree spirits in Khamuan.

"Aha. What's going on here?"

"Are you a nurse?" Nok asked.

"No. I'm a crocodile in a nurse's uniform."

"Have you come to apply?" Manoly asked her.

"What for, darling?"

"To be one of Uncle Siri's wives?"

Dtui feigned a dramatic and very noisy vomit. When Auntie Souk and the guard came rushing in, they found Dtui face-down on the floor, the girls curled up on the bed with laughing aches, and Siri coughing his house up.

Once they'd gone, Siri attempted the telephone again. Instead of getting the Security officer, he found himself talking to the hospital clerk.

"Hello. What happened to the soldier?"

"He's gone. I suppose there was no point in staying here once he got the call he was waiting for."

"What call's that?"

"From Vietnam. I was just on my way home yesterday evening when it came through. Dr. Nguyen something. Don't you remember?"

"I didn't get a call."

"That's odd. The officer said he was going to transfer the caller."

"He didn't transfer it in this direction. Interesting. Look, can you put me through to Police Headquarters? And I want you to look up the number for the central morgue in Hanoi."

"That's in Vietnam."

"It was the last time I saw it."

"You'll need to fill in four forms before I can let you phone internationally. You have to have the director's signature and—"

"All I need is the number. We'll worry about signatures later. And could you send a message for my morgue technician, Mr. Geung, to come here as soon as possible?"

Siri eventually got through to the same gruff-voiced inspector at Central he'd spoken to the day before.

"Hello, Dr. Siri. This is Inspector Tay. After we talked yesterday, it occurred to me who you were. You're the coroner, right? I keep meaning to send someone over to see what you're doing over there. I'm afraid your man still hasn't been in."

"That's all right. I was just wondering: yesterday you said Phosy didn't have a desk?"

"That's right."

"How can one of your detectives not have a desk?"

"Ah, well, he isn't actually one of ours, you see?"

"No?"

"No. He's sort of on special assignment. He's down from Viengsai working on a case. He comes in now and then. He's always running around."

"From Viengsai?"

"Is there a problem?"

"No. It's just that he didn't mention he was based in the north."

"You don't get much information out of that one. Hardly talks to anyone. Secretive bastard, if you don't mind me saying."

"No. Er, thanks anyway."

"Welcome."

Siri slowly put down the phone. Geung had arrived and was standing beside the door, rocking slightly. Siri looked up at him but forgot for a second why he was there.

"Mr. Geung? Ah, yes. I want you to take this note," he wrote as he spoke, "and give it to Comrade Civilai at the Assembly office. You've been there before."

"Yes."

"Don't give it to anyone else. Not even if they rip out your toenails. You understand?"

"Yes." He snorted and loped out of the room, laughing.

"Based in Viengsai? How could he be?"

It was early afternoon when Civilai arrived with a well-preserved old man in a crumpled suit. They both looked drained, as if they'd been up all night.

"Siri. How you feeling?"

"Did you get my note?"

"Your morgue Igor almost got himself shot delivering it. They didn't let him through the gate, so he stood outside the fence and yelled my name till I came to the window."

"He gets the job done." Siri fell into a coughing fit. If anything, he was feeling worse than the previous day.

"Siri, this is Dong Van, the Commander General of the Security Section. He wanted to meet you before you choke to death."

"Looks like you're just in time. How are you, Commander?"

"I'm a little frazzled, Dr. Siri. This has been a very difficult time for me. Major Ngakum has been one of my most trusted colleagues for many years."

"We got him?" Siri punched his fist into the air. Civilai put up his thumb. Dong Van obviously wasn't viewing it as a victory yet.

"When your friend Comrade Civilai first came to see me about this, I didn't believe a word of it. It didn't help that he wouldn't divulge his sources. Even when he started to come up with evidence, I was very defensive; I didn't want to believe it. But he's a very thorough man. He spent the whole night cross-checking the files, getting people out of their beds to give statements."

"Good for you, Ai."

Civilai couldn't wait to explain. "It was all too much of a coincidence. The major was assigned to the Operations Headquarters when Hok was there. He knew the details of the Vietnamese

covert mission. His unit was responsible for security arrange-
ments when the Trans and Hok came over. He had access to all
the communiqués.

"And as if that weren't enough to circumstantiate him into
jail and throw the key away, guess who was doing a survey of traffic to the islands at Nam Ngum? I bet we could get a positive ID
from the district chief."

"And now," the commander added, "we have evidence that
he had your call from Vietnam diverted to his office. What we
don't know is what that conversation was all about."

"So we need you to call Hanoi." Civilai picked up the phone.

"I expect the girl has the number for the morgue already, but
I think I know what Nguyen Hong will have to tell me."

The call took an age to put through. Siri spoke to several confused Vietnamese before locating his colleague.

"Hello, Nguyen Hong."

"Dr. Nguyen Hong? It's Siri." There was a pause. "Nguyen
Hong?"

"I was told you were dead!"

"I'm not. Did you call me yesterday evening?"

"Goodness, you've given me a start. Yes, but the call was transferred to your, what do you call it? Your Security Section."

"Who to?"

"Ah. He did say his name; your Lao names all sound the same
to me. But he said he was the commander."

"I bet he did, and he told you I was killed in an explosion."

"Yes. Then he took down all the details I wanted to give you
and told me they'd be very useful. He gave me his direct line if
I had anything else for him."

"Perfect. That should be the last nail in his coffin. The man
you spoke to was the one Hok was coming here to identify."

"No!"

"I'll write you all about it. But before we get cut off, give me
everything you've got."

Ten minutes later, Siri hung up. He looked at the two men at his bedside and smiled.

"Brilliant. Absolutely brilliant. They should have got away with it. It was just their misfortune to come up against me and Nguyen Hong."

"Come on, little brother. Out with it."

"Here's the way I see it. Major Ngakum received the secret communiqué from Hanoi telling him Hok and his team would be coming to identify the traitor Hok had seen at the massacre. Ngakum couldn't let them get as far as Vientiane, so he got his Black Boar gang to waylay the jeep. He knew the route and the guard postings, so it shouldn't have been difficult.

"They found themselves with three Vietnamese. They could have just killed them and dumped the bodies. But someone had an idea."

He was talking too fast without rest, getting too excited, running out of breath. He took some gulps of oxygen and kept the mask handy.

"It was an ideal opportunity to create a bit of a diplomatic stir. If they could convince the Vietnamese that their men had been arrested and tortured, it wouldn't take a great leap in logic to assume that Laos had been responsible for the earlier massacre as well.

"So the Black Boars killed the three in a way that wouldn't be easy to recognize and then set it up to look like they'd been tortured to death. They flew the bodies to Nam Ngum near the correctional facility, and dropped them into the reservoir. They anchored them to old shell casings, and used cheap string on two of them so they'd eventually bob up to the surface. The second Tran they tied with flex so someone would have to go down and discover the Chinese shells. They knew that would upset the Vietnamese.

"Ngakum 'just happened' to be at the reservoir doing some fictitious survey when the first two bodies were found, and *he* 'recognized' the Vietnamese tattoos. He's the one who made sure the Vietnamese embassy was involved. Of course, the bodies had been set up. When Tran left Hanoi, he didn't have any tattoos."

"No?"

"Not a one. His wife knew nothing about them. They tattooed the poor fellow after he was dead."

Civilai shook his head. "How did they actually kill them?"

"Nguyen Hong believes two of them had air pumped into their veins. It causes an air embolism that blocks the flow of blood through the heart. After a few weeks in the water, there wouldn't be much to show what had happened. It was very professionally done, except for one small error."

"Which was?"

"Tran, the driver, appears to have died from a massive tear in the artery in his chest. There's only one way that could make any sense, but it's too horrible to imagine. Tran didn't die with his countrymen. He was a little fatter than the other two. What if they missed his vein when they injected the air?"

"Then he would have been alive when they electrocuted the bodies?"

"I pray he was unconscious, and not just playing dead. But apparently not even the torture killed him. Civilai, when he arrived at the morgue, we all noticed the expression of horror frozen on his face. There was only one thing that could have caused that look."

"The fall from the helicopter."

"It's quite conclusive that he was still alive when they pushed him out."

"I can't imagine a more horrific death," the commander said.

"I doubt whether it was intentional. I don't think cruelty was the Americans' aim. I mean, they could have *actually* tortured them to death if they had wanted it to look authentic."

The commander sighed. "We have to track them down. I

don't want mercenaries rampaging through the land. But first things first. I want to get my hands on that damn traitor. You've convinced me, gentlemen. God knows how many lives have been lost as a result of the bastard's crimes. If you'll both excuse me, I have a very painful duty to perform."

He shook hands with them warmly and left, taking the guard with him. The two old friends remained there in silence. Civilai sat scratching his head, exhausted. Siri sucked on his oxygen. Neither spoke for several minutes. Slowly their smiles turned to laughter. Civilai moved to the bed and grasped Siri's right hand in his. They squeezed each other's fists so tightly their knuckles turned white, and they laughed as if the funniest thing in the world had just taken place.

"What are we laughing for?" Siri asked through the tears.

"It's a nervous reaction. We're both scared out of our wits."

"You think this was scary, you wait till I tell you about the *other* case."

The Other Case

K hen Nahlee had never failed so ingloriously. He ached with humiliation. Revenge was an unprofessional desire, but he wanted nothing more.

He could have been excused the first miss. It was dark. Siri was a shadow against the front door. He should have gone to check the body, but the woman was always there behind her curtain. It wasn't until the next day that he'd heard the doctor had survived.

By then, Siri had gone, left the capital. So he had to end it some other way. He'd dated the girl from the hairdresser's. It was nothing serious. He used the Vientiane grapevine to spread the rumor that she was Comrade Kham's minor wife. It traveled so fast, he heard it back almost at once. Mai didn't know the comrade from a bowl of noodles, but that didn't matter. She had enough old men chasing her. No one would be surprised.

The suicide method he selected was one he'd seen a few years earlier. The wife of some man he'd killed slashed her wrists and plunged them into boiling water. It was dramatic enough, suitable for a lover filled with remorse. He set up the crime scene exactly as he remembered it. Exactly. The Vientiane police were there, taking pictures, asking questions. When they found the note, there wasn't a doubt in anyone's mind that she'd killed her lover's wife, then taken her own life.

It was all perfect. Nobody questioned it until *he* came back:

the detective pensioner. That interfering old man. He couldn't leave it alone. He had to poke his nose in. He stripped away the layers of deceit and exposed the truth. He was so damned proud of himself, gloating there by the river as he told his story.

Khen Nahlee thought he couldn't have hated Siri any more than he did that night. It had gone beyond an assignment. It was a personal matter. No shriveled old quack was going to make a mockery of him.

He went to his arsenal and found a remedy for the doctor's inquisitive disease. He was patient. He knew what time Siri had come home, so he gave him time to settle down. The old man had been drinking, so he'd tire quickly. Khen Nahlee walked through the silent temple grounds and looked up at the open window. The light was out. He was asleep. Too bad there wouldn't be those few seconds of panic as he saw the bombs.

He pulled the pins and tossed his farewell in through the window. He didn't need to wait. He knew what devastation they'd cause. He'd almost reached the temple gate when the explosion came, but he still didn't bother to look back.

He considered killing the girl and the imbecile at the morgue, as his boss had suggested. But who would ever listen to them? No. All that remained was to remove the evidence. The hospital kitchen was unlocked. The cheap cooking oil burned well. The flames lapped upward to the library and soon took hold of the dry old books. He watched, because it was a satisfying end to a good evening's work. Finally it was all over.

He even went to report to his boss. Comrade Kham met him in the gazebo behind his house. It was one A.M. But the senior comrade rarely slept anymore. These two men had taken part in hundreds of early-morning debriefings, but never one so personal.

Comrade Kham had set up the Discreet Operations Unit some twenty years earlier, when he was still in uniform. Initially, it had been a small department that collected and analyzed data: a humble LPLA version of the CIA. Although very few knew about it, files were compiled on all the senior officials and anyone displaying "uncooperative" or "unhealthy" behavior.

From time to time, the bad mango in the bunch turned out to be so rotten that extreme measures had to be taken. Initially, they were careful to only eliminate those elements likely to cause damage to the movement. But power corrupts, and there were rumors that the only reason Kham was able to rise so rapidly through the ranks was because one or two political rivals "disappeared."

As the Lao Patriotic Front grew and turned into a political force, so the DOU became more organized. One wing became a semi-autonomous death squad, and Khen Nahlee was named its head in 1970. He was ideally suited for the work. He was intelligent and dedicated to the party, and had been killing on its behalf since his early teens. Most important, he was a master of undercover work. He had gone through so many names and identities over the years that not even his own men could say they knew him.

He was a devoted disciple of the group's founder, and carried out whatever assignments Kham gave him without question. He knew that any work he did was for the betterment of the Movement. But when Kham told him his secret at the chilly airstrip in Xiang Khouang, their relationship was forced to change. The comrade had killed his wife, and he wanted Khen to make it all right.

There had been no traditional motive, no crime of passion, no insurance claim. Kham had just grown to hate her. He hated what she had become since they moved to the capital. In peacetime, the Lao Women's Union was developing into a political force. She was the one interviewed by the Khaosan News Agency. She was the one who spoke on the radio. It was her they invited to talk to the students at Dong Dok. And, suddenly, who was he? He was the husband of Comrade Nitnoy. They didn't even remember his name.

So he killed her. The cyanide tablets came into his possession as a sort of incentive. It was fate. The unhappy couple had returned drunk from a Party reception where he was the senior comrade, but she was the star. He'd been her escort. She passed out drunk on the bed, and he went to his study and put the doctored tablets into her bottle.

But it wasn't until she'd gone off with them in her handbag the next morning that he started to think it through. Doing it wasn't enough; he also had to get away with it. Kham left for a week in Xiang Khouang, where he met Khen Nahlee and explained what he'd done. His henchman, ever faithful, promised to make everything turn out right, as he always had. Khen went to the capital and waited. Three days later, word of Mrs. Nitnoy's death reached Kham. All Khen Nahlee needed to do was put on a uniform and pick up the evidence from the LWU.

But things didn't go as smoothly as the comrade had hoped. The pill bottle wasn't in her bag, and Khen didn't want to attract attention to it by going back a second time. Kham had to hope things would work out in the course of events. But he hadn't taken Siri's skill into account. He'd assumed the reluctant coroner was untrained and incompetent, but that was no longer true. If he'd noticed the doctor's determination, he might not have underestimated him so badly.

He knew. Somehow the little coroner knew, and Kham was afraid he wouldn't be able to keep him quiet. There was little choice. He ordered Khen Nahlee to kill him before the findings became public.

The comrade had always been a staunch believer in Fate. He began projects only on auspicious dates and consulted the stars. It was Fate that he'd been given the cyanide, and it was Fate that she'd taken it so soon. Up to that point, fortune had been on his side. The assassin had never known failure; so when his bullets flew over Siri's head that night, it was the first indication that Fate had gone against him. Siri had been given a second chance. Kham looked for another way.

He had Khen Nahlee set up a suicide. One murder of an insignificant girl and it could be all over. It was no scandal for a powerful man to be adored by his mistress. It would be no surprise that she'd killed her rival and taken her own life. The police were satisfied. He gave a tearful statement to the Press. It was all over.

Then Siri came back and screwed it all up again. There really was only one way to challenge Fate. All the logic on the earth dictated that Siri couldn't escape a second assassination attempt. Nothing human could keep him alive.

But now the senior comrade sat in mid-afternoon in his empty house, drunk. He'd walked out of the Assembly in the middle of the ceremony for heroes of the revolution, ignored all questions. He'd shooed away the driver and driven the limousine home himself. He'd gone four nights without sleep; the journey home had been a blur.

He could compete with men. He'd shown that time and time again. But here he was up against something far beyond anything he'd ever known. His enemy was spiritual. Mrs. Nitnoy wasn't going to let him forget what he'd done to her. She was in his nightmares, and she was at Siri's back, protecting him. Something told him he would probably never spend a restful night again, and he couldn't bear the thought of that.

He turned the radio up to its loudest and tuned it to Thailand. An expert in genealogy was discussing the reasons why Lao communists were so physically unattractive. He listened to find out why he was ugly, and when the music rose at the end of the program, he shot himself in the head.

Thrice Dead

Khen Nahlee hadn't failed. Not yet. Although his nemesis was blessed with astoundingly good fortune, it didn't necessarily mean he'd failed. The boss had told him to go back north. Give it up. But his mission was unfinished. Not failed: just delayed.

He sat in the bare room meticulously oiling his pistol and cleaning the silencer. He went through the plan in his mind. This was the evening of the That Luang Festival. The hospital would maintain a skeleton staff, if they could persuade anyone at all to stay on. The nurses would be made up like porcelain dolls with blood-red lipstick. They'd be parading themselves in front of the boys at the fair. Perhaps he'd go and help himself to one when it was all over.

The Security Section had withdrawn its guards, so Siri should be alone. No luck, no coincidences, could possibly keep him alive a third time.

On his old motorcycle heading down the hill from the Great Stupa, he seemed to be fighting against the current. There were no left and right lanes to the crowds on their way to the festival. They traveled on foot, on bicycles, pushing motorcycles, in one huge colorful herd. He put his scarf around his face and leaned on his horn all the way down to the arch. People laughed and called out names to the strange man who was going the wrong way.

The ride was slow until he reached Lan Xang Avenue, where the police had kept a lane free for Party members returning from the remembrance ceremony. Once he was away from the main roads, he saw no one. He parked his bike near the Department of Education and walked down to the concrete gate posts of Mahosot. There wasn't even a guard on duty.

The sun had recently set and many of the buildings were in darkness. There were distant strip lights in the public ward, and a single bulb glowed in the nurses' quarters. He entered the building that housed the private rooms and kicked off his shoes inside the door. There was a long corridor running down the center, with rooms on either side. The hallway itself was dark. The only lights shone through the glass windows above two of the doors. The other rooms all appeared empty.

Room 2E was halfway down. He stopped outside the door and listened. There was no sound. He turned the knob gently and the door opened without a squeak. He peeked inside. Siri lay on the bed, asleep beneath a white sheet. The oxygen mask was over his mouth. The light came from a bedside lamp that was covered with a red cloth.

Khen Nahlee looked back along the deserted corridor before stepping inside the room. He closed the door behind him. He took the gun from the holster inside the top of his track suit and screwed on the silencer. But on a night like this he could have used a cannon, and there would have been nobody to hear.

He stepped to the end of the bed, aimed at the coroner's heart, and fired. Six times he fired. Professional. No conversations. No confessions or last-minute explanations. Once the chamber was empty, he sighed with relief. At last the man's luck had run out.

He waited for the pleasing sight of blood slowly seeping through the white sheet, but it didn't come. Immediately, he knew that something had gone wrong. He stepped forward, grabbed the bottom corner of the sheet, and yanked it from the bed.

Three pillows—one assassinated—lay along the center of the mattress. At their summit, beneath the oxygen mask, was a mask of a different kind. As a special tribute to the new regime, they were selling papier-mâché masks of the prime minister at the That Luang festival. With a few white chicken feathers added here and there, it bore a remarkable resemblance to Dr. Siri.

Khen Nahlee's stomach turned. He reached into his pocket for another clip, but he instinctively knew there'd be no time to use it. The door crashed open, and Phosy and two other burly police officers charged into the room with their pistols drawn. They were expecting a fight, but they didn't get one. Khen Nahlee dropped his gun, looked up at the ceiling, and laughed. It was a humorless, defeated laugh.

They handcuffed him, searched his pockets, and told him to keep his mouth shut unless he was asked a question. As the Constitution had been abolished, there were no rights to be read. That was just as well, as they didn't intend to give him any.

Phosy put his nose close to the prisoner's. "I've been looking for you. You know that, don't you? I suppose I must have had too much respect for you. If I'd known you were this hopeless at your job, I would have found you a lot sooner." Khen Nahlee glared blankly at Phosy's forehead. He wasn't one to be riled easily. "How about going to say hello to Dr. Siri before we take you to your new home?"

They led him to another room along the corridor where another Dr. Siri, surrounded by an odd collection of visitors, lay propped up on his pillow, smiling. The police stood Khen Nahlee at the end of the bed. He looked at Siri and shook his head slowly.

"Well, Mr. Ketkaew. Nice to see you again. You're such a disappointment. I was hoping to get rid of Miss Vong on you. Now I'm stuck with her." Khen Nahlee smiled. "Oh, but your name probably isn't Ketkaew, is it? I have to hand it to you: you do play the fool very well. You were a most convincing chicken counter. I'm sorry I spoiled everything for you, but you were up against forces that are not of this earth. Don't berate yourself."

Khen Nahlee had nothing to say. He had no questions, and he no longer needed to act. He looked around at the assembly; Dtui, Mr. Geung, Judge Haeng, Civilai, Dr. Pornsawan, and Mai's sister. How had he fallen to such an army of misfits? He turned to Phosy and gestured that he wanted to go.

"I wouldn't be in a hurry to go where you're going," Phosy told him.

Two more officers came in from outside. They gathered around Khen Nahlee and marched him out to the van. His future promised to be very short.

The Dead Coroner's Lunch

A week had passed since Siri's third coming. Civilai was starting to believe his friend really was immortal. So, as Siri didn't want to be deprived of the pleasure, he announced that lunch this Friday would be a wake. He would supplement their usual fare with a bottle of sparkling wine. As a special treat, he also invited Inspector Phosy to join them. There were still one or two things that weren't completely clear about last week's incredible events.

Civilai and Phosy were on time. They'd canceled their appointments for the afternoon and were settling down around the log for a long and leisurely lunch. Civilai was struggling with a corkscrew.

"You don't want to wait for the deceased?"

"Hell, no."

"Then I'd better help you." He took the bottle and started to open it.

"So, Phosy, Siri had no idea what you were actually doing here?"

"He knew I was with the police. He didn't have a clue I was investigating Kham and his gang. I knew he'd just done the autopsy on Mrs. Nitnoy, so I hoped I could get some information from him over a few drinks. That's why the judge introduced me as the police liaison with the coroner's office. It didn't occur to me I'd get so lucky."

"Why did you wait so long before using the evidence?"

"Well, firstly, none of it was conclusive. Secondly, I really wanted to get my hands on Khen Nahlee. I'd been chasing him around for years. But he changed identity and looks so often, I was always too slow. I was sure if his boss killed his wife, he'd get his henchman in to help clean up. I just needed time to find out who he was. He had me fooled for a long time." He poured wine into the four glasses. "Who's the fourth?"

"You'll see. When did you start to suspect it was Ketkaew?"

"Well, things didn't come together until Siri told me they'd sent Teacher Oum from the Lycée to Viengsai."

"Damn. I was supposed to follow up on that."

"Never mind. I did. The transfer paper was signed by Comrade Kham's office, but then again, most of them are. The initial report was sent in by Ketkaew. That was the first connection I found linking the two of them. It wasn't particularly significant. He sent in reports about everyone for the silliest reasons. He was still acting the fool, so I didn't suspect him for a second.

"But then I found a second connection in a roundabout way. I had file photos of Mrs. Nitnoy. These were some old Press pictures, and it occurred to me she wasn't the best-groomed woman in the country."

"That's very polite of you. I've heard her compared to the arse end of a long-haired goat." They toasted with the sparkling wine. It was a rare treat.

"Well, whatever end of the goat she was, I didn't see her being the type of woman who frequented a beauty salon."

"God, no."

"But that's what the report on the murder said. I chased down the officer who wrote it. He said a witness had told him she went to Mai's salon once a week."

"She should get a posthumous refund."

"I checked at the salon, *and it wasn't true.* They'd never seen her there. Now, you realize that chasing down a rumor in this town is like grabbing a wet lizard by the tail. The officer got it from one of Mai's neighbors, and she got it from one of Mai's boyfriends. It struck me as peculiar that he should choose to share that information with a complete stranger, and I became very interested in that particular boyfriend.

"Fortunately, in a dormitory full of single women, there are a lot of accidental-on-purpose sightings of other girls' late-night visitors. I got the girls in a huddle and tried to put together a profile of the fellow I was looking for. One of the others came up with a gem of information. She happened to be going to Mahosot regularly for treatment of a certain condition she didn't want to elaborate on.

"She said that if this was the man the others were referring to, she'd seen him around the hospital a couple of times. He didn't look like a doctor; he certainly didn't come across as a patient either. 'Something official,' she called him. I told her where I was staying and how to get in touch with me if she ran into him again. In fact, I gave them all my address."

"I bet you did."

"Well, it was the night Siri got blown up. I went back to my place and found a note from the neighbor. She'd been to the hospital that day and seen our fellow again. She asked one of the nurses about him and was told he worked behind the morgue and was some sort of government spy.

"This really sparked my interest. Siri had told me about his chicken counter, but I'd never met him. I didn't know what he looked like. I thought I might just break into his office, see if he had some old ID or photos lying around, and take them to show the neighbors.

"But when I got to the hospital, there was one hell of a commotion going on. Half the night staff was out with old buckets and bedpans, trying to put out a fire in the kitchen. I helped them for an hour until it was under control. That's when I learned that the kitchen was directly under the library. I knew that wasn't a coincidence.

"So I went around to the *khon khouay* office behind the morgue. It wasn't the most secure building I've ever seen: bamboo and banana leaf. It was too easy to get into. I wasn't surprised not to find anything incriminating there. But I just had a feeling something was out of place. I sat at the desk and looked around at the layout of the room.

"Then it occurred to me. There were windows front and back, but the desk wasn't in front of either of them. There wasn't a fan, so why didn't he sit where he could get some natural breeze? The desk was squashed up against one wall. I tried to move it, but one leg was stuck. That's when I saw the wire taped to the back leg. It came straight out of the ground. There was only a four-inch section visible, and at the top was a connector, the type you'd put an extension cord into."

"He was bugging the morgue."

"He obviously took the main equipment home with him, but I dug up what was there. The wire went underground all the way to the drain outlet behind the morgue."

"So he knew everything that went on in there."

"All the autopsy dictations, the conversations of the morgue assistants. I knew I had him, but I didn't know where he lived. The only place I could get him was right there. So I woke up a couple of my men and we set up a surveillance. I got the judge out of bed for a warrant and had the place sprung like a rat trap for when he turned up. But the creep didn't come. All day we waited, not daring to go take a piss or get something to eat, in case we missed him. But there was no sign of him."

Civilai noticed they'd finished their wine. He picked up the two other glasses and handed one to the policeman.

"It's going flat." He raised his glass. "Good luck."

"Good luck."

"So, how did you find him?"

"In the end he found us. We'd been watching the office, day and night. I was afraid if he showed up we'd all be asleep. We split into two shifts, and I joined the first rest team to get a little shut-eye. I contacted Judge Haeng to let him know what was happening, and that's when I first found out about the Security Section scandal and the arrest of Major Ngakum, and, to my utter shock, of Siri's house being blown up.

"When I'd last seen the little fellow, he was on his way into the house. God only knows how he escaped the blast. My first reaction was to go and see him. But then I got to thinking about things. Like Siri, I'd assumed the attempt on his life was in connection with the Vietnamese case. I'd never known Khen Nahlee to miss a target.

"But by Tuesday, Siri had shared all his Vietnamese information with so many people that it didn't make sense for them to single him out anymore. There was only one case where Siri was sitting on evidence. Khen Nahlee had no idea who I was or that I was connected to that case. I'd been very discreet. As far as he was concerned, Siri was the only one who could put together a case against Kham. So I had to assume the impossible had happened. The professional assassin had failed, not once but twice.

"I'd been tracking him so long, seen the aftermath of his capabilities so many times, I had started to think like him. I knew how those two failures must have hurt his pride. I was surer than anything else in my life that he'd try again."

"And the night of the That Luang Festival was the perfect time."

"The Security Section guard had been recalled and there weren't a lot of people around. I smuggled my men in—one by one, in case he was watching—and the rest you know."

"The fly dropped neatly into the web. Where is he now?"

"I'm afraid I'm not at liberty to say. But with Kham no longer at his back, and Khen Nahlee out of action, it won't be hard to dismantle the death squad. I guess that's a bad sign."

"Why?"

"I've been so efficient, I've done myself out of a job. I'm unemployed."

"Nonsense. Consider yourself rehired. I've got a hundred jobs for a fellow of your cunning. Let's finish this up and hide the bottle before our body gets here. We'll pretend it was stolen."

They'd just removed the last of the evidence when Siri and another man they didn't recognize crossed the road. The doctor was carrying a plastic bag that clinked as he walked.

"Good afternoon, gentlemen."

"Surely it's evening already."

"Sorry I'm late. There was more muck to wash off him than I expected." The apparent stranger stood beside him in a long-sleeved pink shirt, permanent-press slacks, and almost-new running shoes. His hair was washed, cut, and parted. His dark chocolate face was the only familiar thing about him.

"Good afternoon, Ambassador Rajid. How do you like your new self?" Crazy Rajid looked confused but moderately excited. Siri shook hands with his two friends.

"He passed his medical with flying colors. I was expecting all kinds of diseases. But apart from lice and a few friction wounds, he's a glowing advertisement for eating out of trash cans and sleeping in sewers."

"Perhaps we should try it ourselves." Rajid started to walk away when the others sat cross-legged around the log as if it were a high table.

"Where are you going, Ambassador? Come and join us." The Indian looked back, thought about it, then came to sit with them. He gave them a Rajid silent laugh to show he was happy. Civilai inspected the fine silk shirt.

"How did you find clothes to fit him?"

"I work in a morgue, Ai. Do you need to ask? Waste not . . ."

"How are your lungs?" Phosy asked.

"I just passed a medical that I had to administer myself."

"Good for you. You were lucky."

"Lucky is my middle name. And that reminds me. I went to visit an old witch I know—"

"A live one?"

"Most certainly. And she was so pleased to see me, she gave me a special discount on these." From the plastic bag he produced three bottles of cherry-red liquid in oddly shaped bottles sealed with wax. "Which was just as well, as I see you've finished the good stuff without me. It's plum rice wine."

Civilai upturned one bottle and watched the alien sediment float to the top. "Phosy, under normal circumstances I'd tell you not to accept blood-red liquid in unmarked bottles from a coroner, but in this case I think we have no choice but to trust him. What do you say?"

"I say he takes the first glass and we give him ten minutes."

Siri opened a bottle. Phosy laid out four jumbo-sized baguettes on the log, and Crazy Rajid sniffed and tasted his running shoes. While he was slicing through the bread, Civilai recalled an item of news that had landed briefly on his desk that day.

"I heard the funniest thing today. It appears the Taiwanese have canceled a logging contract they had with the Lao Military Council."

"No!" Siri blushed.

"You wouldn't know anything about that, would you?"

"Me? 'Course not. I don't hear about anything before you do. But—"

"Here we go."

"No, it's just that I hear the Chinese are a very superstitious people. I imagine if they knew about the massive displacement of spirits in Khamuan, they'd be concerned that the timber might be . . . well, cursed in some way."

"Especially if they had a little spiritual demonstration. And how do you think those Taiwanese could have heard of the spirit displacement in faraway Khamuan?"

Siri shook his head. "Beats me."

"H'mm. Not much does, I'll bet." Phosy laughed.

At last, all the guests were in attendance and ready for the wake toast. It was mercifully short. They stood and raised their glasses. Civilai coughed and spoke in his most somber Party voice.

"Gentlemen of the Dead Coroner's Lunch. We're gathered here today in honor of a loyal and sadly departed loved one."

"Hear, hear."

"Shut up, Siri. Although he lived much of his life as a fool, he died, without question, a hero."

"Three times," Phosy added.

"Three times. Dr. Siri Paiboun, coroner, scholar, witch doctor. We salute you. Good luck."

"Good luck."

"Good luck."

". . . good luck."

They all turned in amazement to look at Rajid.

"You talk?"

"Sometimes."

Lunch stretched until five. Rajid's new clothes were piled neatly on the riverbank, but he wasn't anywhere near them. The others finally stood and said their farewells. Civilai had to be home for a family get-together. The other two didn't have families to get together with, so Phosy asked Siri if he'd like to have a drink somewhere else.

"Um. Afraid I can't."

"Can't?"

"I have an . . . appointment this evening."

Civilai yelped and danced up and down. Rock lizards fled for cover. "Would this 'appointment' be with a stunning bakery gal, by any chance?"

"It's only dinner."

"And the Tet Offensive was only a skirmish. I hope you remember where everything goes."

"Don't be so vulgar. It's dinner. In fact, I'm a bit nervous."

"Don't worry. I'm sure she'll lead."

Phosy went to the briefcase that had been sitting at his side all through lunch, and pulled out a thick file that virtually filled it.

"In that case, I'd better give you this now."

"What is it?"

"It's you."

"Me?"

"We found all the confidential files Comrade K and his gang had been keeping on the senior members. We weren't too sure what to do with them. Your judge suggested we should give them back. Let you decide. He said 'Socialism is a great cosmos, but trust is the atmosphere that holds the stars together.'"

"Even with the motto, it appears Judge Haeng is developing some common sense," Siri said.

"I don't think I get it," Phosy said.

"Nobody ever does. Can I borrow your briefcase? I don't want a hernia on top of everything else."

Just When You Think It's All Over . . .

Siri was living temporarily at a guest house not far from the Anusawari Arch. It was nicely landscaped and friendly, and he wouldn't have minded staying there forever. But as a reward for his heroics, his name was elevated on the housing list: in a month, he'd have his own place. He wouldn't have to share a door, or a hallway, or a bathroom. It sounded lonely.

He had a couple of hours before his date, time to rest and get cleaned up. As he only had one change of clothes, he didn't have to spend time deciding what to wear. He lay back on the bed and smiled. The briefcase was beside him, so he unlocked it and pulled out his top-secret file. His life was over three inches thick.

It would afford him some enjoyable reading over the next month. He flipped through it; typed pages, hurried handwritten notes (*'Dr. Siri just called the deputy commander an ass.'*), photographs, news reports, dispatches. And then, in the middle of it all, date-stamped 9.6.1965, was a sheet of paper torn from an old exercise book. The handwriting was as familiar as his own. The consonants were large; the vowels floated around them like balloons. This was Boua's style.

He felt his heart close up like a knot as he read:

My darling Siri,
   What's happening to me? I can't explain. Why have I destroyed everything wonderful we had? Why can I only

reward your love and patience with anger? Why can I no longer speak the words we used to find so natural?

I can't control this depression. It's like a vine that's choking the life out of me. It's a disease that limits what I can see in front of me. I can only see the failures of our political struggle, even though I'm sure there must be successes. I can only see selfish and corrupt Party members around me, but I know there has to be good, somewhere.

But most of all I can only see an irritating husband who constantly reminds me of the hopeful, pretty girl I lost somewhere on the endless jungle treks to nowhere. But I know you are the best thing in my life.

Can you ever forgive me for what I've done to you, and for what I have to do this evening? This is the only escape for us two.

To my dearest and only love,

Boua.

On the back, someone had handwritten "WITHHOLD-NEGATIVE."

They'd found her suicide note. They'd found the key that would have unlocked some of the guilt, some of the doubts, that had shackled him for the past eleven years. And they'd kept it from him because it was "negative."

If only they knew how negative life had been without it.

Tears rolled freely down his cheeks. Some were tears of sadness. He was so sorry that she'd been unable to stop her misery any other way; that he hadn't been able to bring her back from the edge.

But some tears were nothing short of ecstasy. She had loved him. Even at the end she still loved him, and she knew he loved her. That was all he needed to know.

For an hour and a half he cried. It was only the wind against his face that was finally able to dry the tears. The Justice

Department had fixed his carburetor and he sped off on his beloved motorcycle along the Dong Dok road, through the untouched fields that belied their closeness to a capital city. He yelled at the top of his voice in harmony with the engine. He was free.

By the time he turned back for the city, he was at peace. There were no coincidences anymore in his life. The file had found him. The note found him on this day, at this time. Boua was letting him know it was all right. He didn't have to feel guilty that another woman was in his heart.

He turned on to Samsenthai Avenue and immediately saw Lah standing there at the end of the alleyway. When she saw Siri on his sturdy old bike, like some white-haired knight, she smiled more brightly than the tilted streetlights along the roadside. She wore a purple *phasin* with gold trimming and a white blouse moulded around her breasts. Goodness knows how many hours she'd spent combing her hair into the style of Imelda Marcos, complete with lily. She was a picture.

He stopped at the curb in front of her and smiled warmly. She walked over on unfamiliar high heels and kissed him on the cheek. In her left hand was a delicate handbag studded with rhinestones. In her right, she held a small box. It was wrapped in green paper to match his eyes, and tied with a dark green ribbon bow.

"Are you bringing sandwiches?"

"It's a present."

"For me? Can I open it now?"

"You have to. I'm not getting on that bike until you do."

He couldn't stop smiling as he ripped the paper and plucked off the bow. The cardboard box inside had a lid. He looked up at her face, excited like a child at a birthday party. She really was very beautiful. She looked at him, then back at the box. "Hurry up. I'm hungry."

As soon as he opened the lid, his smile faded. Whatever joy

that had surrounded them vanished like incense smoke. Lying in the box, like a charred corpse in a coffin, was the black prism on its leather thong. Not some other black prism, the one worn smooth from years of hands. The one that had been destroyed and scattered on the land in Khamuan.

"Given the bad luck you've been having lately, I figured you could use a lucky charm. Like it?"